THE DIAMOND CHASE

Also by Cap Daniels

The Chase Fulton Novels Series
Book One: *The Opening Chase*
Book Two: *The Broken Chase*
Book Three: *The Stronger Chase*
Book Four: *The Unending Chase*
Book Five: *The Distant Chase*
Book Six: *The Entangled Chase*
Book Seven: *The Devil's Chase*
Book Eight: *The Angel's Chase*
Book Nine: *The Forgotten Chase*
Book Ten: *The Emerald Chase*
Book Eleven: *The Polar Chase*
Book Twelve: *The Burning Chase*
Book Thirteen: *The Poison Chase*
Book Fourteen: *The Bitter Chase*
Book Fifteen: *The Blind Chase*
Book Sixteen: *The Smuggler's Chase*
Book Seventeen: *The Hollow Chase*
Book Eighteen: *The Sunken Chase*
Book Nineteen: *The Darker Chase*
Book Twenty: *The Abandoned Chase*
Book Twenty-One: *The Gambler's Chase*
Book Twenty-Two: *The Arctic Chase*
Book Twenty-Three: *The Diamond Chase*
Book Twenty-Four: *The Phantom Chase*

The Avenging Angel – Seven Deadly Sins Series
Book One: *The Russian's Pride*
Book Two: *The Russian's Greed*
Book Three: *The Russian's Gluttony*
Book Four: *The Russian's Lust*
Book Five: *The Russian's Sloth* (2023)
Book Six: *The Russian's Envy* (2024)
Book Seven: *The Russian's Wrath* (TBA)

Stand-Alone Novels
We Were Brave
Singer – Memoir of a Christian Sniper

Novellas
The Chase Is On
I Am Gypsy

THE DIAMOND CHASE

CHASE FULTON NOVEL #23

CAP DANIELS

ANCHOR WATCH
PUBLISHING
** USA **

The Diamond Chase
Chase Fulton Novel #23
Cap Daniels

Published by:

ANCHOR WATCH
PUBLISHING
** USA **

13 Digit ISBN: 978-1-951021-52-8
Library of Congress Control Number: 2023948349

Cover Design: German Creative

Printed in the United States of America

The Diamond Chase

CAP DANIELS

Chapter 1
Gun Him Down

Spring 2010

Staring into the late-afternoon sun made the battlefield in front of me little more than an orange glare with animated silhouettes moving in old, familiar patterns before me. I was dug in well, and my body armor and helmet would provide far more protection than my adversary enjoyed. The time would come, and I would fire my well-worn rifle to gun down the man desperately trying to improve his position. Defeat wasn't something I would allow, and I had proven in years past that I would sacrifice my mortal body to protect and defend what I held dear, especially when those things were my family and home.

Home was a bit of an abstract concept in my world—a place I felt safe, but where I was rarely alone. When the time came to defend that small piece of ground I considered uniquely mine, I would do so with a fire in my belly and a determination to never surrender and never fail to take the blows that, invariably, came with the defense of such a place, such a concept, such a small, insignificant piece of dirt the rest of the world could never understand. But for men like me and my team, that spot, that entity, that concept of home meant everything.

Keeping score was not something on which we would waste energy. We simply poured our bodies into the fight and left our opponents battle-weary and defeated. Winning wasn't an option. It was the only outcome we would accept, and no sacrifice was too great to walk or drag ourselves from the battlefield only to nurse, heal, and return to fight another day.

My target knew where I crouched. He could see the fire in my eyes, and he even knew precisely the skill set I possessed to gun him down when he devoted himself to the achievement of his next goal—a position of greater threat and lower risk for him. I wouldn't give him the goal easily or willingly. I had a weapon that was far more than capable of ending his quest and sending him slinking from the battlefield if he were lucky . . . and carried off if not. He would make his move, and I would punish not only him, but also every member of his team for the treachery he would un-dertake and for the gall to believe I wouldn't pull the trigger and gun him down just like so many before him.

I wasn't wrong. From my position, I'd long ago stopped being wrong when I believed an opponent was on the verge of attempt-ing to fulfill his unspoken threat to advance while in my sights and challenge a superior player—one of greater experience, skill, and fearlessness. I was his superior both on and off the field of battle. We both knew it, but that wouldn't stop him from risking it all on a fool's gamble born of desperation and ignorant hope.

He sprang into action, and in three strides, reached the peak of his speed. I raised a hand, and in a fraction of a second, the crack of the collision of skin on skin—hide on hide—rang through the air, and I pulled the trigger of the rifle attached to my right shoul-der. The missile I sent wasn't supersonic. Instead, it was silent as it flew through the scalding afternoon air, closing on my target and leaving me with nothing left to do except trust my aim and watch the inevitable unfold in front of me.

My shot was perfect, hitting the precise point at which I'd aimed, and down went my opponent in a cloud of dust and the grinding roar of his body sliding to a dead stop, his eyes still open and his heart beating like a thousand drums. Before his body came to rest, I relaxed for the first time in hours, pulled off my helmet, and took my first stride toward the edge of the battlefield, where I was once again undefeated.

I didn't have to look or listen for the official result of the final shot of the battle, the ultimate declaration of victory. I had done it, and even though I didn't cast my eyes into the torrent of dust and noise and defeat, I knew the second-base umpire would call the runner out, and I'd carve one more notch in my mitt for gunning down another runner who dared attempt to steal against me. I still had the rifle that my right arm had become so many years before, and that felt good. I may have never worn the armor of an Atlanta Braves catcher, but I was undefeated in the Greater Jacksonville, over-thirty, men's amateur baseball league.

Business meetings involving a team of knuckle-dragging gun-toters have always devolved into a rat's nest of twelve-year-old boys and somebody looking for an excuse to kill somebody else. I was determined to manage our upcoming session while maintaining at least some degree of decorum.

On the ride back to St. Marys in our newest addition to our fleet of high-tech tactical vehicles—a 1977 Chevy short bus—had once been the proud possession of the Camden County public school system but had since been relegated to status as a toolshed behind the current school bus maintenance facility. I bought it for $300, towed it to Bonaventure, and put our favorite diesel mechanic to work bringing the old girl back to her former glory.

Earline, "Earl at the End," spent a few hundred hours and twenty thousand of my dollars turning the faded yellow carcass into an ultra-luxurious limo with a seven-hundred-horsepower turbocharged diesel beast beneath the hood, but from the outside, it was still a 34-year-old short bus. A new paint job covered the previous yellow skin and bore the logo and name of a traveling gospel quartet. As my mentor, Dr. Robert "Rocket" Richter, was so fond of telling me, nothing is as it appears, and if it is, we probably perceived it incorrectly the first time.

I spun in my seat and called the meeting to order. "All right, listen up. That was fun, but I'm glad you guys don't have to make a living playing baseball."

Mongo, our personal giant and resident big brain, glared down his nose at me. "Speak for yourself. I went four-for-four with four home runs. How many did you hit?"

I ignored his jab since I'd gone one-for-four with one single and three groundouts.

The woman I adored, my wife Penny, leaned across the seat and planted an extremely enjoyable kiss exactly where kisses like that one belong. "This is the first time I've ever seen you play, Chase, and I've got to say, it was pretty hot from the cheap seats. You did look kind of silly with only one shin guard, though."

The new guy, Kodiak, bounced an aluminum bat off my prosthetic lower leg. "He cheated. He's part cyborg."

"That's it," I said. "My titanium parts are what makes me a great athlete. Is that what you're saying, Juggle King?"

"Juggle King?" he said. "The sun was in my eyes."

"The sun was in *my* eyes and at *your* back," I said. "The only thing in *your* eyes were tears of embarrassment when you dropped three fly balls in a row."

"Hey, it's been a long time since I've played ball. I was soldiering while you were playing in the dirt."

I turned to my old friend and handler, Clark Johnson. "Are you going to let him get away with talking to me like that?"

He shrugged. "The man's got a point, College Boy. We were all soldiering and getting shot at while you were *playing*."

I said, "Well, thank God I'm a lot better at soldiering than you losers are at balling. Now, let's talk about work for a minute. We've got an unorthodox offer on the table."

The banter ceased, and I finally had everyone's attention. "We're going to interview a tech services brainiac from DC and talk about bringing her on, at least part-time, to build nifty gadgets for us to save the world with. That's thing one. Thing two is a contract from Penny's movie studio. They need somebody to provide security in a place called Diamond Beach, and they threw us a bone."

Mongo laughed. "A bone? I've got a different name for it. We're not rent-a-cops. We're operators."

"I know, but I told the guy I'd listen. We're not committed yet."

Stone W. Hunter, former Air Force combat controller turned chief dive officer and conditioning trainer for the team, asked, "Is this one of Penny's movies?"

My wife, the wild-haired North Texas beauty turned world-famous screenwriter, wrestled her strawberry-blonde mane into something resembling a ponytail. "No, this one isn't mine. It's an action-adventure film. I read the script, and it's not bad."

"Where's Diamond Beach?" Hunter asked.

Penny shrugged. "Beats me. I'm not the geography expert."

Mongo spoke up. "The only Diamond Beach I've ever heard of is in Iceland at the southern end of a glacial lagoon called Jökulsárlón."

Clark Johnson, my former partner who'd moved up the ladder to serve as our team handler, dispensing assignments as they came down from the Board—a shadowy organization of seasoned geopolitical operatives and multi-millionaires—said, "Jökulsárlón.

That's one of those words with a bunch of crazy dots and squiggles above the letters, isn't it?"

Mongo rolled his eyes. "It's a good thing you can shoot, pretty boy."

Clark feigned offense. "What's that supposed to mean?"

The giant patted our handler on his head. "Nothing. Just find something shiny to play with while the grown-ups talk."

Skipper, our hot-shot analyst and practically my little sister, crossed her arms as if skeptical. "So, where'd you find this so-called brainiac techy we're going to interview?"

A knot the size of Siberia roiled in my gut. "I didn't really find her. She came highly recommended."

"Who recommended her?"

Skipper wasn't going to let it go, and I was standing on the precipice of a hole of my own creation.

I said, "The Department of Justice."

Skipper raised an eyebrow. "Wow! The whole department, or just the attorney general?"

I feared the scowl and disappointment from Penny, but coming clean was the only avenue of escape from Skipper's probe. "Anya gave Dr. Mankiller my number."

"Anya? Oh, really?" Skipper said. "So, Anya had this Dr. Mankiller—made-up name, by the way—give you a call to recommend herself for a job with you. Is that how it went down?"

"Let's talk about it later, okay?"

It was Penny's turn to cross her arms. "I think I'd like to talk about it right now, especially the part that has anything to do with *our* ex-girlfriend."

That drew a cacophony of laughter and jeers from the team, and Skipper joined in. "What does *our* ex-girlfriend mean?"

Penny rolled her eyes. "I've accepted the fact that she's never going away, so now I consider her part mine as well."

I took a long, dreadful breath. "Anya called me and put me on the phone with Dr. Mankiller. That is her real name, by the way. I did some research. Her mother was the first female chief of the Cherokee Indian tribe."

"That's interesting," Skipper said. "Let's get back to the part about Anya calling you. Did she whisper sweet Russian nothings in your ear?"

Beads of sweat formed on my forehead, but there was no chance I was going to wipe them away. "No, there was no whispering. It was all business."

Penny lowered her chin and gave me the hairy eyeball. "I'll bet."

If I thought I could squeeze through the window, I would've jumped out of our short bus right there on Interstate 95, but before I had to make my leap, Penny and Skipper burst into uncontrollable laughter, and my forehead ceased its production of sweat beads. "I'm going to drown you two. You had that whole episode planned, didn't you? Why do you insist on torturing me like this?"

Penny mussed my hair. "It's not torture, my dear. It's entertainment. Besides, I spend more than half my time with actors who look like . . . well, movie stars. If you're not jealous of those guys, I'm certainly not worried about some former Russian spy."

Chapter 2
Cute

The following morning, I assembled the team in the op center on the third floor of the house at Bonaventure Plantation, a piece of property that had been in my mother's family since the 18th century. An arsonist destroyed the original brick home in which my ancestors had lived for two hundred years, but thanks to a little involvement from the federal government, we rebuilt the new house to look nearly identical to the original two-story brick structure that had survived countless hurricanes, tropical storms, Civil War musket balls, and scorching Southern summers . . . at least on the outside.

The inside was a horse of a different color. Where two stories and a shallow cellar had once been now stood a three-story structure with a full subterranean, watertight armory. The third floor of the home boasted one of the finest and most technologically advanced operation centers on the planet. From inside the op center, Skipper could run missions with the computing and communication power of the White House Situation Room. We didn't have the authority to deploy a naval carrier battle group, but we had something almost as deadly: the ability to be anywhere in the world and ready to conduct any small cell covert operation in less than 24 hours without the fear of losing the next election. The voters would never know our names nor see our pictures on the covers of the *Times* or *Journal*, but they would sleep every night beneath the warmth of safety and security that teams like ours provided for the millions of unsuspecting, unknowing, and sometimes, ungrateful citizens.

I opened the meeting in my typical laid-back fashion. "Now that everyone is awake, clean, and hopefully fed, let's get started."

Clark put on his patented pitiful face. "Does that mean there's not going to be snacks?"

Skipper launched a granola bar across the conference table, landing it only inches from Clark's knuckles. "That'll have to do. Now, shut up and listen to Chase. We've got a lot to cover."

I shot a thumb toward our analyst. "Yeah, what she said."

Clark tore into the foil wrapper and made short work of the goody.

"Let's talk about the security job first," I said. "It's not really our thing, and that's why Penny is in here with us this morning."

It was rare for her to be inside the op center, especially for mission planning. Keeping a degree of separation between her world and mine kept her from losing her mind worrying about what might happen to me on the next assignment, and it kept me from trying to understand the make-believe world she lived in on the West Coast. It's still a toss-up between which world is more dangerous. As far as I was concerned, Tinseltown would never be a realm I wanted to understand.

"Let's have it, Penny. You've spent a lot more time on movie sets than any of us, so what are the security requirements, and who typically provides that service?"

She cleared her throat and cast her eyes to the ceiling for a moment. "That's not really part of my job, and to be honest, I've never really thought about it much. Security is just one of those things most people on set take for granted. There are always overzealous fans who want to sneak onto a shoot to get a glimpse of their favorite actor, and on rare occasions, those fans fall a little closer to the rabid than the zealous. You've all heard of stalkers. Every actor has his or her share of those, and that's usually what the security people have to deal with."

Hunter said. "So, it's site access and perimeter security. Is that what you're saying?"

"Mostly, but there's always the after-hours personal security for the major actors. Sometimes, they have their own private security —you know, bodyguards—but I guess there might be some of that involved, too."

I tapped my pencil against my legal pad. "Do you know of any credible threats to the actors of this particular movie?"

"No, but like I said, it's not my movie. I didn't write the screen-play, so I'm not in the know."

Hunter asked, "How many guards do you typically see on a shoot?"

"I don't know. Maybe eight to ten, not including the personal bodyguards after hours."

I stuck my pencil in the air. "Okay, let's do it this way. This isn't our thing, and it's not the kind of thing we want to do for a living, but if we turn down the job, will that have a negative im-pact on your position with the studio?"

Penny grimaced. "It's not a case of negative impact, but I would love to get a multi-picture contract with the studio. I love working with them, and I've got a bunch of ideas that would be perfect for their lineup."

"Does that mean you want us to take the job to help get you a contract?" I asked.

"It's selfish of me to say yes, but it wouldn't hurt."

Hunter said, "I've got an idea. Now that Tony's a big-time crime buster with the St. Marys PD and out of the shoot-'em-up game, he's gotta be pretty bored. Aren't you, Tony?"

Skipper answered before Tony could. "Absolutely. He's bored out of his mind, and he's driving me nuts. If you can get him out of my hair, I'll pay whatever it costs."

Tony landed both hands in the center of his chest. "Ouch!"

Skipper bounced a pen off his shoulder. "Don't pretend like I'm making it up. You know it's true."

"Okay, maybe a little. What are you thinking?"

Hunter said, "I didn't get the best of reports from the doctor."

I leaned forward and glared at him. "And you're just telling me now?"

He lowered his chin. "I know. I've been putting it off, but I guess it's time to come clean. My left lung isn't doing great. The shots we took in Cuba weren't exactly welterweight blows. I got hit pretty hard, and I'm not eighteen anymore."

I said, "But you're going to heal, right?"

He shrugged. "We'll see, but it won't be any time soon. I'm going to be off the starting lineup for at least another couple of months, depending on how the lung heals."

I closed my eyes and leaned back. "You can't keep this stuff from me. I can't run the team if I don't know who's up and who's down. You know that."

He nodded. "Yeah, I know. I'm sorry."

In multi-voice stereo, the team said, "Don't be sorry. Be better."

Hunter ignored the blast. "Anyway, if it'll help Penny land the full-time gig with the studio, Tony and I could put a team together and pull security for the shoot. It's not like we'll be running and gunning. It's just a rent-a-cop gig."

I turned to Penny, and she said, "Don't do it just for me. Getting a contract with the studio would be great, but you guys are serious operators, and this feels like it's a little beneath your skill set."

Hunter chuckled. "We *used* to be serious operators. Now, we're shot-up, beat-up old men. Maybe we'll heal and get back in the game, but this'll give us something to do while we're convalescing."

"*Convalescing*?" I asked. "Where did you learn a big word like that?"

"I think I read it in a comic book once. Did I use it right?"

I turned a sheet of notepaper into a missile and launched it at his head. "Close enough. So, I guess that settles it. Hunter and Tony will spearhead the new rent-a-cop division and get Penny the contract she wants while the rest of us . . ."

Clark made a face, and I said, "What does that look mean? You've got a mission for us, don't you?"

"Maybe," he said. "It depends on a lot of variables, but there's something in the works."

"Let's hear it."

He shook his head. "Not yet. There's no reason to get it in your head until we're sure it's going to happen. Let's talk about little Miss Mankiller."

Skipper's fingers danced across the keyboard, and soon, a photograph filled the monitor over her head. She said, "That's her. Dr. Celeste Mankiller. And it wasn't her mother who was the Cherokee Indian Chief. It was her grandmother, Wilma Mankiller."

Clark said, "She's cute."

Skipper bored a hole through his head. "Cut it out, playboy. You're married, and that's sexist."

Clark threw up both hands. "What? That's not sexist. It's an observation. You're cute, too."

Skipper rolled her eyes. "And you're a dinosaur. Just take it from me. Don't make observations like that about coworkers and potential coworkers. Can you manage that?"

"I'll try, but Chase is cute, too."

My responsibility as ringmaster for the Bonaventure Circus was often more than I could bear, but reclaiming control of the op center was necessary. "Thank you, Clark. I'm flattered to hear you think I'm cute. You're not bad yourself, but let's get back to work."

"Great idea," Skipper said. "There's a copy of Dr. Mankiller's CV in front of each of you. If you flip through it, you'll see that she's more than qualified to be and do whatever she wants. Under education, you'll notice a pair of PhDs—one in mechanical engineering, and one in materials science and engineering, both from MIT."

Clark bounced my paper wad off my forehead. "She's got more learnin' than you, College Boy. How does that make you feel?"

Ignoring Clark rarely worked, but I gave it a try. "Has she accomplished anything other than stacking diplomas?"

Skipper flipped to the second page and shook the CV. "Thirty-one patents, recipient of eight prestigious engineering and design awards, and she finished eighteenth in last year's Iron Man Triathlon."

"Eighteenth in the women's division?" I asked.

Skipper shook her head. "Eighteenth overall."

"How much?" I asked.

"How much what?"

I dropped Dr. Mankiller's CV onto the table. "How much will she cost us?"

"She's a GS-thirteen, step-six on the DOJ special salary scale. That puts her around one fifty to one sixty per year, plus federal government benefits."

I grimaced at the relatively low salary for such an accomplished scientist. "Do we have enough work to keep her busy?"

"That's up to you," Skipper said. "Something tells me she and Mongo would be inseparable."

"Irina might have something to say about that," I said, but our giant jumped in.

"My wife's got nothing to worry about. She knows I've only got eyes for her."

"That's because she'd kill you in your sleep if she found out you were cheating . . . even with a mankiller."

Clark chimed in. "Irina's cute, too!"

Skipper sighed. "You just can't do it, can you?"

"Do what?"

"I've got an idea," the analyst said. "How about telling us what you can about the potential mission without calling anybody cute? Can you handle that?"

"I'm not ready to brief it yet. I've not been fully read in, so anything I know is superficial at best."

I tapped on the table in front of me. "Just give us a little taste, and we'll fill in the blanks with our imagination."

He took a long breath and slowly let it out. When he looked up, his eyes fell on Penny.

She stood. "Okay, I get it. I don't have a need to know, so I'm out. I'll be in the barn with Pecan. It's time for a little grooming anyway."

Pecan was one of the beasts from Hell that came with Bonaventure when I inherited the property from my great uncle, Judge Bernard Henry Huntsinger. My detestation of horses was not only bottomless, but well-deserved. Nothing about the beasts appealed to me on any level, but if I wanted to keep waking up next to my beautiful wife every morning, the horses were permanent fixtures, and there was nothing I could do about it.

Clark rolled his pen between his knuckles. "I'm sure you've all seen the news out of Central Asia, so I don't need to bore you with the basics."

Kodiak, former Green Beret and the newest member of the team, threw up a finger. "Hang on a minute. I haven't seen any news in a week or more, so I'd appreciate some of those boring details."

Clark spun his legal pad, sketched a rough map of Central Asia, and pointed toward the northern border of Iran. "These two little countries, Turkmenistan and Uzbekistan, have started a shooting war."

"Over what?" I asked.

"Keep your pants on, College Boy. I'll get there. But first, we need a little geography lesson."

Skipper said, "I can help with that."

In seconds, a color-coded map of the region replaced Dr. Mankiller's photo on the screen above the console.

Clark said, "That's much better than my drawing. We're all familiar with Iraq and Afghanistan. Most of us have been there and still have sand in our boots, but this particular pissing match doesn't involve them . . . yet."

He pulled a laser pointer from the well and motioned toward a border town between the two former Soviet states. "Prior to nineteen ninety-one, all of this belonged to the good ol' USSR, but when the wall came down, everybody ran for the hills and started renaming themselves."

He drew a circle around the area in question. "This is the city of Urgench in Uzbekistan. Four days ago, the city befell mortar fire from Turkmenistan forces. Early reports of casualties were initially light, but the Uzbeks weren't expecting trouble from their neighbors, so they were caught on their heels. Turk forces rolled across the border and invaded the city, killing just over eight hundred civilians and possibly as many as two hundred military."

I said, "I thought Turkmenistan was officially neutral."

Clark shrugged. "Just because they wrote it on the wall doesn't mean they're living it. There's nothing neutral looking about the invasion."

"But that still leaves my question of why."

He nodded. "Yes, it does, and the official answer is, we don't know."

I chewed on my lip. "So, what's the unofficial answer?"

Clark groaned. "Rumors are floating around about a massive oil reserve in southwestern Uzbekistan. If the rumors are true, it boils down to black gold, and all we have to do is follow the money, like always."

I let the words wash over me, and a thousand questions sprang up. "What would be our role if this potential mission becomes a real one?"

Clark said, "That's exactly why I wasn't ready to brief this thing. I have no idea what our mission might be. We're not a conventional fighting force. We can't run in and scare the Turkmen out of there. The Board told me to stay up-to-date on the action in preparation for a potential assignment. That's all I know."

I turned back to our analyst. "Do you have anything else?"

She glanced at the clock. "Just picking up Dr. Mankiller for her interview."

Chapter 3
First Impressions

Disco, our chief pilot and retired A-10 Warthog driver, returned from DC in the *Grey Ghost*, our Gulfstream IV, with Dr. Celeste Mankiller reclining in luxury on one of the plane's plush captain's chairs.

When she stepped from the plane, I stuck out a hand. "You must be Dr. Mankiller."

She stuck her hand in mine and glanced over her shoulder at the Gulfstream. "You must be Mr. Fulton. And if you were trying to make a good impression with the Gulfstream, it worked."

"I don't make impressions, ma'am. This just happens to be our preferred means of long-distance transportation."

She smiled and brushed a long strand of raven hair from her face. "Perhaps you don't try to make impressions intentionally, but you make them, and from what I hear, some of them stick around a long time."

I cocked my head. "What's that supposed to mean?"

She smiled up at me through the bright morning sun. "You seem to have left an indelible impression on a mutual friend of ours."

A thousand fleeting memories danced through my head of the beautiful Russian who'd almost been my undoing. "If this morn-

ing goes well, you'll meet my wife this afternoon, and I'd really appreciate it if you wouldn't bring that up."

She made a face. "Ooh, sorry. I didn't mean to . . ."

"It's okay. Let's go have a chat."

I ushered her into my ancient VW Microbus and buzzed our
way back to Bonaventure.

"What's the story on this van?" she asked.

I said, "It's classified."

She laughed out loud. "So, the Gulfstream is public information, but the ragged-out van is classified."

"You're catching on. Come with me, and I'll show you my favorite place on Earth."

I led her to the gazebo in my backyard overlooking the North
River in St. Marys, Georgia.

She slid her hand down the long, worn cannon resting atop its
heavy oak cradle. "Nice centerpiece."

"Thank you. I pulled it out of the mud about four miles from
here. I've never been able to determine its exact origin, but it came
from a French or British man-o'-war during the War of Eighteen
Twelve. I'd love to know its full history, but like a faithful warrior
should, she just sits there, holding her silence while the world plays
on all around her."

Celeste then did something I would've never anticipated. She
leaned down, pressed her cheek against the centuries-old weapon
of war, and closed her eyes as if listening for the whispered voices
through the ages. When she opened her eyes, she said, "My
brother is a history professor at the Naval Academy in Annapolis.
I'll bet he could tell you everything there is to know about your
cannon."

"She's not mine," I said. "She belongs to a British naval captain
who likely died two hundred years ago. I'm just charged with

keeping her warm and dry. I would love to hear your brother's thoughts on her, though."

"All the more reason to hire me."

I motioned toward an Adirondack chair. "Have a seat. Would you like something to drink?"

"No, thank you. I'm fine. Will it just be you and me for the interview?"

I slipped into my slightly oversized chair. "For now, but if it goes well, you'll meet the rest of the team at lunch."

"Okay, then. I'm ready when you are."

I crossed my legs, and Celeste's attention flew to my carbon fiber prosthetic. "Sorry. I should've warned you."

"No, it's fine," she said. "It's just that I didn't notice anything wrong with your gait."

I tapped on the appendage. "It's not your run-of-the-mill prosthetic. It was custom-designed and built for me and the life I lead."

"If you don't mind saying, what happened to your real leg?"

I gave her a smile. "It was just a little boating accident overseas. Let's talk about you. Why do you want to leave the DOJ?"

She sighed. "I was afraid that was going to be your opening question, and my answer sounds corny, but it's true."

"Truth is what I want to hear, Doctor."

She waved a hand. "Please call me Celeste."

"Okay, then. Celeste it is, and I'm Chase. Now, back to the question."

She bounced her index finger against her thumb. "The truth is, I'm bored. There's just not that much to do, and living in DC on a government salary isn't a lot of fun."

I made a mental note and said, "Tell me about your patents. Are they yours, or does the government have a claim on them?"

"They're all mine with one exception. I designed and built a prototype boot sole that morphs between three designs for use in varying terrain. The prototype implemented a sand sole, a mud sole, and a mountain sole. That was one of my early designs, so I did the R and D on government time. It wasn't great, but it worked. I originally thought it would be invaluable to operators in Afghanistan, but it turns out that it may have a better use in covert operations to make it nearly impossible to leave identifiable boot tracks at an op site."

I couldn't stop the smile. Anya Burinkova, the woman who could've been the death of me, had just deposited a golden-egg-laying goose right in my lap. "Dr. Mankiller . . . Celeste. I think you're going to fit right in around here."

"Let's not get ahead of ourselves. I'm still not exactly clear on what it is you do here."

I propped my feet on the carriage of the cannon. "I've got a little office downtown where I practice clinical psychology. Outside of that, we collect toys like the Gulfstream and spend as much time as possible doing as little as possible."

She rolled her eyes. "That explains why you need a technical services officer. There's nothing like covert ops gadgets for a psychologist's office."

"You're catching on. So, tell me what you want to do since government service isn't holding your attention."

She didn't hesitate. "I want to design and build technology that's more advanced than anything that's currently available. I've got a billion ideas and no budget."

"How about commo gear?"

"Covert or overt?" she asked.

"Unless we say otherwise, consider everything covert."

She leaned forward as if bursting to tell me a secret only she knew. "You've heard of a Molar Mic, right?"

"Sure, but you didn't invent it. That's been on the market for years."

She shook her head. "No, I didn't invent the Molar Mic, but I've got something in the works that's a thousand times better. There's way too much that can—and does—go wrong when you stick a piece of electronics in somebody's mouth."

She paused as if it was my turn to talk, but I was hanging on every word.

"So, anyway, you know about bone conduction hearing, right?"

"A little."

She kept talking. "Bone conduction hearing devices have been around for years, just like the Molar Mic, but what no one has ever been able to do is use bone conduction to transmit instead of just receive. Sound is a simple thing. It's just vibrations, and turning vibrations into transmittable signals is hundred-year-old technology. The problem is in capturing those vibrations. That's where my device comes in. It's a tiny receiver implanted in the mandible. That's the jawbone." She ran her fingertips across her jawline.

"I know what the mandible is."

"Of course you do. I didn't mean to imply that you didn't."

"Relax," I said. "You're not going to offend me, or any of us for that matter. How far along are you in testing this device of yours?"

She grimaced. "That's the thing. The government won't agree to test a medical implant without FDA approval, so I've never actually tried it on a living human."

"Have you tried it on a dead guy?"

She blushed. "Well, yeah. I tried it on a cadaver, but getting vocal cords to create sound without a beating heart or operational lungs isn't so easy. I tried it on a chimpanzee, but their vocal range is so much different than ours, so it was a waste of time."

"Were there any adverse side effects on the chimp?"

"None. She's fine, and she's had the implant in place for over a year."

I watched a bald eagle dive on a baitfish twenty yards off the bank of the river. "Did you see that?"

Celeste looked over her shoulder. "See what?"

"The eagle. She just caught a fish."

"No, I didn't see it, but that's really cool."

"A pair of eagles moved in about a year ago, and they spend a lot of time fishing off my dock. The amazing thing about them is their tenacity. They miss their mark at least twenty times for every catch they make, but they don't get discouraged. They just keep trying until they come up with a fish. You're starting to sound like one of those eagles to me."

"Oh, yeah, definitely. I don't give up. If I know something works conceptionally, I'll follow it to the ends of the Earth to prove it works in practice."

I asked a few more questions and spent a lot of time listening to the perfect addition to our team. When my brain was incapable of ingesting one more tidbit of high-tech gadgetry, I said, "Listen. It's not entirely up to me, but I'm going to recommend that we give you an operating budget and the facilities to put your concepts into practice. What we do, as I'm sure you've figured out, is a lot more than practice psychology and fly airplanes. I've got a whole zoo full of chimps who'd love to be your crash test dummies, with or without FDA approval. If you're interested, I'll introduce you to the team, and they can take a few shots at you this afternoon."

Her eyes turned to saucers. "For real?"

I couldn't stop myself from chuckling at how the brilliant scientist sitting in front of me sounded so much like an excited little girl.

Introductions were made over lunch, and the continuation of Celeste's job interview played into the afternoon. When everyone, including Skipper, was adequately impressed, I said, "Let's talk brass tacks, Doctor."

"I told you to call me Celeste."

I held my expression. "We'll keep it formal for the next few minutes, if you don't mind. Tell me about your salary requirement."

She seemed to shrink into her chair. "I made one sixty-two last year, and even though that sounds like a lot of money, it's really not when you live in DC. It's crazy expensive up there."

I ignored her commentary. "What about facility requirements, not including the real estate?"

She cocked her head. "You mean, like a lab?"

"Yes. We have the real estate, but I need to know how much it'll cost me to build you the lab you need."

Her face took on the look of a frightened child. "That's a pretty big number. I mean, probably like half a million dollars."

"And how quickly are you going to be ready to start?"

"You mean, like full-time?"

"Yeah, that's how we work around here. We don't use part-time folks. I need everyone in this organization to focus on our missions without worrying if they can get off work from another part-time job to go somewhere and blow something up."

She dug her toe into the carpet in front of her chair. "I'd need to work out a notice. I've got a lot of irons in the fire back at the DOJ, so maybe like three or four weeks."

I said, "Okay. Step outside for a few minutes so we can talk about you behind your back, and we'll call you back inside when we're ready."

Without hesitation, she stood, walked through the door, and left my team in awe.

"Pretty impressive, huh?"

Everyone agreed, and Mongo said, "I guess that means I'm the second smartest one on the team now."

Skipper shot him a look. "You're already the second smartest. When she comes on board, you'll barely make honorable mention."

I said, "Is there any need to take a vote? Is anyone opposed to bringing her on board for a year?"

Heads nodded, and I asked, "What about a salary?"

When the discussion was over, I called Celeste back into the op center.

"You look nervous," I said.

"I am . . . a little."

"Don't be nervous. We want to make you an offer. We own seven empty buildings at what used to be the St. Marys Municipal Airport. It now belongs to us, and we operate it as a private airport. You can pick the building you like best, and we'll have it remodeled and equipped with whatever you need, but we disagree with your estimate of half a million."

She shrank again. "I was just guessing, and that was probably a little high. It's just that doing cutting-edge R and D requires a lot of—"

I held up a hand. "Relax. You've got the wrong impression. We don't think half a million is enough, and we're willing to foot the bill for whatever you need as long as you produce quality products that are directly applicable to our mission."

She appeared to relax. "Oh . . . wow."

I have another question before we talk about your salary. "Do you have anything keeping you in DC other than your job with the DOJ?"

She bowed her head. "I did, but not anymore. I was dating this guy who was a special agent, but a mission went south, and his career didn't survive. He broke it off with me, so to answer your question, no, there's nothing keeping me in DC."

"In that case, here's our offer. We'll pay for your move to St. Marys or this general area. You're not required to live in the city. We'll provide a house or apartment for one year so you don't have to make a financial investment right off the bat. We'll pay you two hundred thousand for one year. In that year, you'll design, develop, test, and implement technical equipment specifically suited to the operation of our team. You'll report directly to Mongo, sign an NDA, and work only on our projects during that year. We'll provide an operational budget for you to hire a small staff as needed. Oh, and I almost forgot. There's one more requirement."

She raised her eyebrows. "Yeah? Let's hear it."

"You put the bone conduction transmitter/receiver in my head first."

She grinned. "You've got a deal!"

Chapter 4

Welcome Aboard

Three weeks later, I followed Dr. Celeste Mankiller, formerly of the U.S. DOJ, into the freshly remodeled building that had been, for the first twenty years of its life, an aircraft hangar, but now looked more like a physics lab than a storage barn for somebody's aeronautical mistress. "Not bad, huh?"

She let out something akin to a combined sigh and grunt at the same time. "Not bad? That's the understatement of the century. It's fantastic."

I motioned toward an open door near the back corner of the lab. "The computer techs are finishing up the network installation now. Skipper designed the computer system. There's a secure off-site mainframe and five terminals here. You can have the techs get your personal laptop talking with the local network, and you'll be ready to go."

She stared in wonder at her new playground. "Is this seriously all for me? I mean, I didn't ask for anything this elaborate."

I motioned toward a low sofa and a pair of chairs around a circular coffee table. "Have a seat, Celeste. We need to have a little talk."

Her look of excitement morphed into instant discomfort. "Have I done something wrong already?"

"No, not at all. We simply need to understand each other. Your life has just changed more dramatically than it's possible for you to know. You're not a civil servant anymore. You're a servant of a much higher calling."

The intellectual inside the lighthearted scientist took over, and she nestled onto the end of the sofa. "I've been expecting this conversation."

"I'm sure you have," I said. "But it's probably not the pep talk you thought you'd get. Would you like some coffee or a drink?"

She shook her head as if eager to dive in, so I said, "There are no more time clocks to punch and no more bureaucracy to deal with. We're independent, and in many ways, invisible. Do you understand what I'm saying?"

She licked her lips. "It sounds like you're telling me I'm in for long hours."

"That's part of it, but that's not the important part. What I want you to take away from this little talk is that rules are out the window. Don't stifle your creativity. If you've got an idea, do it. If you want to try something, do it. If you want to test something on a human, you've got a whole team of willing guinea pigs at your disposal. If you want to test something potentially lethal, the world is full of bad guys in our sights, and we'd love to pull any trigger on any device you can dream up. Ultimately, I need you to stop thinking like an employee and start thinking like a mad scientist with a nearly unlimited budget."

Her look of concern turned diabolical as the parameters of her new career grew clearer. "What *are* you people?"

I gave her a wink. "We're nobodies from nowhere who don't exist, Dr. Mankiller, and now, you're one of us. Welcome to the island of misfit toys."

"This is going to be fun."

I stood. "You have no idea. Now, about your first order of business. When will you be ready to perform my surgery?"

"Surgery? I'm not that kind of doctor."

"Mad scientist," I corrected her. "And you promised me an implant in my jawbone."

"Oh, that. That's not surgery. It's just a tiny incision and some adhesive, but the FDA—"

I took her by the shoulders. "FDA? I've never heard of them. How does tomorrow at eight a.m. sound?"

* * *

While Celeste settled herself into her new playground, Clark called the meeting I'd been anticipating for weeks. To my surprise, though, he convened the gathering aboard *Aegis*, our 50-foot custom sailing catamaran. His opening shot made it clear why we weren't in the op center.

"It's on, gentlemen . . . and lady."

Skipper gave him an appreciative nod, and he continued. "It has become clear to the intelligence community that Turkmenistan has, without question, launched an unprovoked attack against their formerly friendly neighbor, Uzbekistan."

"Is it about the oil?" I asked.

Clark shrugged. "The NSA thinks so, but I'm not convinced."

The National Security Agency had never lived up to their title, as far as I was concerned. They did a lot of listening and pontificating, but I'd never seen an agent of that so-called agency draw a knife or pull a trigger to help me win a fight. "So, what do you think it's about?"

He sighed. "I don't know, but it doesn't taste like oil to me. My guess is the NSA knows what it's about, but they won't tell the

CIA, who, in turn, won't brief the Pentagon, who doesn't want to touch a shooting war in Asia."

"That's why the Board is involved, right?"

Clark gave me his slow nod. "You're getting better at this gig all the time, College Boy. Pretty soon, you won't need me at all."

"I'll always need you," I said. "Somebody has to keep my refrigerator cleaned out."

He checked his watch. "Speaking of groceries . . . I'm getting hungry."

"You're always hungry," I said. "But I just happen to have a secret that'll take care of that little problem."

Clark raised his gaze. "A secret?"

"Indeed. We're having a very special guest for dinner, and that's not all. We've invited a world-class chef to cater the affair."

Clark instantly forgot all about a land war in Asia. "Maebelle's coming?"

His wife and my cousin, Maebelle Huntsinger Johnson, was well on her way to her first Michelin Star for her masterful cuisine at el Juez, her showstopping restaurant on South Beach.

"Yep, I suspect she'll be here by the time we finish our briefing."

"In that case, let's get this thing in high gear," Clark said. He refocused and continued. "We're going in, but not as shooters. We're escorting a case officer from Central Intelligence while he gathers on-site hum-int."

I recoiled. "You mean the CIA doesn't have a case officer who can watch his own back while he works human intelligence?"

Clark pointed directly at me. "That's why I don't think this is about oil. The Agency is scared of something or somebody, and they can't dispatch SEALs or Delta with this guy. That means it's an off-the-books, completely black op."

Singer, our continual voice of reason, asked the question I wasn't smart enough to bring up. "So, we're taking assignments from the CIA now?"

Clark held up two fingers. "That's reason number two I don't think this has anything to do with oil, and the answer to your question is, I don't know. The assignment came to me through the Board, so on the surface, it looks legit, but we've never been assigned a babysitting mission for an Agency guy, so that leaves a weird taste in my mouth."

"Does the case officer know we're tagging along to keep him alive?" I asked.

"I'm still working on details, but I have to say yes to that one. Those guys are sharp enough to be spies, so there's no way we could sneak a team like ours into the country to watch their backs without knowing we were there."

Disco said, "Especially Mongo."

The giant covered his heart with both hands. "That's size-shaming, and it's hurtful. Take it back."

Clark cleared his throat. "That's enough. Here's the timetable. We'll filter in two by two through Kazakhstan, Kyrgyzstan, and Tajikistan over the next ten days and rendezvous with the case officer in-country."

"Whose idea is that?" I asked. "Do we know anything about this guy? Can he fight? Can he shoot? Does he have any language skills? Can he run if this whole thing goes to hell?"

Clark gazed across my shoulder and into the marshland across the North River. "That's not how things like this work."

"Things like what?" I asked. "Things like a team of civilian operators escorting an American CIA case officer into a warzone where he's got no business being and where he'll be denied by everybody in Washington if he gets caught? Just how many operations like this have you been on to know how they're supposed to work?"

Singer turned to me. "What's eating you, Chase? This isn't like you. What's going on?"

I ground the toe of my boot into *Aegis's* deck. "I'm one hundred percent in when we know and understand a mission that will make our country safer or save the lives of innocent American citizens, but I can't see either of those things being associated with this mission. The CIA can't send a clandestine service team because there's no official national interest, but they can send one case officer with us, a bunch of expendables. If we get screwed up over there, no one's coming to get us. You understand that, right?"

The quiet man of God softened his tone. "When was the last time we went on a mission believing we had backup if it went south?"

"This isn't the same," I said. "This is sticking our nose in somebody else's war we don't understand, and we've already picked a side based on a faulty assumption of oil."

"How do you know it's a faulty assumption?" Clark asked.

I leaned back and took a few deep breaths. "Look, I'll go. I just want to know who and what the CIA case officer is. How's he getting into the country?"

Clark stared into the overhead, apparently to gather his thoughts. "She's already in-country."

"She? The case officer is a woman? You can't be serious! This isn't an escort mission. This is a hostage rescue. They're sending us into a pair of Muslim countries where over eighty percent of the sane people practice Hanafi Sunnism, and the leftover crazy ones are still cutting heads off chickens and smoking opium."

I squeezed my eyelids closed and tried to hold my tongue, but I couldn't. "I need you to tell me you're on board with every aspect of this mission, and I need you to look me in the eye when you do it."

He couldn't, or wouldn't, but what he did say made more sense than I wanted it to. "She's an American, Chase, and she's in trouble. Her name is Teresa Lynn, and she's from Jacksonville, Florida. She was the acting COS in Tashkent."

"She *was* the acting chief of station?" I asked. "Tashkent is about as far away from Urgench as you can be and still be in Uzbekistan. Keep talking."

Clark pulled at his beard. "Okay, here's the dope as I know it. Ms. Lynn was the deputy chief of station in the embassy in Tashkent. Don't let that get you too excited. There were six case officers and two clerks on the CIA staff in Tashkent, so it's not like she was second-in-command of the Moscow station in nineteen sixty-five. She just happened to be the most senior case officer, so she fell into the DCOS role. She's got a good sheet—solid experience—and like I said before, she's got pretty good language skills. She's had her share of hard knocks along the way, but she kept her head above water. She's a good, loyal officer with a good track record."

"I thought you said she was the acting chief, not the deputy."

Clark said, "I did, but that changed while she was on assignment to Urgench. She'd apparently been in the field for eight days before the Turkmen attacked. After the attack, she was presumed dead but apparently went to ground and started working her local contacts and staying alive. She was finally able to make a call back to the embassy four days ago."

"I'm starting to like her," I said. "But we're still a long way from her becoming acting chief of station. Did they pick her up?"

"No. In fact, they did the opposite. The former chief left her out in the cold. That's when the ambassador stepped in and made a priority call to the secretary of state. The chief was immediately dismissed for cause and recalled to DC. However, he never made it home."

Clark had my full attention. "What do you mean?"

"I mean he vanished. The official flight he was supposed to be on landed in Stockholm, where he was supposed to change planes for the second leg to DC, but he never made the connecting flight across the Atlantic."

Kodiak, the newest operator on our team, had finally heard all he could take without jumping in. "So, this guy's in the wind?" Clark nodded, and Kodiak said, "I know I'm the new kid here, but I've been around the world killing bad guys for twenty years, and this sounds like some puredee bureaucratic BS to me. The chief of station dispatches his most senior case officer—who just happens to be a woman—undercover into a city that gets blown off the map a few days later, then refuses to dispatch a team to recover her when she reports in alive. SecState fires him and promotes the agent who's still out in the cold to replace said former chief. Am I on track so far?"

Clark nodded, and Kodiak kept talking. "Let me guess. When she finally got back to the embassy, she wasn't welcomed with open arms."

"That's where it gets tricky," Clark said. "She never made it back to the embassy. The three case officers who were dispatched to pick her up were found dead on the outskirts of Dashoguz, a border town northwest of Urgench on the Turkmenistan side."

Kodiak leaned back and ran both hands through his hair. "I'm starting to feel like I've finally found my people. It sounds to me like you guys just got handpicked to go kill a rogue CIA officer in Central Asia."

I slowly shook my head. "No, not *you* guys. *We* guys. Welcome to Team Twenty-One."

Chapter 5
Pocket Dump

The meeting aboard *Aegis* broke up, but I wasn't finished with Clark. "Hang back a minute. We need to talk."

He deposited himself back onto the sofa. "Yeah, I know . . ."

With the rest of the team back ashore, I poured three fingers of Angel's Envy and put a tumbler in his hand. "What was that about?"

He stared into the glass as the amber bourbon slowly devoured the ice. "This is no excuse, but I was ordered to limit the briefing to keep the intel compartmented."

"Compartmented? Is that what you call it when you hold back critical information from a mission brief? Information the team needs to know and understand before jumping into Hell in gasoline underwear?"

"I know . . . I know. It won't happen again, okay?"

I swallowed my first taste of the whiskey, savored the craftsmanship, and felt every year it spent in the white oak cask somewhere high in a rickhouse in Kentucky. "We've been through too much together for you to hold back critical intel."

He swirled his glass. "This one is different, Chase. I've never worked a mission like this one. This is a true national security situation with possible worldwide impact. If Case Officer Lynn is rogue, she has to be stopped before she kills more Americans."

"Do you think she's rogue?"

He took another sip. "No, I think she's on the run from a rogue station."

"Was Kodiak right? Are we supposed to kill her if we find her?"

"No. We're supposed to bring her in out of the cold."

"And if she doesn't want to come in?"

He said, "We're not delivering an invitation. We're bringing in a potentially rogue case officer."

I emptied my tumbler. "So, it's an apprehension."

"Maybe."

I leaned back and crossed my legs, exposing a few inches of my prosthetic. "There's no oil, is there?"

Clark placed his empty glass on the table between us. "There's probably some oil in the ground, but that's not what this is about. It's just a convenient cover story for what may be the defection of a senior American intelligence officer."

I ground the heels of my hands into my eyes. "Every new mission is a little more complex than the last one."

"That's how it works, kid, and it ain't gonna stop until we fail."

"I know. They'll keep pushing until we reach the limit of our capability, but why did they pick us for this one?"

"I don't know, but I can guess. We have operational knowledge of the region. We've got a stellar track record of completing missions at all costs. I mean, look at Hunter and Tony. We almost had to get the two of them killed to complete two separate missions. We're dedicated, competent, and proven. Isn't that the team you'd want on this assignment if you were calling the shots?"

I refilled our tumblers. "Who *is* calling the shots on this one?"

He raised his glass. "As far as I know, it's the Board. The president isn't going to authorize military boots on the ground until a direct threat to America is clear and present. Two former Soviet republics lobbing mortars at each other doesn't rise to that standard."

"But I was right about the government disavowing any knowledge of our presence if we get caught, wasn't I?"

"Probably," he said. "But that's why I'm glad this one is coming from the Board and not the Pentagon. The White House may not send anybody to get us, but the Board will."

"Is that everything you know?"

He took a sip and let it slide down his throat. "Yeah, that's all I know, but you're holding something back. Who's this mystery guest of ours that warrants Maebelle coming all the way up from Miami?"

I raised my glass and smiled. "You'll see. Just be prepared for a pocket dump."

He stood. "That sounds like fun."

"It will be."

The team spent the remainder of the afternoon mostly in the op center, poring over maps of Central Asia and committing the geography to memory. Just when every mountain started to look like every other mountain, the chime on the secure door pulled us from our misery.

Skipper flipped on the monitor, and Penny's face appeared on the screen. "Our guests are here, so come down when you find a stopping point."

I pressed the button on the mic built into the table in front of me. "We'll be right out."

Mongo stopped me at the door. "Who are these people, and why are you playing it so close to the vest?"

I planted a hand in the center of his two-acre back. "You'll see. Let's go."

I followed him down the stairs and watched his sullen demeanor explode into immeasurable excitement. Just inside the front door of the house stood a breathtaking beauty with eyes as blue as the sky and features nearly identical to those of her flawless mother.

Mongo lunged toward the young woman and lifted her into his arms. "Tatiana! Why didn't you tell me you were coming home?"

Tatiana, Mongo's stepdaughter and light of his life, was a senior at the Juilliard School of performing arts and one of the most talented ballerinas on any stage anywhere in the world.

She was so tiny in his arms, making it almost impossible to see her inside Mongo's bear hug.

"Mom knew I was coming. Why didn't she tell you?"

Mongo turned to Irina. "Yeah, why didn't you tell me?"

Irina tilted her head into the look that never failed to make the big man melt to his knees, and she pointed to the young man who'd been standing beside Tatiana before she'd been yanked from her feet. "Him."

Mongo looked down at the boy. "Who's he?"

Tatiana squirmed. "If you'll put me down, I'll introduce you."

Mongo lightly lowered his princess back to her ballerina toes, and she reached for the boy's hand and said, "Grayson, this is my dad, Mr. Malloy. And Dad, this is Grayson Knox. He's sort of my boyfriend."

"Your boyfriend? Why didn't I know you had a boyfriend?" Mongo spun to Irina. "Did you know? You knew, didn't you? You knew, and you didn't tell me because you thought I'd do something crazy."

He didn't wait for an answer. Instead, he turned back to the young man who was trembling in his loafers beside the girl Mongo adored beyond description. "Grayson? Is that what she said your name is? Grayson?"

"Yeah, Grayson Knox."

Mongo shot a look at me and quickly back to Grayson. "Yeah? It's yeah, and not yes, sir? Do you not understand the dynamic here?"

Tatiana stepped in front of him and laid her hand against his chest. "Dad, can you give him a chance? I think you'll like him."

Mongo couldn't take his eyes off Grayson. He studied every inch of the man-child, and I imagined him wondering if the boy even shaved yet. Finally, he said, "So, Grayson, what do you do?"

"I'm a classical pianist."

"A classical pianist? Is that a real job? Do you earn a living playing classical piano?"

"Well, no, not really . . . not yet. I won't graduate until later this year, but I hope to play for a theater company on Broadway."

"You hope?"

Irina reached for my arm. "Chase, please do something with him. This is thing I almost feared most."

"Almost?" I asked.

Her Russian accent grew even thicker. "Yes, first thing of fear was he might kill boy and sink body inside ocean."

Mongo raised a finger. "That option is still on the table."

"Chase, please," Irina pleaded.

I laid a hand against Mongo's shoulder. "Come on, killer. Let's go for a walk. I've got a tree stump you can yank out of the ground out back."

He turned with hesitance, but turn he did, and then followed me through the kitchen and to the gazebo.

"She's got a boyfriend, Chase. What am I supposed to do with that? Did you know?"

Suddenly, the fear that Mongo might sink my body inside ocean became a real possibility. "Well, Irina told me Tatiana was bringing a friend home, and she asked me not to mention it."

"Not to mention it? What? I saw you steaming in that briefing three hours ago. You were furious because Clark had intel he wasn't sharing, and you obviously felt like he didn't trust you with it. Sound familiar?"

I swallowed hard. "You're right. I should've told you, but I didn't want to break Irina's trust."

"A little heads-up would've been nice. Did you see that kid? What is he, like twelve? And a classical pianist? What kind of man makes a living playing classical piano?"

I leaned forward and gazed around the muzzle of the cannon at my injured friend. "I'm sorry I didn't tell you, but Tatiana obviously cares about Grayson, and having a little faith in her character judgment might go a long way. You don't want to push her away because you don't instantly love her boyfriend."

Mongo pounded on the arms of his oversized Adirondack chair. "I just can't deal with the thought of any boy touching Tatiana. You know . . . that way."

"I'll never have a daughter," I said. "But I get it. You fell in love with that little girl the instant you met her, and she'll always be that tiny little princess who wrapped you around her pinky finger. But you have to let her grow up."

He growled. "Yeah, but with *that* guy? He's a buck thirty, tops, and you can look at him and tell he's never been in a gym a day in his life. What's he going to do when somebody tries to mess with Tatiana? Play them a classical piano tune and hope they're afraid of a B-flat minor chord?"

I let him steam for a moment before saying, "Would you rather see her with a knuckle-dragging gun-toter like one of us?"

"Of course I would. Well, maybe not exactly a knuckle-dragger. Maybe not a soldier. Maybe somebody like Singer or Disco—somebody who's soft on the outside and rock hard in his gut."

"Have you ever told Singer or Disco that's how you see either of them?"

He shook his head. "Don't change the subject. We're still talking about you keeping me from killing that Garret kid for touching my daughter."

"His name is Grayson, and maybe Tatiana's right. Maybe you will like him when you get to know him."

Mongo lowered his chin and stared through my face. "We're doing a pocket dump at dinner, and there's nothing you can do to stop it."

I couldn't resist chuckling. "I'm already loaded, and so is Clark. I'll make sure to tell the rest of the gun-toters."

Maebelle stuck her head through the kitchen door and yelled across the yard. "Dinner's ready in fifteen, so you boys come get washed up. You don't want to miss what I've whipped up."

I pushed myself from my chair. "Don't kill the boy at dinner, okay?"

Mongo groaned. "I'll try not to, but if he drinks with his pinky in the air, I can't make any promises."

Clark beat me to the prep work for the planned pocket dump. Everyone, including Irina and Penny, was well prepared.

Dinner was a five-course masterpiece, and Maebelle was a brilliant master of ceremonies. She'd hired two waiters from the local bed and breakfast downtown to serve so we could all relax and enjoy ourselves around the family table.

There had been a time when such dinners were quite common at Bonaventure, but as our lives grew more complicated, the dining affairs fell by the wayside. It was nice to have so many people I loved around the table, but I couldn't quiet the devil's laughter in the back of my mind at the terrible prank we were about to play on young, innocent, unsuspecting Grayson, and I prayed Tatiana would find as much humor in the moment as me.

Dessert and coffee arrived, and Grayson raised a hand. "None for me, please."

Mongo had done relatively well up until that moment. "None for you? What's that supposed to mean?"

Grayson said, "I don't drink caffeine or eat sweets."

"You don't drink coffee?" Mongo asked, disbelief glaring from his face.

"Uh, no, I don't. I take care of myself, and I don't put things in my body I'll have to overcome."

Mongo shot a look at me. "It's time."

I cleared my throat. "Listen, Grayson . . . We've got a couple of questions. You don't really know us yet, but we're the kind of people who believe in some things that a lot of people consider old-fashioned, and maybe even archaic, but we still think they're pretty important." I motioned toward the women around the table. "We love these women, and we feel an enormous responsibility to protect them from everything and everyone who might ever try to harm them."

Grayson followed my outstretched hand, apparently waiting for one of the women to protest, but no such argument came.

I continued. "You see, we love Tatiana just as much—"

Mongo interrupted. "I'll take it from here, Chase."

I suppressed the coming smile, but barely.

Mongo said, "What Chase is trying to say is that there's a long history of chivalry in the South and especially in this family. Nobody gets away with threatening the women we love, and God forbid that any man should ever lay a hand on any of them. Am I getting through to you, Gregory?"

"It's Grayson, sir."

Mongo's face lit up. "Ah, there's the sir I've been expecting. Now, let's get back to the point at hand. I'm sure you agree that a good man should protect the woman he loves at all costs, right?"

"Well, yes, within reason."

"Reason? Indeed. Just what may I ask is the reasonable limit a man should go to in order to protect his wife?"

"Well, resorting to violence would certainly be out of the question," Grayson said.

Tatiana buried her face in her hands. "Don't do it, guys. Please."

Her plea was genuine, but we were undaunted.

Mongo said, "We believe you can tell a lot about a man by what he carries in his pockets on any given day. There's even a phrase for that stuff in our world. It's called EDC, or everyday carry items. Let's see what you're carrying, Grayson."

Tatian's boyfriend looked as if he'd just been asked to explain quantum mechanics, and Tatiana shook her head. "Go ahead, Grayson. Get it over with. Show them what's in your pockets."

Hesitant but compliant, Grayson pulled his wallet from a hip pocket and laid it on the table.

Mongo leaned toward the wallet and examined the leatherwork. "Who's that supposed to be?"

Grayson spun the wallet so the silhouette was upright. "That's Beethoven. He's sort of my favorite composer. Did you know he was completely deaf when he composed Symphony Number Nine?"

Mongo slid an enormous finger across the wallet. "Deaf? Really?"

"Yeah, he started going deaf in his late twenties and was completely deaf by his early forties. He died young like a lot of people in the early eighteen hundreds. He was fifty-six. How old are you, Mr. Malloy?"

Mongo shoved the wallet back toward Grayson. "What else have you got?"

The boy dug into his pockets and withdrew a handkerchief, seventy cents in change, and a cell phone. "That's it. I don't usually carry change, but Tati wanted a drink at the airport."

"Tati?" Mongo roared.

"Yes, sir. That's kind of what I call her most of the time. It's meant to be—"

"Just stop," Mongo said. "I don't see how you're going to protect anybody with a wallet adorned with the shadow of a dead deaf guy, some change, and a cell phone. I'll give you credit for the handkerchief, though. A gentleman always carries a handkerchief, but carrying a handkerchief doesn't make you a gentleman."

"Okay," Grayson said, dragging out the word as if he had no understanding of what Mongo was talking about.

I reclaimed the floor. "You see, young man, if somebody came through that door right now who wished to do harm to any of us, especially the women we love, I'm afraid the contents of your pockets would be lacking in terms of your capability to prevent such violence. We, on the other hand, are not lacking in either capability or willingness to stop those who may wish us harm. Gentlemen, shall we empty our pockets?"

Without a word, the warriors at the table produced fourteen handguns, eleven fighting knives, eighteen pieces of paracord, cigar punches and lighters, over ten thousand dollars in cash, four pairs of handcuffs, and a dozen keys.

Grayson stared in wide-eyed disbelief at the display of weaponry on the table before him, but the show was far from over.

Penny said, "Just so you'll know this isn't a sexist little game our beloved men like to play, we're well prepared to defend ourselves while they're on the far side of the world keeping freedom ringing. Show him, girls."

Penny, Irina, Maebelle, and Skipper dumped their pockets, revealing their own impressive arsenal of personal protection equipment.

I expected Tatiana to be at least a little embarrassed for her boyfriend, but to my surprise, she gave him a smile and motioned toward the open space in the dining room. "Go ahead, Grayson. Show them."

He ducked his head. "I don't think that's a very good idea."

"Oh, it's a great idea," Tatiana said. "Show them why my man doesn't have to carry all that stuff."

Grayson sighed and slowly rose from his seat. "Okay, but which one? Please not your dad."

Our pocket dump had just turned interesting, and Clark said, "I'll volunteer."

Grayson eyed him. "I don't want to hurt you. I mean, you're like the oldest guy here."

Clark curled a finger. "Bring it, piano boy."

Tatiana giggled. "Go ahead, Clark. Take him down."

My handler folded his napkin and placed it beside his dessert plate. "Okay, but remember . . . You asked for it."

He lunged at the boy, but Grayson sidestepped the advance and wrapped his arms around Clark's head and neck as he slid behind him and drove a knee into the back of Clark's thigh, sending him to the ground with the pianist's choke hold locked in place. Clark squirmed and tried to roll, but the more he moved, the more Grayson improved his position, and the more Clark's brain demanded oxygen.

Finally, Clark tapped out by patting Grayson's leg several times in rapid succession.

Grayson released my handler and even helped him to his feet. "I didn't hurt you, did I?"

Clark adjusted his shirt and reclaimed his spot at the table at the same instant Tatiana said, "Grayson is a fourth-degree black belt in Brazilian jiu-jitsu."

Mongo scoffed. "Yeah, but somebody still needs to teach him to drink coffee like a man."

Chapter 6
But Not with Your Ears

After dinner, I caught Clark on his way out of the dining room and leaned in to whisper, "You just got choked out by a piano player."

His knuckles against my ribs reminded me that it's not a great idea to poke the bear when the bear happens to be Clark Johnson.

We settled in the great room, and those of us who drank coffee did so. Grayson did not. Tatiana nudged her boyfriend and motioned toward the grand piano consuming more than its share of the room.

His eyes lit up. "May I?"

Penny jumped up and immediately cleared the bench of the notes she'd been working on. "Yes, please! This old thing would love to have somebody play it correctly. I just play around with some melodies when I'm writing."

Grayson stood. "Do you compose?"

My wife shook her head. "Oh, no. What I do is more like compost than composition. Sometimes music pops into my head when I'm writing a scene, and I like to see if I can play it."

Grayson smiled. "That's called composing, and I'm sure you're great at it. What do you write?"

Penny almost blushed. "Screenplays mostly, but some poetry and short stories. I've got a novel bouncing around in my head, but I don't know if I'll ever get it on paper."

"Screenplays? Awesome. Do you have an agent?"

Penny gave me a look and turned back to our guest. "Yeah, I've got an agent and four major motion pictures under my belt."

Grayson recoiled. "Oh, wow! That really is awesome. I didn't know I was going to be playing in front of a real live celebrity."

"Oh, I'm no celebrity. Nobody knows the writers' names. We're just faceless shadows way in the back."

The young man took a seat on the bench and stretched his fingers over the keys. When he began to play, the room fell silent of every sound except the beautiful music resounding from the piano I'd considered nothing more than a useless piece of furniture before that moment. The instant he finished the first classical piece, he broke into a raucous rendition of "Great Balls of Fire," and the mood of the room changed in a snap.

Ten minutes later, Singer had taken our breath away with a soul-stirring version of "How Great Thou Art" over Grayson's hypnotic mastery of the piano. Applause came, and Singer took a small bow.

Grayson spun on the bench and asked, "Do you guys have a set of noise-canceling headphones?"

The looks on our faces must've appeared strange because he chuckled. "They're not for me. I want to show Mr. Malloy how Beethoven could compose even after he went deaf."

Penny pulled out a set of Bose and tossed them to Mongo.

Grayson said, "Perfect. I know this is going to seem weird, but put on the headset and turn on the noise canceling while I play softly."

Mongo followed the instructions until Grayson made the hand signal to remove the headphones. "You couldn't hear what I was playing, could you?"

Mongo said, "I could hear it a little, but not much."

Grayson scooted to one end of the bench and patted the empty space beside him. "Come sit here. This is when it gets really weird, but stick with me. You're gonna love this."

Mongo slid onto the bench, leaving me wondering just how much weight the seat could support.

Grayson said, "Okay, now put the headphones back on and lean forward until you can rest your upper teeth on the edge of the piano."

Mongo spun toward Penny and yanked off his headset. "Are you okay with me putting my teeth on your piano?"

She smiled and gave him a nod, so the big man replaced the headset and touched the rim of the piano with his two front teeth. Grayson played softly, and Mongo jumped back as if he'd been shot. "That's crazy! I can hear it through my teeth."

Grayson said, "Yep. Sound is a pretty cool thing. Nobody knows for sure if Beethoven did that while he was composing, but it's one of the ways it might've been possible for him to create such beautiful work, even while trapped inside his own silent world."

I don't think Clark was on board yet, but Mongo was clearly warming up to the idea of accepting Grayson into the family.

* * *

Young Grayson wasn't the only one at Bonaventure who understood precisely how sound works. I strolled into Dr. Celeste Mankiller's little shop of horrors the next morning with Disco and Clark in tow.

Celeste looked up from her computer as if she'd been asleep. "Oh, hey. I'm sorry I didn't hear you come in. I was engrossed in something. Are you ready for your implant?"

I said, "Yes, ma'am, and I brought a couple of additional volunteers. We figured the more data you can gather, the quicker this thing will be ready for the field."

"You're right about that," she said. "But we have to make some decisions first. This device is an extremely short-range transmitter, so it has to be associated with an external transmitter to broadcast the signal via whatever means you want. If you want it to work through a satellite network—and that would be my recommendation—you'll have to run a sat-phone or secure uplink as part of your kit."

"I thought that might be the case," I said. "For now, let's set it up for satellite-coms because that's our most common method of communication."

"Already done," she said. "Now, let's get you on the operating table."

"Operating table? I thought you told me it was just a simple injection."

"I'm messing with you. Just have a seat and relax. I promise not to hurt you too badly."

She pulled a small bottle of topical anesthetic and sprayed it on the skin of my jaw. Next, she withdrew a terrifying syringe from its packing. A few seconds later, she was finished, and I was fitted with my own personal commo device.

"How long will this thing work without being recharged, and does it have to come out to be recharged?"

"That's one of the best parts. I designed and built it to run off the energy within your body. It's not a perpetual motion machine, but, in theory, it could work for ten years or more without being replaced. That wouldn't make any sense, of course, because technology will change over the next decade, and this thing will be obsolete in a year."

I said, "As long as it works, we'll take it."

She repeated the procedure on Disco and Clark, and we were soon communicating through a secure satellite uplink without an exposed microphone. It took several minutes to adjust to the ethereal sounds playing in our skulls, but even after listening to each other for several minutes, something still wasn't right.

Clark put it best. "We sound like ghosts trying to talk underwater. Is this as good as it gets?"

Celeste grabbed a contraption that looked more like a twisted coat hanger than anything else and stuck it on her head. After several seconds of warping and shaping the wire tiara, she said, "Give me some conversation. Just say anything."

We talked about nothing for several seconds as she listened and typed furiously on her laptop. Without a word, she leapt to her feet and nabbed our sat-com transceivers. She had the plastic cases off in seconds and worked furiously with tiny screwdrivers inside some of the most expensive portable coms gear on the planet. I wanted to trust her, but that screwdriver inside those critical pieces of equipment made me more than a little nervous.

I wasn't the only one.

Clark said, "Do you see what she's doing? Are you sure about this?"

"Let's give her a little latitude and see what happens."

"She's retuning our sat-coms is what she's doing, and those things are ten grand a piece."

I stepped toward her bench, ready to share our concerns, but before I could open my mouth, she shoved one of the transceivers into my hand.

"Here. Try it now."

I stuck the radio on my belt while she passed the remaining two to Disco and Clark. The next sound I heard bouncing eerily inside my head was Clark's crystal-clear voice, followed by Disco's. It was almost as if we could hear each other's thoughts before they became words.

I shut down my radio and hopped onto the corner of the workbench. "Dr. Mankiller, you've just earned your first year's salary. These things are amazing."

She leaned back with a look of utter satisfaction. "If monkeys or cadavers could talk, these things would've been on the market two years ago."

I said, "For our sake, I'm glad they can't. The rest of the team will be here before close of business for their implants. We've got a little field trip planned to Central Asia, where these babies will come in quite handy."

She froze. "Oh, no. They're not ready for fielding yet. We've still got months of trials to conduct before I'm ready to release them."

That gave the three of us a good chuckle. "We just did your trials, and your baby works. What better way to test it than to put it into real-world use? If they fail, we'll have backup coms."

"Are you sure?" she asked.

"We're absolutely sure, and now we're even more convinced that we made the right decision bringing you on board. Keep working, Doctor. You're going to save the world one day, and you don't even know it yet."

* * *

To our surprise, we found Mongo at the range with Grayson, and he wasn't pointing a gun at the boy.

"What's going on here?" I asked.

Mongo looked up. "The kid's never shot a gun. Can you believe that? Do you know anybody who's never shot a gun?"

I said, "I hope we made it in time to see his first shot."

"You did," Mongo said. "We've been working on manipulation, mechanics, and dry-firing. You're just in time."

Mongo's gentle nature made him one of the greatest dichotomies on our team. In spite of his strength and massive physique, he could be the most calming voice in the room.

"Don't think about the bang," he said just above a whisper. "Just think about steadily pressing the trigger. When it breaks, try not to flinch. Just pin that trigger to the rear and maintain your firing position. Got it?"

"Yes, sir."

Seconds later, the 9mm Glock cycled, fired, and bucked in Grayson's hands.

Almost before the resounding roar quieted, Mongo said, "Good . . . Very good. Now, slowly release the trigger until you feel it reset, then press it again. Do that three more times, just the way you fired the first one."

Mongo stepped behind Grayson, and the pistol roared and recoiled three more times.

"Well done," Mongo said. "Now, drop the magazine, eject the round from the chamber, and lock the slide to the rear."

The pianist's fingers appeared to be equally at home on the controls of the Glock as they had been on the keys of Penny's piano.

He pulled his hearing protection from his ears and laid them on the bench. "That was amazing. I've always thought guns were scary and dangerous and even a little evil."

Mongo pulled the plugs from inside his ears. "Guns are just machines, son. They don't have the capacity for evil. Evil exists in the hearts of men, not in the polymer and steel of a pistol. That gun can't hurt anybody. It's an inanimate object with no will or agenda of its own. When a person with evil intentions picks up a gun, it's the person who is evil, not the tool. That person can do the same damage and more with a car, or a baseball bat, or a knife. Evil lives in the hearts of men, Grayson, not in the weapons those men choose to use."

Clark took over Mongo's teaching duties while I rounded up the rest of the team for their visit with our new doctor.

Chapter 7
Downrange

There's a place inside the warrior's soul that can never be seen or understood by those who live their lives blindly ignorant to the true nature of good and evil. In the loving arms of his family, the warrior sees the epitome of innocence and the beauty of a life untouched by evil, and those are the anchors that tie him to his ultimate responsibility to boldly step between all he loves and the forces that would destroy them. He's drawn to the field of battle, be it the sodden trenches of Europe or the body-strewn beaches of Normandy, the seething jungles of Southeast Asia or the endless foreboding mountains of Afghanistan. He's drawn to these hellish places because he's one of the chosen, the select, who must never beat his swords into a plowshare, who must never lay down his armor and cast off his boundless debt to those who've bled and died before him to preserve what they loved when the sun shone on their faces. Those mortal men shed their life on the bloodthirsty ground to blaze the path he must now follow so those who'll come after him will know that he stood in the face of the beast, without the weakness of fear in his heart, and drove his dagger into the breast of tyranny to pay the awful price that must be paid by every generation if the things we love and hold dear are to endure another day, another hour, another timeless instant.

Such was the soul of the men and women around me the morning Clark Johnson looked into my eyes and gave the order none of us could deny. "It's time."

Our Gulfstream IV *Grey Ghost* would be the steed on which we would ride into battle, but she could only take us so far. We packed the gear that would keep us alive and provide the tools we'd need in the uncertainty of a warzone halfway around the globe, and we spent priceless moments holding the ones we loved.

I took Penny's hands in mind. "I don't know when I'll be back, but this has to be done."

She pulled her hand from mine and laid it on the center of my chest. "I cry for you and for myself every time you leave, but that heart beating inside your chest is the purest love I've ever seen, and although I'll never understand why it has to be you, I'll always love knowing you're the kind of man who'll always answer that call. Come home to me, Chase. Don't make me a widow. Not this time."

I pulled her against my chest and felt her sobbing as a thousand words poured through my mind, but none of them were worthy of the breath I'd waste if they came from my lips. The love and honesty between us were enough. The embrace was enough. The moment was enough to express the pain that would come while we were apart, while I was chasing a ghost in the name of finding truth and pursuing ever-elusive peace.

I imagined every soul on my team feeling and experiencing something similar in the arms of their loved ones in the moments before we shed the light, soft clothes of a man of peace to don the weighty armor a warrior must bear.

Some men laugh or joke as the miles between themselves and the fight melt away and they draw ever nearer to the moment they'll pay the ultimate price, but the gladiators around me sat mostly in silence as we cut through the frigid, high-altitude air over the North Atlantic.

Disco and Clark flew the *Grey Ghost* with the precision of surgeons. Mongo sat, stoically peering through the window at the endless expanse of icy water in every direction. Kodiak mindlessly ran the blade of his knife across a whetstone, slowly polishing away everything that wasn't razor-sharp. Perhaps we were all doing the same to our minds in preparation for what was to come. Singer appeared to sleep, but anyone who knew him understood that he was lost in the midst of prayer, pouring out his heart to his god and reveling in that communion of soul and spirit.

I was lost in my own world, peering from deep within to bring the reality of what we'd soon face into clear focus. Was I walking blindly into a scene I'd never escape? Was CIA Case Officer Teresa Lynn running for her life, or was she the threat from which everyone else was running? Did she kill the three officers sent to pluck her off the war-torn street, or had she watched them die at the hands of their common enemy as she escaped into the night? Would I make the same escape, or would my corpse come to rest just as those three had done so far from home? With every thundering tick of the second hand, I drew an instant closer to every answer, especially the ones I lacked the courage to ask.

Disco finessed the wheels of the *Grey Ghost* onto the runway at Reykjavik, Iceland, and we rolled to a stop outside a massive hangar on the north side of the airfield.

Clark twisted himself to peer into the cabin. "Sit tight, guys. They're going to pull us inside."

I leaned around to see Clark in the seat in front of me. "Why?"

"Just sit tight, College Boy. You'll see in a minute."

Just as Clark had predicted, the tug clamped onto our nose gear, and we moved slowly through the enormous hangar doors. A fuel truck followed us into the space, and someone closed the doors behind us. To my surprise, the cabin door popped open, and a man in an open-collared shirt and sport coat stepped aboard.

Mongo slipped from his seat and consumed the space in front of the man. "Who are you?"

The man studied Mongo and held up both hands. "Relax. I'm on your team. The name's Ben from Langley."

Mongo didn't relax. Instead, he said, "Clark, do you know this guy, and is he supposed to be on our plane?"

Clark said, "He's okay, but close the door behind him."

Instead of making room for Mongo to get to the door, the man who claimed to be Ben pulled it closed and secured the latch. When he turned back around, he seemed to take note of every detail inside the *Ghost*. "Nice."

"Thanks," I said. "What do you want, Ben from Langley?"

The man checked the cockpit. "You two might want to join us back here."

Disco and Clark crawled from the drivers' seats and nestled into a pair of plush captain's chairs.

Before getting too comfortable, Clark stuck out his hand. "I'm Clark Johnson."

Ben ignored the gesture. "I know, and I have some uncomfortable news for you. The Shymkent Airport is closed."

Clark asked, "What does that have to do with us? We're not going to Shymkent."

Ben said, "I know where you were going, Mr. Johnson, and I'm telling you the airport isn't available."

Clark crossed his legs. "Well, thanks for the update, Skippy, but you don't know anything about us, where we're going, or what we're doing, so that leaves you with only two options. The first and better option would be for you to turn around, walk back down those stairs, and disappear back to Langley or wherever you really came from. The second is for you to tell me exactly who you are, what you want, and who sent you."

The man didn't flinch. "I told you. I'm Ben from Langley, and that's all you need to know. The Shymkent Airport is closed, and your little band of merry tooth fairies can turn around and flitter back to your little compound down in Georgia. The so-called *Board* isn't running this operation, so step aside and let the grown-ups handle our business."

Clark turned on his canned laughter and slapped his knee. "Oh, Benny Boy, that's a good one. Tooth fairies . . . Now, that's funny."

Clark froze, turning his laughter to a piercing stare. "Listen closely, Ben. Get off our airplane and out of our way. We're not your enemy unless you decide to make us exactly that, and if that's what you do, you likely won't live long enough to regret the decision. You see, here's how I've got it figured. You're either an ambitious young case officer looking to make your chops in the Agency, or you're somebody's pawn sent to do a job you're not smart enough to understand. Either way, you're of no value to me, and I don't have time to deal with no-value elements, so walk away, Benny Boy."

He pointed a finger directly into Clark's face, and everyone aboard the plane, except Ben, knew precisely what was about to happen. Clark may have put a few birthdays astern, but he was anything but slow. The speed and violence with which he broke Ben's pointed finger would've been terrifying if Clark hadn't been on our side.

Mongo was on his feet in an instant, and Disco already had the door open before Ben realized how badly he was hurt. The collision of the back of his head striking the concrete floor of the hangar would only add insult to injury, but the man wasn't yet convinced he was out of the fight. With his one healthy hand, he reached inside his jacket and discovered an empty holster where his pistol should've been.

Clark held up the Sig Sauer by its trigger guard. "Looking for this?"

"You don't know who you're messing with, Johnson!"

Clark examined the pistol. "I suppose you're right, but we'll know everything there is to know about you as soon as we run your fingerprints from your Sig and a DNA panel from the blood your broken finger produced. Nice work, Ben. Now, crawl on back to Daddy . . . whoever that is. And keep your nose—and your broken finger—out of our business. Oh, and one more thing. Tell your daddy the tooth fairy won't be leaving any change under your pillow."

Without looking up, Clark gave the order. "Set security."

We poured from the plane and spread out to protect our position. With the *Grey Ghost* inside the hangar, we were far more vulnerable than I liked, and our environment was almost entirely out of my control. I've never been good at submission, and I wasn't going to change that day.

The fuel truck driver stepped from the cab and stared at the scene in front of him. I tried to imagine his confusion if he were innocent. A man with a broken finger lying on his back beneath another guy holding a pistol inside a service hangar in Iceland is not an everyday scenario, so I didn't want to shake things up more than necessary.

Planting a boot in front of the fuel guy, I stopped him in his tracks. "What's your name?"

"Paul. And what's going on?"

I leaned down to his line of sight. "Listen to me, Paul. I don't know you, and you don't know me, so we're going to work together to change that." Pointing to Ben, still on his back, I asked. "Do you know that man?"

Paul shook his head.

"Have you ever seen him before?"

Paul nodded. "He's been here for an hour or maybe more, but I never saw him before that."

"All right. I believe you, but not enough to let you touch my airplane, so here's what's going to happen. You're going to take a seat on the ground beneath the tail of my plane so I can see you. Got it?"

He turned toward his truck. "But what about the fuel?"

"I'll take care of the fuel. You just sit on the floor beneath the tail. We're the good guys, Paul." I pointed to Ben. "He is not, and I don't have time to determine if you are, so I have to control you while I fuel my airplane. Make sense?"

He nodded and planted himself exactly where I wanted him. With Paul sitting in that spot, I could see him from almost any position around the plane. The perimeter was covered by the rest of the team, but we were just six men, one of whom was occupied by fueling the plane, and a second who had his hands full babysitting Ben.

It took just over fifteen minutes to fuel the Gulfstream, and I stuck more than enough cash into the fuel truck to cover the bill.

"Let's go!" I yelled.

Clark and Disco ran backward toward the plane with their eyes and weapons still trained on the exterior of the hangar.

"I've got the door," I said as they passed me on their way up the stairs.

Seconds later, the engines whistled themselves to life, and the plane began its long, lumbering turn to the left. I shoved the hangar door controls to their limit and watched the forty-foot-tall doors glide apart. I jogged at the tip of the right wing as Clark and Disco taxied the plane from the hangar and onto the tarmac. The rest of the team collapsed toward the plane as it continued its taxi until we'd reached the edge of the parking ramp. With the *Ghost* still rolling, we climbed the stairs one by one until we were all safely aboard.

I secured the door and yelled into the cockpit, "Let's roll!"

We climbed away from Reykjavik and back over the North Atlantic until the island was little more than a speck on the horizon astern.

I stuck my head into the cockpit. "What was that?"

Without looking up, Clark said, "That was proof that whatever we're walking into ain't what it appears to be."

Chapter 8
It's Classified

When we reached our cruising altitude, Clark emerged from the cockpit and took a seat in the main cabin with the rest of the team. "Nice work back there, guys. That could've gotten ugly, and it definitely means it's time to come up with a new plan. We're obviously on somebody's radar, and that somebody doesn't want us on this mission. Any ideas?"

I said, "I think we have to assume they know our plan, regardless of who *they* are."

Mongo said, "That's the beauty of having a terrible plan. Everybody's happy to change it. We've never talked about our boots-on-the-ground plan, so all they could know is which three airports we have in mind."

I said, "I agree, so those three airports are out. They'll obviously track us. In fact, they're probably already doing so. We need some options."

"I'm on it," Kodiak said.

Soon, Skipper's voice rang through the speakers, and a map of Central Asia appeared on the monitor. "Okay, guys. Listen up. Kodiak briefed me on what we know so far. Obviously, that means we have to pick another hard spot to land, but that's not a challenge. We've got a lot of options. Take a look at the map."

Every eye turned to the monitor, and from her perch back in the Bonaventure op center, Skipper zoomed in. "Option one is Nukus International in Uzbekistan. It's a nine-thousand-foot run-way, and nobody seems to care that it's still an airport. There's a flight every other day from and to Moscow, but that's about it."

"I like it," I said. "Do you have any other options as good as Nukus?"

"No, I started with the best one, but just know if you get there and have to abort, the range of the *Grey Ghost* and availability of long, hard strips of concrete will make bailing out a breeze."

"It almost sounds too easy," I said. "Figure out the Russian flight schedule and what the flight numbers are. We may be able to use the Russian flight as a cover if we need it."

"I like where your head's at," she said. "I'll get on it. In the meantime, I'll start listening for leaks. Somebody let the cat out of the bag on our planned infiltration points, and we need to know who it was."

"I agree, and the fact that the Board was so insistent on Clark keeping us in the dark on the details probably means the pool of possible culprits is quite shallow."

Skipper said, "I'll find them, whoever they are."

Disco had been listening through his headset in the cockpit and said, "I like what you're thinking about hiding behind the Russian flight, but we're going to need a plan to get on the ground without whoever Ben works for knowing where we are. I've got an idea, but I'm not saying it's the best one."

"Let's hear it," I said.

"We're still headed for Shymkent, but we obviously can't land there."

Clark said, "I doubt that it's really closed."

"Closed or not," Disco said, "we can't go where they're expect-ing us to go. That's tradecraft one-oh-one. I do like Skipper's idea of Nukus, though. I've actually been there, but that's a story for another day. There's enough questionable ATC service between here and Nukus for us to legitimately get lost in the system. If we can get on the ground at Nukus under a Russian call sign, that would be a killer cover story."

"Can you pull that off?" Skipper asked.

Disco paused as if playing through the possibility. "Maybe, but not without you. We're going to need a fictional flight departing from somewhere plausible and landing at Nukus."

Skipper said, "Give me a minute."

We waited in silence as the wheels inside her head spun up, and she finally said, "Got it! Sevastopol in Crimea."

Disco said, "I love it. There's plenty of dead air between here and there. Getting lost will be a snap, but we'll have to play the presto-change-o down to the minute."

Skipper said, "Don't you worry about that, Fly Boy. I'll take care of the timing. You just take care of getting lost."

"Oh, I'm good at that," he said. "I'll give you a thirty-minute window when I find a way down the rabbit hole."

"That's more than enough. I'm on it now, and I'll be standing by."

Clark said. "That changes the ground game. We're not splitting up anymore, but we're inserting into a blind LZ."

Disco said, "It's not as blind as you might think. I told you I've been in there before, so I know the lay of the land, and if the whole place hasn't been blown off the map, there's a nice little hangar where the old *Ghost* will feel right at home."

Clark clicked his tongue against his teeth. "I think I'd like to hear the story of how you ended up flying into Nukus the first time."

Disco chuckled. "It's classified."

Clark stood to return to the cockpit, but I stopped him. "Don't you think we need to talk about what's going to happen when we hit the ground?"

He said, "We don't have enough information to make a plan, but if you want to throw one together, I'll listen."

I studied the best aerial photo Skipper could find of the airport and surrounding area of Nukus. Thankfully, the airport appeared to be usable, in spite of the shelling from Turkmenistan.

"How recent is this shot?" I asked.

She said, "It's about forty-eight hours old, but there will be an NRO satellite overhead in ninety minutes. If the weather is good, I'll grab up-to-date shots."

"Let me know as soon as you have them. In the meantime, I need some background on Teresa Lynn. If you can get a lead on anybody who might be one of her contacts in or around Urgench, that would be a great start."

Skipper said, "Oh, sure. I'll just hack into the CIA's network and dig around until I find her notes on who she hangs out with when she's having a holiday in Urgench. Seriously, Chase, how do you expect me to get those answers for you?"

"I don't know how you do any of the stuff you do, but you've never let me down. I'm sure you can figure it out."

She huffed. "Is there anything else I can do for you while you're making wishes, Your Majesty?"

"I think I like the sound of that. Maybe you should keep calling me Your Majesty."

"Oh, I've got some names for you, but that isn't on the short list."

"You're the best, Skipper. Thanks."

I stepped into the small galley and threw a few sandwiches together to feed the restless natives while my brain ran through a thousand scenarios on what might happen within seconds of us hitting the ground in Nukus.

Kodiak took a sandwich from my hand. "You're worried about what kind of mess we're falling into, aren't you?"

"A little," I admitted. "I've never been a fan of the unknown, especially when it could involve incoming fire."

He patted the seat beside him, and I took it. "I know I'm the new guy, and I'm not trying to overstep my bounds, but I've worked for some of the best military leaders on Earth, and I've led some of the best operators anybody's ever seen, so I know a little bit about team dynamics and leadership. This outfit you cobbled together is full of some of the most brilliant and fearless hitters I've ever met."

"We've got a good team," I said.

"It's more than that. It's a creature far more powerful than the sum of its parts. Clark is one of the best adaptive shooters I've ever seen. He'll find a way to stay alive and keep you alive when it looks like you've fallen through the ceiling of Hell."

"I learned that about him a long time ago. He's taught me more than everybody else in this game combined."

Kodiak took a bite of his sandwich. "Not bad. If this secret agent gig doesn't pan out for you, I think you've got a future in the deli business."

"Thanks, I'll keep that in mind."

He wiped his mouth. "Mongo back there has one of the best reputations in the special ops community. He's fearless and unstoppable like a big hungry bear."

I took my first bite. "I get that. For some reason, he appointed himself as my personal bodyguard not long after we met."

Kodiak laughed. "Yeah, he does that. And Singer . . . he's another story altogether. He doesn't remember it, but I put him on a Chinook from the roof of a burning building in Northern Africa on his first deployment as a young Ranger. I put the body of his best friend on that same helo. I knew way back then that he was something special. I can count on one hand every other sniper in the world with his level of skill."

The makeup of my team flooded through my head. "You know what they say about everything happening for a reason. Maybe every one of us is exactly what the rest of us need . . . including you."

He crammed the rest of his sandwich down his throat. "I just got lucky when you guys picked me up, but listen . . . Stop worrying so much about what's going to happen on the ground. We'll roll with the punches and find that spy lady. We've all been shot at before, and it'll happen again. It's what people like us do, and sometimes the things that happen just happen, and there ain't no explaining it."

Clarity and simplicity rarely coexist in a world where every day grows more complex. The core of what my team and I did was the epitome of simplicity. We stood in the faces of the bad guys and punched them harder than they were capable of punching us. When the fight was over, most of the time, we were still on our feet, and our opponents were left licking their wounds . . . if their immortal souls hadn't abandoned their mortal bodies in the mele.

I don't know if Kodiak was imparting wisdom or just making an observation through his window on the world. Either way, his confidence and willingness to wade into the fight with me and the men around me cleared the fog from my head, and I stopped overthinking the coming mission. The plan wrote itself. We'd land, defend our position, hide our magic carpet, and find our target. If she were rogue, we'd put her down. If not, we'd fight beside her and chalk up another victory for the good guys. The variables would come, and we'd even take a few body blows in the fight, but ultimately, we'd come out on top or die trying.

Clark stepped from the cockpit and slapped me on the shoulder. "You're up, College Boy. We need somebody who can sound like a confused Russian on the radio, and you're it, comrade."

Chapter 9
We're Committed

I slipped through the cockpit door and onto the right seat. "Let's have it."

Disco gave the cockpit briefing as professionally as any airline captain, and in seconds, I felt like I'd flown every minute of the route up to that moment.

I said, "I have the picture. What's next?"

He cleared his throat. "Back in the States, what we're about to do would cost us every license we ever had, so I hope you're up for some shenanigans."

"If I knew how to spell it, *shenanigans* would be my middle name."

His finger landed on the moving map on the multifunction display in the center of the panel. "We're right here, essentially on the border between Moldova and Romania, but we're favoring the Moldovan side and working with Chisinau Radio because their radar and comms are significantly poorer quality than Romania's. We're going to use that to our advantage."

I followed his finger and studied the map as he continued.

"Out there, about two hundred miles, is the Black Sea. A hundred miles northeast along that coastline is Odesa, Ukraine. They have radar that's just as good as anything we have in the States. In

fact, it may be a little better. Thankfully, though, it's not aug-
mented by GPS. Are you following?"

"I'm still with you," I said.

He tapped the screen. "Good. Here's the illegal part. I'm going
to declare an emergency and dive for the deck. There's a convenient little mountain range just west of Chisinau. That'll make a
nice shadow for us, and we'll disappear from what little radar coverage they have."

I played through the scenario in my head. "That's a terrible
plan, and I love it!"

"Don't judge me yet," he said. "I've not gotten to the good
part."

"Keep talking, brother. This is starting to sound like some A-
Team stuff, and I love it when a plan comes together."

He growled. "I pity the fool."

I shook my head. "No, you're flying, so that makes you Mur-
dock, not B.A."

"Whatever. So, when we get the Moldovan authorities convinced we dumped it in the mountains, we'll go screaming across
the Black Sea as fast and as low as this thing will go, and when we
show up on radar in Odesa, we'll be somebody new, and you get
to put on an Oscar-worthy performance as a Russian-speaking jet
driver."

The more I thought about Disco's plan, the more I loved it.
"I'll get Skipper on the horn."

With the touch of a few switches, I had our analyst's voice ringing in my headset.

"It's all set up and ready to go, Chase. When you start your
climb over the Black Sea, your Russian call sign will be BE-
GOVOY-Two-Two, a Russian Air Force call sign that's typical near
Sevastopol. Your flight plan is already in their system, and if I did it

right, it'll appear perfectly routine. Just try to sound Russian, okay?"

"*Spasibo! Ty luchshiy.*"

She groaned. "No, Chase. *Sound* Russian, but *speak* English."

Disco turned and peered into the cabin. "It's showtime, guys. We're going to dive for the deck, but hopefully I'll get us leveled off before we become part of the Moldovan landscape."

He resituated himself in his seat and grabbed his emergency oxygen mask from behind his left shoulder. I plucked my mask from the bracket on my side as well, and the curtain went up on our acting debut performance.

Disco donned his mask so his radio transmissions would sound like an authentic emergency, and he pushed the nose of the *Grey Ghost* toward the countryside six miles below. "Chisinau Radio, this is *Grey Ghost One* declaring an emergency. We've experienced rapid decompression and possible structural failure. We're descending out of flight level three-seven-oh for one-zero thousand while we work the problem."

The accented air traffic controller said, "Roger, *Grey Ghost One*, advise if you need assistance."

Had I not been sitting three feet away from him, I could've believed Disco was in the middle of an actual emergency. The tension in his voice coupled with the muffled radio transmission through the oxygen mask made his charade even more effective than I expected.

Descending at nearly 7,000 feet per minute, we screamed toward the world below. I kept one eye on the altimeter as it wound down and the other on the rapidly rising earth looming ever larger through the windshield.

Disco yelled into the cabin, "Is everybody okay back there?"

Clark said, "I spilled my martini. Could you bring me another one?"

"I'll get right on that," Disco said.

I continued scanning the expanse of green fields and trees in every direction with the mountains rising to the east.

A quick scan of the instrument panel told me Disco was flying the *Ghost* by hand instead of allowing the autopilot to do its job. The upcoming maneuvers weren't in the autopilot's bag of tricks.

As we passed twelve thousand feet, Disco pulled the control yoke toward his lap, and the nose climbed toward the horizon over the Black Sea. The maneuver slowed, and eventually, stopped our descent, but our pilot in command kept pulling until the nose climbed above the horizon, and the *Ghost* traded airspeed for altitude.

"What are you doing?" I asked.

"Convincing whoever will review the radar data that I stalled the airplane and sent her into the trees."

The nose continued to rise until the airspeed bled off and approached the 105-knot stall speed.

His voice showed even more feigned anxiety when he keyed the radio again. "*Grey Ghost One* is in an uncommanded climb with control surface failure."

Barely above stall speed, he shoved the controls full forward and began the final phase of our disappearing act. We accelerated through 250 knots with the nose well below the horizon until the mountains to the east rose above our altitude. Disco gently pulled the yoke and added power until we leveled off less than 500 feet above the terrain. As the miles between us and the Black Sea melted away at five miles per minute with the world roaring only feet beneath our wingtips, I got my first real look inside the skill set the man to my left possessed.

The thousands of hours he'd spent at the controls of the A-10 Warthog showed as if gleaming from his eyes. His focus bore the intensity of a surgeon while his hands and feet finessed the sixty-thousand-pound Gulfstream as if it were an extension of his own mind and body. I don't know how many hours I've spent at the controls of countless aircraft through the years, but I'll go to my grave knowing I was never half the aviator Disco was.

The dark line of the landscape giving way to the Black Sea flew beneath us almost too quickly for me to see, but the turn Disco made was impossible to miss. The G-forces pressed me into the seat as we rolled left, and Disco pressed the throttles forward. Our speed increased over the water, and I tried to imagine the wake behind us on the surface of the sea so close to our belly that I feared we might soon become a submarine.

Without looking my way, he pulled the yoke and sent us racing into the sky. "Do your thing, Chasechka."

I tried to pretend my Adam's apple wasn't about to fly out the heels of my boots, and I keyed the mic and gave it my best Russian accent. "Odesa Center, is BEGOVOY-Two-Two, one hundred miles south. You should have for me clearance to Nukus."

The Ukrainian air traffic controller cleared us direct to Nukus at twenty-seven thousand, and Disco surrendered the *Ghost* to the autopilot.

He gave me a look. "I think it's working."

I pretended to wipe a bead of sweat from my forehead. "I wonder how long they'll look for the wreckage."

We leveled at our assigned altitude for our 1,500-mile flight, and Disco said, "Something tells me the Moldovans aren't terribly concerned about a lost American airplane in the Black Sea."

"I hope you're right."

I called Skipper and said, "Nice work! The Ukrainians bought it, but I'm not sure how aggressive the Romanian response to our apparent crash will be. Is there anything you can do to keep them calm?"

"I'm already on it," she said. "The chief controller at Chisinau Radio sends his congratulations for landing safely at Bucharest Băneasa - Aurel Vlaicu International Airport."

"You're the best, Skipper. We couldn't do this without you."

She said, "Sure you could. You'd just get caught a lot."

"Touché."

"Speaking of luck, I have what may sound like bad news at first, but ultimately, I think it may work to our advantage."

"Let's hear it," I said.

"Nukus is closed to civilian operations."

"How can that possibly be good for us?"

She said, "Think about it. That probably means there are no air traffic controllers, and there definitely won't be any civilian passengers wandering about on the airport when you arrive."

"Why are they closed?"

"According to local reports, the departure end of runway one-five got a little love from an artillery round or two."

I sighed. "Oh. That doesn't sound good. How much usable runway is left?"

"I don't know. There was a cloud layer over the airport the last time a usable satellite flew over, so I couldn't get a look. How much length do you have to have?"

"Fifty-six hundred for takeoff, and three thousand to land."

"I wish I had better intel, but I'll stay on it."

Disco said, "All we can do is take a look, but we need an alternate if we can't get into Nukus. We burned a lot of fuel during our little 'emergency maneuvering.'"

I flipped through the charts on the MFD. "There's an airport called Muynak a hundred miles north of Nukus."

"That'll have to do," Disco said. "We'll be stretching our fuel reserves just to get there."

We flew the rest of the route as conservatively as possible to keep what fuel we had in the tanks as long as possible, but when we arrived over Nukus, the field was completely obscured by clouds, and Disco got his serious look again.

"What are you thinking?" I asked.

"We don't have much choice. We have to shoot the approach, but I need you to run the fuel numbers. It's tight."

I asked the fuel totalizer to run the numbers, but I broke out the calculator to run them myself as well.

Disco maneuvered the *Ghost* onto the GPS approach to runway 1-5 and began our descent.

After running the numbers twice, I looked up to see nothing but a wall of white clouds outside the windshield. "We're committed."

Disco sighed. "We don't know how much runway is left down there."

"It doesn't matter," I said. "We're on fumes."

Without looking away from the instrument panel, Disco said, "This would be a really good time to get Singer talking to God."

Chapter 10
Not Today

On a normal day in the cockpit of the *Grey Ghost*, almost every task is a team effort. The workloads are divided into those completed by the pilot who's actually flying the airplane and the pilot who is monitoring and supporting the other guy. I had been so consumed with fuel calculations in the previous three minutes of my life that I'd left Disco practically alone to fly the approach in zero visibility while managing the typical two-man workload by himself.

He pulled me from my doomsday mathematical pit and back into the cockpit with his gear call. "Gear down, please."

I heard the call, but inside my head, it sounded as if it were coming from a thousand miles away and was meant for someone else.

"If it's not too much trouble there, Chase, I'd prefer to land on some tires instead of our belly if you've got time to put the gear down."

I shook my head as I forced my brain back inside the cockpit and lowered the landing gear handle. "Sorry. Gear in transit."

I worked my way back into the flow of the cockpit after breaking a cardinal rule of instrument flight. My first flight instructor had a sign above his desk that read, "Never put your airplane in any place your brain hasn't already been." Things happen quickly at three miles per minute, and staying mentally ahead of the airplane is crucial for survival. Once a pilot gets behind his airplane, it's nearly impossible to catch up, but Disco's skill and experience gave me a cushion and room for error that would be impossible with most other pilots.

Three green lights glowed beside the gear handle, and the enunciator showed no warnings, so I said, "Gear down. Three green. No red. Two hundred to minimums."

Disco chuckled, and that caught me off guard. Laughter during an instrument approach just five hundred feet above the ground was no time for comedy. As we descended ever closer to the minimum ceiling and visibility limits for the GPS approach, Disco came clean on what made him giggle.

"The minimums don't matter on this one. I'm flying this thing all the way to the concrete, even if I never see the runway. We don't have the gas for anything else."

He was right, of course, but the thought of craters the size of Rhode Island left by artillery rounds wouldn't leave my head.

It was our procedure to have the pilot flying to execute the approach while the monitoring pilot watched for the runway environment to appear outside the windshield. That allowed the flying pilot to focus only on the instruments and flying the approach as precisely as possible. When and if the runway came into sight, it would be my responsibility to make the announcement so Disco could look up from the instruments and execute the landing in visual conditions. With plenty of fuel in the tanks, if we never broke out of the clouds, Disco would fly the missed approach procedure and make the decision to either hold while waiting for conditions to improve or fly to our alternate destination. We had no fuel for either, so the *Grey Ghost* would land and roll to a stop regardless of what we saw, or didn't see, outside the airplane.

The pucker factor increased exponentially as we descended below minimums, and I strained, hoping against hope, to catch a glimpse of anything that resembled a runway somewhere in front of us. Gradually, the solid white wall of clouds outside the cockpit turned to wispy, gray puffs, and a flash of earth appeared. The tension melted from my spine, and I called, "Runway in sight. Continue."

Disco calmly looked up, raised the nose ever so slightly, and pulled back the throttles. The main landing gear chirped, and the nose gear settled to the concrete as if everything about the landing had been routine, but nothing about the scene in front of us resembled routine of any kind.

Massive craters big enough to swallow a house dotted the landscape of the airport. Entire buildings were demolished and rendered nothing more than piles of still-smoking rubble. Half of a Russian Antinov cargo plane lay on the parking apron, with the other half blown to cinders. We'd just landed on the front lines of a war no one on Earth fully understood and no one on our airplane would ever forget.

Disco taxied us across the ramp, dodging debris and pitfalls every few feet. He pointed through the window. "See that pile of ash and trash?"

I followed his finger. "Yeah, I see it."

"That used to be the hangar I wanted."

I shook my head. "I think it's safe to say it isn't available."

He chuckled. "You think?"

I turned to give the order for the team to gear up and be ready to pull security when we came to a stop, but I was, once again, well behind the power curve. Instead of seeing my team lounging in the captain's chairs, I saw a column of warriors, kitted out from helmets to bootheels with tactical gear, standing in line by the cabin door.

Clark was first down the stairs, even before the turbines stopped spinning. Singer trailed Clark by mere inches with Kodiak right on his heels. Mongo, the beast of a man, filed out in his typical position at the back of the pack. If we put him anywhere else in the column, his size would blind the man behind him.

They surrounded the plane with weapons at the ready while Disco proceeded through the shutdown procedure, and I donned my gear to join the security detail. I hit the tarmac and scanned the environment for potential threats, but the airport was a ghost town. It felt like we'd landed on the surface of the moon until the rumble of artillery fire echoed from the southeast.

Disco was the last man down the stairs, and he took full advantage of the rest of the team's protection as he sprinted for the closest hangar. He returned seconds later on a tractor with a tow bar, and soon, the *Ghost* was parked inside one of the few remaining hangars on the field.

He shut down the tractor and hopped from the seat. "Did anybody see a fuel truck?"

Kodiak motioned to the north with the muzzle of his M4. There's two of them about five hundred meters that way. The pilot sprinted toward the trucks, and Kodiak looked up at Clark in a wordless request for permission to run with Disco to cover him. Clark gave the nod, and soon, Kodiak was in locked step beside Disco with his eyes scanning everything in the environment. Whether it was training, instinct, or a combination of the two, I had enormous respect for the new guy's incessant need to protect and defend. With every step, he became a more valuable and integral part of our team.

We refueled the Gulfstream by pumping every ounce of jet fuel from the two trucks before jamming the hangar doors closed. Short of posting a round-the-clock armed guard, there was no way to ensure our airplane would still be there when and if we got back, but we did everything in our power to give her the best possibility of survival in our absence.

Formal rank structure was never a practice of our team, but Clark made a point of surrendering control after he led the security team from the airplane. "It's all yours, Chase. What's first on the agenda?"

I ran through a mental checklist and prioritized everything we needed to accomplish in the next hour of our lives. "First, let's stay alive. Everything else falls way down on the list. We need at least one vehicle, preferably two. The heavier the better."

Kodiak motioned toward the fuel trucks. "How about those?"

"They'll do if we can't find anything else, but I'd rather have something more maneuverable with a few more seats. Take Disco, and see what you can beg, borrow, or steal."

I called the op center back at Bonaventure, and Skipper answered almost as if she could sense the call coming in. "Are you down and safe?"

"Yes, we're safely on deck, and your satellite was right about the cloud cover. It was nasty getting in, but we made it. There's probably seventy percent of the runway left usable, but the ramp and most of the buildings are shot up. It had to be artillery fire. We need an inventory of military assets for both Turkmenistan and Uzbekistan. Can you get that for us?"

She said, "Sure, but it won't be accurate. There's no way to know what they've used up."

"I don't want you to count bullets. I want to know generally what each side has to fight with. How many tanks, planes, artillery pieces . . . Stuff like that."

"I'm on it. What else do you need from me?"

I said, "As always, track everybody, and we'll report prior to separation whenever possible. With Dr. Mankiller's new coms, we should be able to stay in touch a lot better, but we've still got backup coms in case something goes wrong."

"I always track each of you. That's standard operating procedure."

"I know. I'm just running through the list. We need to know how many people know the truth about what's going on over here. Somebody knew enough to try to intercept us and keep us from making it into the country. Get on that first. If we can figure out who's on whose side in this thing, we'll be way ahead of the game, and we may even be able to use some misinformation tactics to our benefit."

"Got it," she said. "What else?"

"Do you have any sightings of Teresa Lynn?"

"None. It's like she's a ghost. I'm starting to think she might be dead."

"If she's as good as I suspect she is, that's exactly what she wants us to believe. We're reconning for vehicles now, and as soon as we can commandeer some, we'll move toward the border and start sniffing the ground. If she's here, we'll find her, but it's not going to be easy. Is there any chance there are any public cameras good enough for facial recognition in this part of the world?"

She groaned. "No, not hardly. Things are a little primitive over there. I suspect you'll find out soon enough."

"There's one more thing . . ."

The crack of small-arms fire yanked me from the conversation.

Normal human beings don't run toward gunfire. They run as fast as possible in the opposite direction, but there was nothing normal about anyone on the operation. As if connected by some primordial psychic tie, the four of us sprinted toward the sounds of the fight as the familiar crack of 5.56mm rounds filled the air.

I switched my coms from the phone to the sat-com. "Disco, Kodiak . . . report!"

It took only a second for Disco to respond. "We're taking small-arms fire at the northeast end of the field. We're trying to keep enough lead in the air to dissuade the aggressors, but they're closing on us. I don't want to have to shoot these guys."

"Do you have good cover?"

"I do, but Kodiak is exposed a little. Hang on a minute."

The firing from both sides increased, and I didn't like anything about it. "Clark, you and Singer flank from the right. Mongo and I will go left."

We split into two elements and used the cover of the remaining buildings to our advantage. Mongo and I had farther to run, so Clark and Singer made contact first. The full-auto fire of their rifles quieted the guns of the aggressors, but I couldn't know if they were dead or retreating.

I got my answer the instant we rounded the corner of a massive hangar. A squad of twelve men armed with AKs was kneeling in the sand with their rifles held over their heads. Clark's pressure had been too much for the squad, and they hit their knees in surrender before Mongo and I could send a single round downrange. With my rifle shouldered and trained on the ground in front of the kneeling squad, two enormous questions popped into my head simultaneously: First, what language did our new prisoners speak? And second, does anyone on my team speak that language?

Being a former Soviet republic, I guessed at least some citizens of Uzbekistan still spoke some Russian, so that's where I began. "*Polozhite svoye oruzhiye na zemlyu.*"

It worked. Every man laid his weapon on the ground and returned his hands back over his head. As I drew closer, a man who was likely the leader of the squad cocked his head and stared up at me with confusion all over his face. "*Russkiy?*"

Answering questions with questions is always fun, so I gave it a try. "Turkmen?"

He recoiled and answered in Russian. "No, Uzbek. *Amerikan-skiy?*"

Not ready to show my cards, I said, "Israeli. Why were you shooting at us?"

The man's confusion continued. "This is war. It is what happens in war. Surely, an Israeli understands this."

Unwilling to give up the thin cover I was enjoying behind the veil of a Russian-speaking Israeli, I relaxed my posture and continued in Russian. "Put down your hands. We are allies."

I won't lie and say I wasn't enjoying messing with him, but I was on the verge of taking it too far when he said, "You do understand that we are Muslim."

I pointed to the southwest. "So is everyone on the other side of that border. Would you prefer if I were his ally instead of yours?"

For the first time, perhaps in weeks, the man smiled. "Not today, friend. Not today."

Chapter 11
Picking Sides

The deeper I fell down the well of my own creation, the more I wished I'd chosen any lie other than being Israeli, but I was too far gone to change my story. Mongo and Singer gathered the weapons of the Uzbeks, checked the men for anything concealed, and segregated the squad based on who seemed to be senior and not just a foot soldier. They guarded the junior fighters while Clark and I had a chat with the old guys.

The language barrier was a problem since Clark spoke precious little Russian, so I asked, "English?"

The apparent leader of the squad said, "No, but I speak Hebrew. Do you?"

I was busted, or so I thought, but Clark apparently saw a spark in the man's eyes I hadn't seen. He whispered, "This guy doesn't know a word of Hebrew. Throw something on him, and we'll see."

I panicked, but I didn't lose my composure. Not a single word in Hebrew would come to mind, so I made a play at pretending to be a native speaker by making up words that sounded close enough to Hebrew to me. "*Yadu beiusha totomu anna sadfir.*"

My gibberish worked. The man ducked his head and continued in Russian. "I am sorry for the deception. I don't speak Hebrew, but I did not believe you were Israeli."

"We're here to help you, but in order for us to do that, you have to be honest about who and what you are." I pointed toward his men. "Those men aren't well-trained soldiers. In fact, I think most of them are not soldiers at all. You're some sort of Uzbek militia, aren't you?"

The man allowed his eyes to meet mine. "We were once soldiers, but now we are merely men defending our home."

I caught the nuance of the word *dom*, singular for *home*, instead of the plural, *doma*. Such subtlety is difficult to fake, so with every word the man spoke, I believed we were drawing nearer to the truth.

He asked, "Are you here to help us fight the Turkmen?"

"We're here to find a woman," I said.

The man's confusion turned to temporary amusement. "You chose a terrible time to come here in search of a wife."

"Not a wife," I said. "A woman. This woman."

Clark held out a staff photograph of Teresa Lynn. The man took the picture and studied it closely. After showing it to the other two men beside him and speaking a language I didn't recognize, he placed the picture back in Clark's hand. "She is American."

"Maybe," I said. "But that doesn't matter. She's on your side, too, so it's in your best interest to tell us everything you know about her."

He shook his head. "We don't know anything about her, but the picture is American. She's a spy, isn't she?"

"What's your name?" I asked, changing gears.

"I am Anvar."

I extended my hand. "It's nice to meet you, Anvar. I'm David."

"David? I don't believe this is your real name, but it's a nice Jewish name. I admire your dedication to your lie."

It was time to come clean, so I took a knee in front of Anvar. "My name is Chase, and the woman is not a spy. She does, however, have some information my government needs. We will find her, and we will reward the people who help us find her. We'll also punish those who try to stop us from finding her."

"This is a threat?"

"No. I have no reason to threaten you. I believe you are who you say you are, and if you say you've never seen the woman, I'll believe you."

Anvar placed his palm on his chest. "I have never seen her, but my friend, Zafar, says he sold her a map, a compass, and a cellular telephone maybe ten days ago."

"Where?"

"Near Urgench"

Clark's expression never changed, probably because he couldn't understand a word either of us was saying. I liked his stoicism. It played well into my desire to appear to have the upper hand.

I kept my attention on Anvar. "What area did the map cover?"

"Dashoguz."

I said, "That's a town on the Turkmenistan side, right?"

He pointed southeast. "Yes, about fifty kilometers that way."

"What do you need from me?" I asked, but the question seemed to baffle him. "What do I have that you need to help your fight?"

He bowed his head as if ashamed and whispered, "Food."

"Don't look down, my friend. You're not a beggar. You're a leader, and there's nothing more important than feeding your men. We have food, but we need vehicles."

Anvar's eyes brightened. "We have an old Gorky. It's a surplus Soviet truck. It isn't comfortable, and it doesn't look good, but it is dependable."

I turned toward the hangar where we'd stashed the *Grey Ghost*. "Come with me."

Anvar and Zafar fell in locked step with me, and I tossed down eight cases of MREs and five cases of bottled water. With every new box, the men appeared more pleased. When I'd shared every-thing we could afford to spare, I said, "That should last you and your men a few days."

Anvar said, "We can kill goats and sheep when we find them, but with this food, we can survive more than a month without fear of starving. This is your airplane?"

"Yes, it's my plane."

He studied the long, sleek fuselage. "It is not safe here, but I can protect it."

"How much?"

He seemed to envision the piles of cash the rich Israelis must have if they can afford such an airplane. He shrugged. "How much is your airplane worth to you when it is time to go back to America . . . or Israel?"

I dug into our stash of Uzbek cash and produced forty million som. If my math was right, that was somewhere around three thousand bucks. Dropping the money at his feet, I said, "We'll be back in one week. If the plane is still here in the same condition, I'll triple the cash and give you every morsel of food we have."

He said, "And weapons?"

"Yes. And a nice stash of Western weapons and ammo."

Negotiations were apparently over. "The truck is beside the building where you ambushed us."

I huffed. "We didn't ambush anybody. You shot first, and we didn't shoot to kill any of your men. We could've mowed you down in seconds, but we didn't."

"Fair enough. Your plane will be safe in our hands, but we can-not defend it against more artillery."

"I understand, and I wouldn't expect you to stay in an artillery barrage. Now, how about the Gorky? I can't promise we'll bring it back. We tend to destroy equipment in the field."

Anvar smiled. "Thank you for not shooting us, my new friend. The Gorky truck is yours. If you do not come back in one week, your airplane is ours."

I stepped close to him, forcing him to look up at me. "If I'm not back in a week, I don't expect you to stay, but no matter what happens, the airplane is the property of my government, and you seizing it would be an act of war against my country. And, Anvar, you don't want that."

To my surprise, he closed what little distance remained between us. "And what country would that be, Chase?"

I laid a hand on his shoulder. "Shalom, my friend."

* * *

Anvar was right. The Gorky wasn't going to win any beauty pageants, but it started. Once the plume of white smoke floated away, we climbed aboard and made our way to the fuel farm on the airport, where we topped off the tanks with avgas and commandeered all the fuel cans we could find. We couldn't know what resources existed on the border, and the Gorky would become a five-ton chunk of useless steel if her tanks ran dry.

Back at our airplane's temporary home, we loaded the rear of the truck with all the gear we could carry. Weapons, ammo, food, water, and backup communication gear made up the bulk of our load, and the fifty-year-old springs on the Gorky creaked their disapproval of their new burden.

As we pulled away from the hangar, Anvar waved us down and leaned against the side of the battered truck. In our common language, he said, "You shouldn't go alone. I will send two men with you. You will need them for local knowledge and security."

"Thanks," I said, "but we're well qualified to pull our own security, and we learn quickly, so we'll be fine. You just take care of my airplane."

"*Your* airplane?" he said. "You told me it was property of the American government."

"No, I didn't. I told you it was the property of *my* government, but that was a nice try."

He took a step back and pointed up at the registration number on the tail of the *Grey Ghost*. "Israel does not register their airplanes in America, but that was a nice try."

In a cloud of dust and smoke, we roared away from the airport, and I phoned home. "Hey, Skipper. Things are moving along nicely after our little skirmish with the locals."

"That's good to hear," our analyst said. "By the looks of your GPS track, it looks like you found a vehicle."

"We found part of a vehicle, but it'll have to do for now. It's an old Soviet–era utility truck, but it runs, and everyone fits, so it's better than riding a donkey." She burst into laughter, and I said, "Are you okay?"

She got herself under control. "I'm sorry, but I'm trying to picture Mongo on a donkey."

"Maybe a Clydesdale donkey."

She said, "Okay, I can breathe now. I have an update for you. There's heavy fighting near the tiny town of Dzhambaskala, just northeast of Urgench. I'm sending you the GPS coordinates."

I attempted to picture the local maps I'd tried to commit memory. "What are they fighting over?"

"That's unclear," she said, "but according to local reports, it began as an artillery barrage by the Turkmen, followed by an infantry push. I'm a few minutes behind in gathering information, but at the last report, it was a brutal small-arms fight."

"Who's winning?"

"I hope it's the good guys."

I considered what a gunfight of that magnitude would look like. "How do we know which side is the good guys?"

Chapter 12

A Helping Hand

The roads leading into the town of Dzhambaskala were better than I expected. Sandbags and makeshift barricades lined the roadsides and littered the entrances to businesses that were, no doubt, flourishing only weeks before. My inability to understand why the two fledgling countries would take up arms against each other continued to haunt me. Most wars have a definitive catalyst, but so much about the conflict around me made no sense. I feared the truth I might discover as my mission played out.

Clark wrestled the steering wheel of the ancient truck as if battling a bear. It appeared to require constant effort to force the dilapidated vehicle into submission, and I wasn't sure if Clark was winning.

I leaned toward him in hopes of being heard over the roaring engine. "What are we going to do when we get to the fight?"

"What do you mean, when we get there? Can't you see I'm already in a fight? I'm going to be exhausted before this day is over."

"Maybe we should have Mongo drive. He could probably frighten the truck into submission."

Clark groaned. "I'm afraid this old rattletrap isn't afraid of the devil, let alone Mongo."

"I'll drive a while if you want."

He wiped sweat from his face. "I've got it for now, but I can't stay on it all day. We'll have to swap out."

"No problem. But the question remains . . . What are we going to do when we get to the fighting?"

He said, "I don't know yet. In fact, I don't really know why we're running toward the gunfire."

"It just seemed like the right thing to do."

"If you say so, College Boy. But remember, we're noncombatants here. We can't get directly involved in the fighting. We're here to find Teresa Lynn, not pick a side and start shooting."

I braced against the dash and the door as we bounced across a pile of debris on the road. "I think we should be overly cautious when we approach the fight. We make a pretty soft target in this hunk of junk."

"How far out are we?"

I checked the GPS. "Just over a mile to the center of town, but I don't know where the fighting—"

Before I could finish my sentence, a massive explosion filled the air with dust, smoke, and debris only a few feet in front of us.

Clark battled the steering wheel and brakes until he'd wrangled the beast to a stop. He shifted out of gear and relaxed against the seat. "I guess we found the fight."

Sounds of boots hitting the ground behind us reminded me of the quality of soldiers I'd brought with me into the middle of the unknown. In seconds, the team established a security perimeter, set up a hasty machine gun position, and dug in to fight.

I dismounted the cab of the truck and took cover behind an overturned car. Clark was soon at my side and staring down the winding street with his binoculars.

"See anything?" I asked.

"Not yet, but it's the ones you don't see that'll get you."

As Clark glassed the ground in front of us, I scanned left and right just in time to see Singer, our Southern Baptist sniper, scampering up the side of what had once been a three-story building that likely served as home for a few dozen Uzbeks. What remained of the building was a jagged and grotesque pile of concrete, rebar, and detritus that might have been furniture, appliances, and personal effects of the now-displaced refugees of a war they neither began nor understood.

Hide-and-seek is a timeless child's game we've all played, but when Jimmy "Singer" Grossmann played, the rules were a little different and more than a little skewed in his favor. The best sniper I'd ever seen nestled himself into what men like him call a *hide*. It's a nook or crack or void in which not even a skilled contortionist could make himself comfortable. Singer, though, wormed his way into the concrete crevice, snaked the barrel of his rifle through an opening the size of a coffee can, and started the clock on his lethal pursuit. Snipers are, by definition and necessity, spies. They find positions from which they can observe everything that matters in the environment around them. With minds like black holes, they absorb every detail of the world around them and identify and catalog threats, potential threats, and countersnipers.

I'll never possess the intellectual capacity for the work our sniper mastered in his youth, but I had enormous respect for him and his brothers-in-arms who could pull it off.

After having been inside his hide for less than two minutes, Singer's voice rang inside my head. "I count seventy to eighty aggressors from the southwest. I can't get a good count on the number of troops who are pinned down. Nobody's wearing a uniform, but based on their relative positions, I'd say the Turkmen are the aggressors, and the Uzbeks are trying to hold what's left of the town."

"Roger," I said. "Snipers?"

"Affirmative. I have one deceased sniper at eleven o'clock and a thousand yards and two more still active at two o'clock and twelve hundred yards. I have the angle if you want me to quiet their guns."

"Quiet their guns" is a phrase that sounds far more innocuous than it is. Guns don't make any noise by themselves; therefore, to quiet them, the source of their noise must be eliminated. When a human heartbeat ends, so does the activity of that human's trigger finger. I've known a lot of snipers, but never have I met one more skilled at quieting other guns than Singer.

"Stand by."

"Roger."

I waited for Clark to lower his binoculars, but he never flinched. He said, "Stop thinking what you're thinking, College Boy."

"How do you know what I'm thinking?"

He continued scanning. "You're thinking Singer can take out those two snipers, thus taking the cuffs off the Uzbeks who are pinned down in their own city. You're thinking about leveling the playing field, and that's not why we're here."

"Then what are we doing?" I demanded. "Are we supposed to sit by as spectators while the Turkmen kick the crap out of the Uzbeks in their own country? I mean, look at this place. It looks like something out of World War Two. If we can save the lives of innocent people, what's wrong with picking off a couple of invading snipers?"

Clark finally lowered his binoculars. "Invading snipers? Is that what you said?"

"Yeah, that's what I said."

He puffed out his cheeks and sighed. "Do you want me to run it up the chain?"

I considered his question. If he asked the Board for permission to put down two Turkmenistan snipers, there were two possible outcomes. They could approve the request, and Singer could flip the switch that would turn the tide of the battle the locals were fighting on their home court, but if they denied the request, I would be in an impossible position. Everything inside me wanted those two snipers dead. My desire to protect the innocent Uzbeks outweighed any moral considerations I had about the remainder of the snipers' lives. I held the power to end the terrifying afternoon the locals were experiencing. We wouldn't fight their battle for them, but giving them a gift from the other side of the world didn't feel like a bad choice.

I gave the order. "Silence those guns, Singer."

Before the second hand ticked three times, two rounds of Lapua .338 Magnum thundered from the barrel of Singer's rifle, and the war just got a lot safer for the Uzbeks. In the minutes that passed before our eyes, fighters moved from cover inside buildings, behind vehicles, and beneath rubble. They didn't have a sniper of their own, but lending them ours changed everything, and soon the Turkmen were in full retreat, their brothers falling as chase gave way to retaliatory fire and the good guys were once again on top.

That's when Singer offered another option that only he could accomplish. "They're retreating to vehicles, Chase. If there are more vehicles than runners, we can trade in our wheels for something a little shinier."

I didn't hesitate. "Hit 'em!"

When bodies stopped falling to the thirsty ground, fourteen of seventeen trucks retreated for the Turkmenistan border, leaving us three hardened vehicles. The Uzbeks celebrated with hugs, shouts, and relief. The marauders who'd laid siege to their town had been pushed back, and that was more than a mere victory. It was a victory of will, morality, and determination. We wouldn't always be secretly pulling the trigger on their behalf, but on that day, that one afternoon the fighters would never forget, we were there, and we did the right thing at the right time for the right reason, and I beat myself up for hesitating in making the decision.

As the Uzbeks returned to their city and homes, I called our sniper. "Stay on overwatch while we retrieve the vehicles. We'll pick you up."

Singer said, "Roger."

We remounted our half-century-old trusty steed and moved carefully to the staging area where our three new vehicles waited, careful not to look or behave like Turkmen. I didn't want that celebratory mob sending 7.62mm rounds into our backs, but I couldn't simply announce our presence, steal the trucks, and vanish. Every move I made had to be done as covertly as possible. Remaining invisible wasn't possible, but I would do everything in my power to protect the Uzbeks without them seeing our faces. My team couldn't win the war for them, but if we could make concentrated, surgical strikes on their behalf while still finding and recovering Teresa Lynn, the American CIA case officer, amid the destruction and chaos, that would be the epitome of a successful mission.

My sins are many, and my weaknesses abundant, but loving freedom and making the necessary sacrifices to preserve and protect it across the globe will be the single redeeming quality of my life spent on Earth. Seeing a peaceful, resilient population attacked and slaughtered will never be a transgression I'm capable of accepting. I'll fight for those who can't fight for themselves. I'll sacrifice for those who have nothing left to give. I'll die for the perpetuation of goodness, freedom, and peace. And I know, without the slightest doubt, that every man beside me would gladly do the same. That, above all else, is humanity and love and our highest godly purpose.

The abandoned vehicles left behind by the retreating Turkmen militia changed our capabilities, but more importantly, they changed our level of comfort for the coming days. To our delight, the keys were left hanging in the ignition switches, and the fuel gauges read full. We left our sniper in position while we offloaded every piece of gear from the Gorky and carefully positioned each item into our new vehicles in an orderly fashion.

Rummaging through piles of gear to find the right tool at the right time has gotten a lot of warriors killed. When organizational discipline is maintained, there's never a moment of missing-gear panic when incoming fire fills the air. Although my team and I qualified as the inhabitants of the island of misfit toys in our downtime, when bullets flew and lives hung in the balance, we were swift, efficient, and deadly. Something about our mission told me every element of our capabilities would be tried, tested, and pushed beyond every limit we could imagine, and if there was a team of operators ready to face that challenge, it was the six of us.

Chapter 13
The Battle and the War

Thanks, perhaps, to the post-battle euphoria of the Uzbeks in the tiny town of Dzhambaskala, we managed to commandeer the three abandoned trucks, transfer our gear, and retrieve Singer from his hide without being intercepted . . . or shot.

Pulling away from the town, I turned to the man who taught me more about soldiering than everyone else combined. "You think I made the wrong call, don't you?"

Clark Johnson continued staring through the windshield. "It's not the call I would've made, but that doesn't make it wrong. This is your team and your operation. I'm not in charge. I'm just a gun-toting grunt who happens to be your link to the invisible men in an ivory tower who hand out terrible assignments like this one."

For some reason I couldn't put my finger on, his words stung. "A lot of those people would've died back there if I hadn't ordered Singer to take out the Turkmen snipers."

"Probably."

"There's no *probably* about it. Those shooters were picking off Uzbeks every time they popped their heads up."

He finally turned to face me. "Those Uzbeks may live a simple life compared to most of the Western world, but they're not stupid. They know somebody helped them today. Who do you think they'll thank for that help?"

I hadn't thought about the psychological effects of my decision on the locals. I merely wanted to keep them alive, but Clark never failed to make me see everything from a different perspective.

I shook off the feeling I didn't like. "Do you think they believe some foreign force showed up to join their fight?"

"I guess that's one way to put it. They're devout Muslims, Chase. Look at it from their point of view. An unseen, all-powerful force arrived in their darkest hour and devoured the enemy right in front of them."

The sickening feeling I thought I'd shrugged away returned in spades, and I was instantly chilled to the bone. "How did I not think of that before I opened my stupid mouth and ordered Singer to pull the trigger?"

He laid a hand on my shoulder. "Do you feel that, College Boy? That's the weighty burden of command. You just became the Sword of Allah in the minds of a few dozen people, in a town nobody's ever heard of, who now believe they're invincible behind God's shield."

"How do we clean it up?"

He leaned back in his seat and propped his boots on the dash. "Have I ever told you the story about the Lone Ranger and Tonto?"

As much as I wanted to pretend the moment wasn't happening, I'd walked right into Clark's trap. "No, you've not told me that story . . . yet."

"It goes something like this," he began. "The Lone Ranger and Tonto were riding along a dusty trail in Apache Country. I *think* it was Apache Country. Anyway, suddenly, they were surrounded by a massive tribe of angry Native Americans with bows, rifles, and every manner of sharpened object. The marauding mob closed in tighter and tighter on the Lone Ranger and his trusty sidekick, Tonto, with every second that passed. The Apache fighters wore their warpaint, and their horses were bedecked with beads and turquoise from mane to tail. Frightened and unnerved, the Lone Ranger nudged his trusty horse, Silver, to move closer to Tonto, and he whispered, 'What are we going to do now, Kemosabe?' Tonto glared back at him and said, 'What you mean *we*, Pale Face?'"

"Point taken," I said. "Let's put this piece of ground astern and see if we can find ourselves a missing CIA case officer."

My insistence on leaving my poor decision in the dust behind us might work geographically, but I'd taste the bitterness of my hasty call for years to come.

About thirty minutes into our silent drive toward the Turkmenistan border, Clark finally said, "When was the last time you learned anything by doing something right?"

I scowled. "What?"

"Screwing up is how we learn, so quit letting that mess behind us kick your butt. Learn from the experience, rub some dirt on it, and soldier on."

"You're quite the wordsmith, you know that?"

He pulled his hat down over his face. "Yep, some of us have got it, and some of us ain't. Wake me up when we get to Disney World."

There's nobody on Earth I'd rather have in my foxhole than Clark Johnson, but he was a study in contradictions. If he told me once, he told me a thousand times that being a Green Beret meant he could operate at 100% on an hour's sleep and a teacup full of raisins. Perhaps it was the truth—at least in his mind—but I'd never seen him pass up the opportunity for a catnap or a Scooby snack.

When my GPS warned us that we were one mile east of the border with Turkmenistan, I hit the brakes and maneuvered our truck behind a stand of scrub trees. The rest of our convoy followed, and we climbed from our borrowed vehicles.

I said, "These are a little nicer than the Gorky, huh?"

Mongo stretched his back. "Oh, yeah."

I laid my map on the hood of our truck and pointed to our position. "We're here, and the border is less than a mile that way. Since we don't know anything about the security on the border, I'm not interested in rolling up on a checkpoint full of armed guards who don't like armed Americans."

Singer said, "I'll go," and slung his rifle across his shoulder.

Kodiak slid from the hood and grabbed his camelback. "I'm in."

I said, "Not so fast, Recon. Before you take off, let's check in with Skipper."

She answered immediately. "Uh, Chase. Why didn't you tell me you added vehicles?"

"I'm calling to tell you now. We picked up three abandoned trucks, and we're holding off about a mile from the border."

"I know where you are, but what you don't understand is how badly it screwed me up to see the six of you traveling at fifty miles per hour several hundred feet apart."

"Sorry. I'll make the future reports timelier."

She said, "Let me guess. You want me to tell you where the border guards are, right?"

"You're a genius. What do you see?"

"Oh, I know, and right now, I can't see anything. The cloud cover is too dense, but I've been plotting border crossing traffic when there were moments of visibility and when I could borrow a satellite. There's a shallow waterway that makes up most of the border, so depending on what kind of trucks you stole—"

"Requisitioned!"

"Fine, whatever. If your trucks can deal with three feet of water, you can probably cross several places. There are two bridges within ten miles of your position, but they're both heavily patrolled. At least they have been heavily patrolled every time I could get a peek."

I scanned our map. "So, you're saying a creek crossing is our best plan, right?"

"Not necessarily, but it's likely your safest option."

"Thanks. We'll put eyes on the waterway and the bridges and let you know what we decide. Keep watching for a break in the clouds. It looks like it's starting to clear up."

She said, "Don't worry. I'm running constant recordings from every satellite I can access in that part of the world, and I'll keep feeding you the intel as I pick up anything meaningful. How was the gunfight?"

"The good guys won . . . at least temporarily."

"That's good enough for me. Is there anything I need to put in the log?"

Clark raised an eyebrow. "Yeah, Chase. Is there anything that needs to be logged about that gunfight?"

I let out a disgruntled breath. "Just log minimal involvement with multiple casualties and acquisition of three capable vehicles."

She said, "Minimal involvement? What does that mean?"

"That means we've got a border to cross, so if there's nothing else you need, we'll get back to work."

"We're not finished discussing this yet," she said.

"Half of *we* is finished. Talk soon."

I cut the connection and said, "Singer, Kodiak . . . find us a nice quiet route into Turkmenistan."

They took off at a jogging pace and soon disappeared amidst the scrub brush and rocky terrain.

I said, "Let's get some food and water in us. We don't know what the evening is going to bring."

Clark was first into the goody bag and tossed granola bars to everyone. We downed bottles of water and shoved calories into our mouths in preparation for the unknown. There are few things worse than being hungry and thirsty in the middle of a gunfight.

Twenty minutes into Singer's recon run, my earpiece clicked.

He said, "We've got bad news and worse news. Which one do you want first?"

"You choose," I said.

"We'll start with the bridge. This one is barricaded with eight men and a heavy machine gun emplacement. It's an old Russian Dushka, so I'm not interested in dancing with that thing."

"Is that the bad news?"

He said, "I'll let you decide. We found several spots in the waterway that are shallow enough to cross in the trucks."

"That doesn't sound like bad news."

"You didn't let me finish. Although they're shallow and narrow enough to cross without any trouble, the bottom composition is muck. We checked half a dozen spots, and we sank up to our knees every time we stepped in the water."

I closed my eyes. "Of course it's muck. Why would I expect a break?"

"What's that?" Singer asked.

"Nothing. Recover back here, and we'll come up with a plan."

"Roger. Moving."

When our recon team jogged back into sight, the black mud caked on their pants confirmed Singer's report and reinforced my fear that I was about to make another haunting decision.

I took a knee beside the front tire of my truck. "Let's talk through a few options. Number one, we could shoot our way through the checkpoint, but that's loaded with problems, and I don't like any of them. Option two is to swim the waterway and take the checkpoint on foot. That's safer and quieter, but that still leaves us with eight more dead bodies to deal with and possibly explain. Number three is more recon. We can check out the other bridge and compare the level of security. Maybe it's softer."

Clark scratched the rocky ground with his fingertip. "Maybe since we're driving the same kind of trucks the border guards are driving, they won't stop us, and we can roll right through."

"That's a big maybe," I said. "And if it doesn't work, we're left with only one option—shooting our way through and risking casualties of our own."

Clark shrugged. "I didn't say it was a good plan."

"A chopper would come in handy," Disco said.

I looked up at our chief pilot. "Have you seen any of those lying around?"

Finally, Mongo took a knee on the sand. "What if I could lure the border guards away from the bridge long enough for the rest of you to cross?"

"I like it," I said, "but can you be a little more specific?"

He chuckled. "Nobody is better at breaking things than me, so I thought I'd just do what comes naturally. I can cross the water three or four hundred yards downstream from the bridge, find something to blow up, and plant a nice, noisy charge. I can follow that up with some small-arms fire and a couple of flash-bangs. If the guys on the bridge are disciplined enough to stand their post while a firefight is happening a thousand feet away, we probably don't want to mess with them anyway."

"I don't hate it," I said, "but you're not going alone. If the guards move in on you, I'm not okay with you being outgunned eight to one with us stuck on the opposite side of the border."

Mongo said, "We've got three trucks, so the best we can do is split the team in half: three on the Turk side and one in each truck."

"Pick your team," I said.

Mongo didn't hesitate. "Kodiak and Singer."

I nodded. "Gear up."

It took only minutes for the three to rig the gear they'd need for the crossing and their task on the other side. I called the op center and briefed Skipper on our plan.

She said, "A helicopter would come in handy, wouldn't it?"

I turned to Disco, who said, "Great minds and birds of a feather."

I rolled my eyes. "I think you're spending too much time with Clark. He's starting to rub off on you."

I cut the connection, and the crossing team set off in a double-time run toward the water and the border.

"Let's mount up. I've got the lead," I said. "We'll reposition close enough to put eyes on the guards so we'll be ready to go the instant they abandon their post."

"*If* they abandon their post," Clark said.

"What's the plan if they don't?" Disco asked.

"Run, and if necessary, gun. Singer will be in position to take out their heavy machine gun if needed, and that'll level the playing field enough for us to fight our way across that bridge."

We mounted our vehicles and moved a few hundred yards until the bridge was visible through a grove of low trees.

Clark climbed on top of his truck with his binoculars and glassed the scene in front of us. "Business as usual. They're smoking and joking like every gate guard all over the world."

Thanks to Dr. Mankiller's implanted device, Singer's voice rang inside my head. "I'm in position with good visibility to the east. Bridge is in sight, and guards are relaxed."

Mongo's voice appeared immediately after Singer's. "The first charge is set, and Kodiak is finishing up number two."

Singer asked, "Chase, are you up?"

"Chase is up," I said. "We're in position due east of the bridge with eyes on the guards. Let the games begin."

Almost before I finished the command, the first explosion rocked everything in my world. I was expecting a satchel charge, but Mongo's idea of a distraction was a little bigger than mine. A three-story building on the Turk side shuddered and leaned as if competing with that tower in Pisa, but unlike that tower, the building succumbed to the second charge and crumbled as if it had been shoved by some invisible giant, and in my mind, that's exactly what happened.

Clark said, "We've got their attention, but they're standing fast."

The echoing reports of gunfire from the vicinity of the toppled building thundered through the air. The fire was coming from at least four rifles. Kodiak, Singer, and Mongo were definitely putting on a show.

Clark announced, "The sergeant of the guard is dispatching four men toward the fire." A second later, he said, "Singer, kill the radio at the bridge."

I had missed it, but Clark did not. The antenna extending above the roof of the guard shack was undoubtedly linked to the radio connecting the border guards to higher command. Almost before I could turn my binoculars to see the bridge, the antenna exploded from its base in a fiery flash, and the two men inside the squatty structure ran as if running for their lives.

That's when the number of rifles in the fight on the western side of the water grew exponentially. Instead of four distinct rifles, a cacophony of cracking, thundering reports sliced through the air.

Singer's calm baritone came. "Chase, we could use some help. There's half a platoon of what looks like regulars moving in from the northwest, and they're doing it right."

"Let roll!" I ordered.

Clark rolled from the top of his vehicle and slid behind the wheel. I cranked my truck and threw gravel in a rooster tail when I crushed the accelerator beneath my boot. Disco fell in right behind me, and Clark accelerated into the trail position.

As we approached the bridge, I yelled, "Singer, kill the Dushka!"

At the same moment, one of the guards leapt behind the massive weapon, and in an instant, the man who'd mounted the gun turned from threat to corpse with the pressure from Singer's trigger finger. A second round split the receiver of the Dushka in half, rendering it nothing more than scrap metal.

Singer said, "Dushka is dead, and the troops are still coming."

"Retreat to the water," I ordered. "We're crossing the bridge in ten seconds."

The single remaining guard stood in disbelief at what was happening around him. His rifle hung harmless around his shoulder, and his head spun back and forth between the firefight and our three-vehicle convoy thundering toward his bridge. I thought I saw the look of relief on his face when he identified the trucks as those of his countrymen and not Uzbek. He ran to the barricade and raised the counterbalanced arm until it pointed skyward, and I pressed the accelerator almost through the floorboard.

As I bounced from the bridge and onto the asphalt road on the other side, I raised my rifle and poured lead through the right front window in the direction of the approaching fighters. Kodiak and Mongo were sprinting from the demolished building toward the border, and I was determined to provide them with all the cover fire I could.

I yelled, "Singer, where are you?"

His breathy reply came. "I'm descending the black building due south of the rubble, and I'm under heavy fire."

I spun the wheel, determined to place myself between the approaching horde and my sniper. Losing Singer would be a blow we couldn't survive. I continued firing through the window while closing the distance between Singer and me as he ran without looking back. His bolt action rifle was the perfect weapon inside the safety of his hide on top of the building, but in the open space between the buildings and my truck, the heavy rifle was little more than a twenty-pound stick.

As I pushed the truck to its limits across the rugged terrain, the soldiers continued pressing closer, and I silently wished for a miracle. It came in the form of Kodiak and Mongo leaning from the rear windows of the other two trucks with Clark and Disco behind the wheels. They poured rounds downrange and angled for the oncoming fighters. Bullets ricocheted off the hardened surfaces of our trucks and tore chunks from the bullet-resistant glass.

Focusing on Singer grew more difficult with the strike of every bullet. We'd announced our presence, and there was no way to deny that we'd become players in a war that was neither ours nor a fight we wanted. The cover of secrecy was well astern, and what lay ahead looked like the worst welcoming party in history. The ground around Singer's running feet roiled with debris as rifle fire struck ever closer to one of the world's most accomplished snipers. I'd give my life to save his, but based on the scene in front of me, giving my life would do little to secure his. Staying alive was everyone's best option.

Bodies fell as Mongo and Kodiak worked with the precision of a surgeon while bouncing so violently their heads crashed against the tops of the trucks. I had little hope of landing a shot with any accuracy while driving and firing one-handed, but the rest of my team was putting lead on target with unmatched skill.

I glanced up just in time to see Singer plummet to the ground and roll like a log. His arms were tucked, and his feet were pointed, so the roll was intentional and his brain was obviously still communicating with his limbs. If he'd been hit, it wasn't a killing shot . . . yet, and I was finally on line directly between him and the oncoming warriors.

I hit the brakes and cranked the wheel to the left until I was bearing directly on our sniper. He came to a stop in the prone position with his rifle pointed directly at me, and for an instant, I believed he'd put a round into the engine of his potential getaway car.

I focused on the muzzle of his rifle, awaiting the orange belch of fire that would follow the massive projectile from the barrel if he pressed his trigger, but the flash didn't come. I leaned across the front seat and pulled the door handle just before I crushed the brake pedal and slid to a stop only inches in front of my target. The door flew open from the momentum of the slide, and Singer dived inside as if his life depended on the move. It likely did.

He tossed his Lapua onto the back seat and yanked my M4 from my hand. As I powered away from the scene, he filled the air behind us with 5.56mm rounds as fast as the rifle would spit them out. The mirror told me the two other trucks were still coming, and the distance between us and our would-be assassins grew with every passing second.

It may have lasted a few seconds, or perhaps a few thousand years, but when Singer withdrew his torso from outside the window and relaxed on the seat beside me, the battle was over, but the war had no end in sight.

Chapter 14
Can You Keep a Secret?

We put three miles between us and the bridge before stopping behind a modern one-story building that showed no signs of battle damage. Singer, Kodiak, and Mongo sprang from the vehicles and established a security perimeter as soon as the tires stopped rolling.

I followed and immediately began the battle damage assessment. "Is anybody hit?"

Singer was first to answer. "I think I took one in my left calf."

I stepped toward Mongo's position as the former Green Beret medic cut away Singer's mud-soaked pant leg. "You're hit, but it's not bad. It was a glancing blow. I'll need to clean it up and dress it when we get somewhere a little more secure, but there's not enough bleeding to be a problem. If you'd been two inches farther to the right, this would be a very different conversation. You and Chase would've been twins with matching prosthetics."

I said, "Sound off. Is everybody else okay?"

Right down the line, every man reported safe, and I moved to the vehicles. Each of the three trucks bore the scars of combat, but all the tires were healthy, and there was no glass too badly broken to see through. "If we live through this, I might want to take these trucks home with us."

Clark said, "Your optimism is encouraging, but it's starting to look like we've painted ourselves onto thin ice."

I shook off confusion the sentence tried to squeeze into my head. "I'm pretty sure neither of us knows what that's supposed to mean, but I don't want you to try to explain it."

"It's pretty simple, really," Clark began, but I cut him off.

"I said, don't explain it. I'm calling home."

Skipper said, "Give it to me. Is everybody all right?"

"Mostly," I said. "Our vehicles got shot up pretty good, and Singer took a grazer to the right calf, but we're still operational."

"Do you have a body count?" she asked.

"Let's stick with our statement of minimal contact for the log. Things are hotter than I expected, but so far, it's nothing we can't handle."

"Whatever you say. You're the boss. And speaking of the boss, you're wanted for a secure call with the Board."

"Me?" I asked. "I thought they only talked to Clark."

"They were very specific. They want a secure line with you, and only you, ASAP."

I turned to Clark, and he held up two palms. "Don't look at me. I have no idea what they want."

"Why would they ask to speak only to me?"

Clark didn't drop his hands. "Again, I've got no idea, but I'd recommend taking that call. It sounds like they're serious."

I checked my watch and scanned the area. "Give us thirty minutes to get somewhere quiet and private, then set up the call."

Skipper said, "Roger. Let me know when you're in position, and I'll make the secure link."

We drove ten miles to the southwest of the town of Dashoguz and found a piece of ground where we felt right at home. The Dashoguz Airport, just southeast of Tezedurmysh, was clean with no sign of damage. An abandoned hangar on the northeast extreme of the airport was more than welcoming and gave us the space to thoroughly inspect our vehicles for damage.

Once inside, Mongo went to work on Singer's leg, carefully cleaning the wound and examining him for more wounds he may not have felt yet. With the bandage in place, he said, "It looks like you're going to live, sharpshooter."

After playing doctor, Mongo installed four temporary cameras to feed live video to our tablets. The technology gave us the freedom to have only one man pulling security at a time. That freed up the rest of the team to inspect the vehicles for unseen damage, and it gave me the time to take the call from the Board.

The hangar had a cramped, cluttered office in the back corner, so I holed up inside the space with my satellite phone pressed tightly to my ear.

Skipper asked, "Are you ready, Chase?"

"Make the connection."

It took a minute or so to route the secure call through the Bonaventure op center, but when it was finally done and Skipper had verified the call was encrypted and secure, a disembodied voice said, "Hello, Chase. Are you alone?"

"I am. What's this about?"

The voice didn't waste any time getting to the point. "It's about conflicting intelligence reports."

"I'm listening."

He said, "We deployed you and your team on this mission under the belief that Turkmenistan was the aggressor. Everything pointed exactly in that direction. Of course, Turkmenistan denied launching the first strike and claimed they were responding to aggression from the Uzbeks."

"Are you saying we don't know who started the fight?"

"That's not exactly what we're saying. We still believe the Turkmen were the initial aggressors, but our initial theory that they were trying a landgrab for oil has turned out to be false."

I chewed my lip for a moment. "I'm starting to feel like we're here under illegitimate pretenses."

"What you feel isn't of anyone's concern, Chase. You are there, and you're under a mandate to act in the interest of the Board. Feelings are irrelevant."

That left a bitter taste in my mouth. "The interest of the *Board*? Don't you mean the interest of my country?"

"No. The U.S. is neutral in the conflict, and we are allies to both countries. What I'm about to tell you is never to leave your mouth. Do you understand, Mr. Fulton?"

From Chase to Mr. Fulton . . . that's interesting.

"Are you ordering me to keep critical intelligence from my team?"

"It doesn't qualify as critical intelligence yet. It's merely a possibility that is growing more likely by the minute. Are you willing and capable of compartmentalizing this information and keeping it from anyone beyond yourself?"

Nothing about the setup felt good. "That depends on several factors," I said. "Chief among those factors is whether I believe the information has potential to put my team in danger. I will not keep information from them if knowing the information increases their survivability."

"I understand your sentiment, but this is information you need to know, and it can go no farther. If at any point you feel the information proves to increase the likelihood of your team befalling misfortune, you may, at that time, but not before, brief the team, but only to the extent that the information may keep them alive. Otherwise, you will take this information to your grave."

"I still don't like it," I said, "but I can live with those conditions."

"If it becomes known to us that you shared the intel with any member of your team or anyone else before the information proves potentially deadly, you will be tried for and convicted of treason. Is that clear?"

"That sounds a lot like a threat."

"It's no threat, Mr. Fulton. It's merely the reality of the weight of this operation."

"Okay, I accept your terms, but I will be the one who decides when and if my team hears whatever you're about to tell me. I will not ask permission. I will simply do what is best for my team. If you expect anything other than that, we've reached the end of this conversation."

He didn't react to my boldness but said, "It has come to our attention that Ms. Teresa Lynn may be an enemy of the United States."

"What? Do you mean to tell me you sent us downrange under the guise of bringing a loyal agent in from the cold, when in fact, we're here to kill her?"

"Not at all, Chase. When you were sent, we had every faith that Ms. Lynn was a victim of circumstances far beyond her control. Your mission hasn't changed. Your orders remain to locate and recover Ms. Lynn, repatriating her and surrendering her to the secretary of state."

"Surrender her?" I said. "That sounds a lot like the phraseology one would use when discussing the disposition of a prisoner. Is that what Ms. Lynn will be when we find her? A prisoner?"

"That remains to be seen. If she comes willingly, she is an American intelligence operative in good standing, but if she resists, you must do everything necessary to remove her from the environment."

I closed my eyes and let the weight of his words bear down on me, crushing me into the ground at my feet. "Do you have any more information on where Ms. Lynn might be?"

He cleared his throat. "We're certain she's gone to ground, and an operative of her experience with her network of connections throughout Central Asia won't be easy to find. Nothing can be done to locate her by traditional means. She's too smart for that. If she is to be found, it will be done by your team on the ground doing what is necessary to turn every rock and peel back every curtain behind which she could be hiding. Nothing short of recovering Officer Lynn is acceptable."

"Is she a threat to me or my team?"

A long silence hung over the conversation. "We don't believe so."

"That's reassuring. Is there anything else?"

He said, "Keeping your word to store this information under lock and key is paramount in this matter. I'm not threatening. I'm merely reiterating. This information is compartmentalized and classified at the highest levels. Do not destroy your future and your career because of a feeling in your gut, Chase. This is espionage at the extremes, and the Board has limitless faith in you and your team to execute in good faith. And Chase, there's one more thing . . . Stop killing people. If you are captured or killed, the United States will disavow any knowledge of your team of vigilantes or your mission. Is that understood?"

By way of an answer, I disconnected the call and stared down at the small, dark screen of my satellite phone with the new burden of a secret I may have been forced to take to my grave ten thousand miles from home.

Eager to hear a friendly voice, I called the op center, and Skipper said, "Did you hang up on them?"

"I did. We'd reached the end of meaningful conversation and begun posturing, and you know how I hate posturing."

"Were they threatening you?" she asked.

"Not according to him. He called it 'stating facts,' but those so-called facts turned out to be a reminder of the punishment for an act of treason."

"Treason?" she blurted out. "Why on Earth would he mention treason?"

"To scare me into submission."

Skipper laughed. "Oh, yeah . . . that always works."

"It may have this time," I admitted. "He laid some pretty heavy stuff on me and then told me I couldn't tell anyone."

"So you told Clark, right?"

"Not yet, but I don't see how we can continue the mission if I don't brief the team on everything I know."

She sighed. "I can't help you with that one, but I'll tell you this. I don't want to sit in the gallery at your trial for treason."

"Thanks for letting me vent. We're going to find a place to bivouac for the night, and I'll check in if anything happens."

She said, "You'll check in even if nothing happens. Don't leave me hanging."

"You got it. There's just one more thing . . ."

"Shoot."

"What's the news saying about this war?"

She said, "The down and dirty is this. Turkmenistan attacked Uzbekistan unprovoked and has killed hundreds of innocent civilians in addition to possibly thousands of militia and regular military. CNN and Fox are at opposite ends of the extreme, of course, but other than that, it's getting very little coverage."

"Has anyone mentioned the CIA being a player in this thing?"

She said, "No, of course not. Even the hard-core extremes aren't barking up that tree . . . yet."

"They will, and when they do, that'll change everything."

Chapter 15

Russian Girls and PBR

Being alone is more about psychology than a physical condition. I sat—alone—in the corner of that tiny office that felt a lot like a closet and let the reality of my life cascade over me. I was the orphaned son of mercenaries who hid behind the veil of missionaries. I was a baseball player shoved from the only world I understood and into a realm of constant change. I was a civilian thrust into the world of covert operations in command of a team of warriors who were, and will forever be, my superior in every measurable way. I had just become the guardian of a secret bigger than both countries involved in a war that made no sense to me. In that moment, I was either Teresa Lynn's truest ally or her most hated enemy, and there was only one way to know on which side of that razor's edge I would fall.

I pocketed my phone and stepped from my seclusion and into the vastness of the hangar. Clark immediately met my gaze, and out of some involuntary sense of shame, I looked away.

The gesture wasn't lost on him, and he wiped his hands and turned from the truck he'd been inspecting. "Are you all right, College Boy?" I nodded without a word, and he said, "Ah, it was one of those briefings."

I continued nodding, and he took a step closer. "It's heavy, ain't it?"

My nodding continued, and he said, "Bear it, Chase. Every man on this team knows you'll never knowingly put any of us in danger because of a piece of classified information. I don't know about Disco, but the rest of us have been where you are. We've been entrusted with knowledge, wisdom, or intel that had to remain locked inside our chests when there was nothing we wanted more than to tell everyone around us."

He paused and tapped the tip of his index finger on my chest. "If we need to know whatever they just shoved inside your head, we all know where to find it, and we all trust you to pour it out no matter what the cost, if the necessity arises."

"What would I do without you?"

He took a step back and laughed. "You'd have been dead a decade ago without me, so that's a meaningless question. Your trucks aren't hurt bad enough to take any of them out of service, Singer's leg is going to be fine, and we're warm and dry right here. That's your status report, chief."

I pushed his finger away. "Everybody needs a Clark in their life."

He shook his head. "Most people couldn't handle it. What's next, boss?"

I said, "Let's get out of this tactical gear and into something that looks a little less threatening. Six American commandos in full battle rattle get a lot of attention when they start knocking on doors in Central Asia."

We stowed our combat gear and pulled on blue jeans and oversized cotton shirts under which we could conceal communications gear and weapons. Dr. Mankiller's implanted coms eliminated the earpiece and microphones we'd used for years. A coiled wire leading to an earpiece is essentially a flashing neon sign that says, "Hey!

Look at me! I'm a spy!" Thanks to our newest big brain in the family, we looked a little less conspicuous.

I called the team together at the hood of my truck and called the op center. A map of Dashoguz filled the screen of my tablet, and I started the briefing. "I just got off the phone with the Board, and they're convinced Teresa Lynn has gone hard to ground and her last known location was right here. We're breaking up into teams of two and doing some old-fashioned detective work. Knock on doors, slip into businesses, talk to the homeless guys on the streets. Show Teresa's picture around and ask if they've seen her."

Clark tapped on the hood of the truck. "Most of us don't speak their language."

"Not a problem," I said. "Mongo and I are the strongest Russian speakers, and Disco isn't bad, so one of the three of us will be on each team. Any questions?"

Kodiak spoke up. "Is that all the Board had to say?"

"No, there's more. They told me to stop killing people, so let's do our best to keep our bullets in our guns on this one, okay?"

Heads nodded, and teams formed. Mongo took Singer, Clark paired up with Disco, and I took Kodiak.

As we rolled into the city of Dashoguz, I was astonished by the modern, Western feel of the city. Mosques bore the old-world look, but most of the office buildings could've been right at home in St. Louis or a suburb of Atlanta.

"I'm afraid I misjudged this place. We're not looking for a needle in a haystack. We're looking for one needle in a thousand haystacks."

Kodiak leaned forward and took in the city through the windshield. "I'm with you. How do we know where to start?"

"We have to think like an American CIA case officer on the run. Where would she go?"

He leaned back. "The *she* part is where I get hung up. I know what I'd do, but an American woman in a Muslim country isn't exactly everybody's favorite surprise guest."

"I get it," I said. "But she's still an intelligence officer with a lifetime of experience. From the briefing we got, she has no shortage of contacts in the region."

"What I don't get is why she'd stay here. Getting out wouldn't be all that hard, and what is there to keep her here?"

"I've got a theory on that one," I said. "I think she has more connections to this city than we know."

He relaxed in his seat. "I would agree, except for one little detail. Why would she buy a map and compass from a band of Uzbek militia if she felt comfortable in the city?"

"That's a good point, and I don't have an answer. I say we forget Lynn is a woman and hunt her as if she were one of the boys."

He shrugged. "It's a start."

I pulled up in front of the Hotel Dashoguz, and a valet leapt from a stool and flipped his cigarette into the bushes. When he leaned down to see through my window, he showed a momentary shock. "American?"

I looked up at the teen and held up Teresa Lynn's picture with a twenty-dollar bill pressed to the upper right corner. He lifted the bill and picture from my hand. After gazing at the picture for a while, he shot a disapproving look at the twenty and shrugged. The man let the picture fall from his fingertips and back inside my truck.

I feigned embarrassment. "I'm so sorry. I didn't realize that was just a twenty." I folded a Benjamin and held it between my fingers. "Would you care to take another look?"

He smiled and pinched the bill, but I didn't let it go. "First, you tell us what you know about this woman."

He glanced over the hood, and I imagined him fearing being caught talking to a pair of Americans in a Turkmen military truck. Probably expecting me not to understand, he spoke in Russian. "I don't know her name, but she's been here. She arrived by taxi five or six days ago."

To his surprise, I answered as if I'd learned to speak in downtown Moscow. "Why do you remember her?"

He tried to hide his reaction to my language skills, but there was no question he hadn't expected what he got. "I remember her because I tried to carry her bag—singular, one bag—for her, but she almost broke my arm snatching it back from me. Whatever was in that bag was important enough to not let it out of her sight."

"How long did she stay?"

"I don't know, but she's gone now. Someone else checked into her room."

"Tell me about the person in the room now."

He stared down at the bill between my fingers. "For that, I will tell you only about guests who are no longer here. Guests who come here expect privacy in a luxury hotel. I can't . . ."

I wrapped a second bill around the first. "Privacy is important all over the world, but so is two hundred bucks American."

Instead of pinching the bills, he held out an open palm, and I laid the cash in the center of his hand. "Two people, a man and a woman, checked into that woman's room four days ago. They wanted everyone to believe they were married, but it was obvious they were not."

"How was it obvious?"

He said, "When the lady pulled her luggage, the handle moved her wedding ring, and there was no white shadow beneath the ring. Unless she takes off her ring every time she goes outside, she wasn't anybody's wife."

"Nationality?"

He pocketed the bills. "American, like you."

"Can you find out if they're still here?"

He turned up his palms. "Both of our hands are empty, my friend. This means our conversation is over."

I peeled two more bills from my folded stash and hid them in my hand. "Have you ever heard of double or nothing?"

The valet slowly shook his head, and I said, "It works like this. You tell me everything I want to know, and if I believe you've been honest and thorough, I'll double your money, but if I get the slightest feeling you're holding back, you get nothing. Simple, right?"

He started talking. "Tom and Joanne Smith. They left two days ago in a government car." He took a step back and appraised my truck. "Not like this one, though. It was a black sedan."

"Chauffeured?"

He nodded.

"How did the woman leave?"

My ploy didn't work.

He screwed up his face. "I told you I didn't see her leave."

"Fair enough. This Smith couple, where did they go?"

"How would I know? I park cars and carry bags."

"You're not winning this game."

He stepped closer and leaned toward the open window. "What else do you want to know?"

"While the woman was here, did you see her leave and return, or did she stay in the hotel the whole time?"

"I'm only here for twelve hours at a time. She may have, but I didn't see her leave the hotel."

I rubbed the two bills together between my fingers. "You're not doing so well. Here's your last chance. Did the woman leave a forwarding address or mention where she was going next?"

He puffed out his cheeks with a long exhalation. "Wait here."

With that, he vanished, and I turned to Kodiak. "Where do you think he's going?"

"I think he wants what's behind door number two, so he's gone digging for anything he can find to entice you to fork over the dough."

Before I could respond, movement at the top of the stairs caught my eye. Two bigger-than-average men in suits and earpieces —a dead giveaway—rushed through the doors and down the stairs, unbuttoning their jackets as they came. Our valet was nowhere in sight, but I wasn't interested in waiting around for his reappearance.

Kodiak pounded on the dash with his fist. "Go! Go! Go!"

I was an instant faster than his demand, and my boot stomped the accelerator almost far enough to touch the ground beneath us. The tires spun, and white smoke boiled as we fishtailed away from the valet stand. I cut the corner as the truck sped through fifty miles per hour and bounced across the curb. The string of traffic behind us honked and swerved, but I was too concerned about what lay ahead to care about the road rage in the rearview.

Kodiak spun and scanned the scene behind us. "That was close."

"It was, indeed. The last thing we need is a physical altercation in the parking lot of the best hotel in the city."

Kodiak let out a chortle. "Besides, they told us to stop killing people, right?"

"I think they might have mentioned something about that, but I don't plan to change my tactics very much to accommodate the whim of suits in soft chairs back in DC."

He nestled in his seat and pulled on his seat belt. "I hate these autolocking things." When he'd won the holy war with a strap of nylon, he said, "Where are we headed now?"

"I'm putting some distance between us and that hotel, then we're going to find the railroad tracks."

"Railroad tracks?"

"Yep. We can't find the wrong side of the tracks if we can't find the tracks."

He grinned like Clark. "I like where your head's at, boss man."

I pulled to the edge of the road and popped open my door. "Trade seats with me."

Kodiak didn't ask any questions. He climbed behind the steering wheel and pulled us back onto the road, then he said, "Let me guess. You want to turn around and hit that taxi stand about half a mile back."

"You're pretty good at this game."

"It's all I've ever done," he said. "I joined the Army when I was seventeen, and the rest is battle scars and MREs."

"You're making a fine addition to the team, and everybody's glad you're here. Do you plan to stick around?"

He looked at me as if I'd asked if he was going to the moon. "What kind of idiot would walk away from this gig? The pay is out of sight. The team is hard-core. And the assignments are something right out of a James Bond movie. If you want to get rid of me, you'll have to throw me overboard and hope I can't swim fast enough to catch up. I ain't going nowhere, boss."

I motioned through the windshield. "Pull over here, and let me out. Keep your eyes on me, and don't let me get rolled up, but try to stay out of sight."

He eased the truck to the curb, and I stepped from the cab. The three taxi drivers leaning against a concrete stand tried to ignore the American, but I persisted in English. When that didn't work, I switched to a language each of them spoke fluently. The crisp one-hundred-dollar bill reminded them how much English they actually knew.

"Now that I've got your attention, I need some information. I'm a long way from home, and I've not seen a woman's legs in six months. Where can I get a beer and a lap dance in this place?"

The man closest to me threw down a half-smoked cigarette and took me by the arm. "Come. I take you."

If Clark were in the truck parked five hundred feet away, I'd never look back, but I'd never worked with Kodiak in an urban environment. Would he follow? Would he attack? Would he lose sight of me and stay where he was?

My gut told me there was enough Clark Johnson wisdom in Kodiak's head to make him pull away from the curb and follow at a comfortable distance, so I followed the cabbie into his car. He seemed a little nervous about having me in the front seat, but my C-note was still doing most of my talking for me. It took a little bit of neck twisting, but I finally situated myself so I could see a tiny slice of what was behind us in the passenger-side mirror. The grill of a blue and white truck bounced in the shaky image, and the dependability of the former Green Beret earned another mark of respect in my book.

"What kind of women you like, huh? Big ones? Little ones? Dark ones? Huh?"

"Russians aren't bad," I said.

The cabbie gave me a punch on the arm. "I have just perfect place for you, friend, but you should know I cannot make change for American dollars."

I looked at him over the rim of my sunglasses. "If you drop me off at the right spot, I won't need any change."

His roaring laughter bounced off every surface of the interior of the smoky car, but I caught his eyes dancing back and forth between the mirror and the road in front of us. As the ride continued, his eyes spent more time on the mirror than the road, and my concern mounted.

"Is everything okay behind us?"

He frowned. "Could it be maybe you are being followed by militia?"

I spun in my seat as if terrified and studied the traffic behind us. "No. I've not done anything to be followed. I'm just an American stuck somewhere he doesn't belong."

He nodded slowly and kept watching the mirror. I let my right arm drape out the open window, and I gave the hand signal for Kodiak to back off. At least, that's what I hoped the hand signal meant. It was easy to forget that the new guy hadn't been with us from day one.

To my enormous relief, the cabbie relaxed and said, "Is okay. He is not following us now. What is American doing in Dashoguz?"

I gave the one-word answer that would end the inquisition. "Oil."

A mile later, after half a dozen turns, he pulled to the side of the road where a curb should've been. Outside the window stood a building that had once boasted a second story.

I asked, "Is this the place?"

He shook his head. "No, but it is near. This was storage place. Maybe in English . . . where house?"

"Warehouse," I said. "What happened to it?"

"The Uzbeks and their damned explosives in dark of night."

"Explosives?"

"Yes, we are in war. This is why you are trapped here. Trust me, friend. Go home any way you can. The Uzbeks are devils, and they will kill all of us, one at time, you also. I will drive you to Tajikistan for three hundred U.S. From there, you can fly to Europe and home."

"Thanks for the tip. How can I find you?"

He looked confused. "You already find me. We go now. You can have all Russian girls you want in Europe."

I softened my tone. "Thanks for the concern, but I'm not ready to go yet. I still have a deal to make, but do you have a phone?"

He reached beneath the seat and produced an ancient flip phone. "Yes, I have phone. You need?"

"I just need the number so I can call you when I'm ready to go."

He fumbled with a scrap of paper and a broken pencil. When he finished, he laid the paper into my hand and let his hand linger near mine.

I pressed the hundred into his palm. "How close is the place?"

He pulled the car into drive and turned down a long, narrow alley. "Just around corner."

I didn't like anything about the situation I was in. There could be no better ambush point than that ten-foot-wide chunk of concrete between two ancient buildings. I was pinned in with a cabbie who knew only three things about me: I was American, had a nice bankroll, and liked Russian girls. Any two of those three was enough reason to leave my corpse behind a pile of trash with empty pockets.

I pressed my elbow against the frame of my Glock beneath my shirt and prayed there weren't a dozen men lurking ahead who were hell-bent on making the American pay for looking for oil so far from home.

As covertly as possible, I unbuttoned two of the buttons near the bottom of my shirt. Accessing my Glock in an instant may have been the only thing that could keep me alive in the coming minutes. With the buttons undone, I slipped my hand inside and pressed the transmit button of my sat-com so Kodiak could hear everything I said in the coming minutes.

I made no effort to hide my movement to check the mirrors. "Stop right here! Where are you taking me?"

He hit the brakes, and I kept my eyes peeled through the windshield. "I don't like this alley behind the blown-out building."

"Is okay, friend. Relax. Is best way to place for Russian girls and Pabst Blue Ribbon."

Chapter 16
Pick a Number

In spite of the cabbie's reassurances, my heart rate continued to rise. "There has to be a better way."

The driver checked the mirrors. "This is best way. Nobody will see you."

"Why would I care if anybody sees me?"

"Are you afraid, American?"

"Not afraid. Just cautious. Let me out here, and I'll walk the rest of the way."

He shrugged. "Okay, but is safe with me. Is not safe with Uzbeks."

"It's not the Uzbeks I'm worried about. It's the thugs hiding in the shadows waiting to take my wallet."

I pulled the handle and stepped from the taxi. Being on foot felt a lot safer than being stuck inside a taxi that smelled like Turkish cigarettes and incense. As soon as I closed the door, the driver pulled away as if nothing out of the ordinary had just occurred—like hundred-dollar tips happened every day in the city of Dashoguz.

I drew my pistol and approached the corner where a smaller, darker alley joined the main branch. Carefully cutting the pie around the corner with my pistol extended, just as I'd practiced thousands of times in the shooting house back at Bonaventure, slices of the alley came into view with every tiny lateral movement.

That's when I heard Kodiak's grizzly voice. "I've got your six, Chase. It's clear in every direction."

It sounded as if he were standing only inches behind me, but thanks to the bone conduction receiver glued to my jawbone, he could've been anywhere on Earth.

"Say position."

"I'm on overwatch at six o'clock high."

I turned and caught a glimpse of my newest teammate nestled in the debris of the mostly demolished second floor of the building behind me. "Nicely done. Can I interest you in a beer?"

He stepped to the edge of the building. "Nah, but I wouldn't mind a Russian girl if they've got enough to go around."

I holstered my Glock. "I know a beautiful helicopter pilot back in the States who wouldn't approve of you and a Russian girl."

He scampered down the wall using the remnants of a down-spout and landed a few feet away. "Ah, she and I are separated."

"Separated? What happened."

"Nothing. We're just separated. I'm in whatever country this is, and she's on a ship somewhere."

"You're a funny guy," I said. "I'll be sure to let her know that's how you feel."

He gave me a wink and changed the subject. "Nice job on the coms."

"Thanks," I said. "I wanted you to know where I was."

"Yeah, I figured. Did the cabbie see me on the drive over here?"

I said, "He did. That's why I waved you off."

Kodiak peered around the corner as if looking for the driver. "That guy might come in handy."

I held up the wrinkled piece of paper. "I got them digits."

"Of course you did. Now, let's put eyes on this world-famous beer joint of his."

We rounded the corner to see a squatty building with bars over blacked-out windows and a massive padlock on a steel hasp on the door.

I checked my watch. "It must not be happy hour yet. Where's the truck?"

We walked back to the borrowed vehicle and did a little recon in case we needed a hasty escape from the shady side of town. Kodiak pulled behind a box truck that looked like it hadn't moved in years and shut down the engine. "How's this?"

"I like it," I said. "While we're waiting for them to swing open the gates and invite us in, I guess we should check in with the rest of the team."

Clark answered first. "We're getting shot down everywhere we go. Either nobody's seen this Teresa Lynn woman or they're not talking."

Mongo said, "We're striking out, too."

I said, "We're running down a lead. I'll send you our coordinates in case this turns into the O.K. Corral. According to the cabbie, it's safe here except for trouble with the Uzbeks. He seems to have a special kind of hatred for those guys."

Clark said, "Hmm. That's interesting. We'll start moving your way, and I'll see if I can round up Wyatt Earp and Doc Holliday, just in case."

Darkness slowly consumed the city, and one by one, dim lights filled a few of the visible windows. A man about Mongo's size pulled a ring of keys from his pocket and fumbled with the padlock on the door. After several unsuccessful attempts, the lock fell open, and he propped the door against the concrete wall of the building. The mountain of a man disappeared inside and returned minutes later with a stool and a baseball bat.

"Would you look at that?" I said. "He and I've got something in common. I guess there are baseball fans all over the world."

Kodiak said, "I'm not sure that guy's ever heard of baseball."

"You may be right, but if he swings that thing at me, I expect you to put a bullet in his head before I start bleeding."

"You know it," Kodiak said. "How's this going to go down?"

"I figure business will be slow for a while, so maybe I can talk Mr. Baseball out of a little local intel."

Kodiak stared at the bouncer. "He doesn't look like the local information booth, but I guess it's worth a try. We might have more luck with the bartender if we can get inside."

"You keep using the pronoun *we*," I said. "I'm going in there alone unless the rest of the cowboys show up in time to cover both of us. If they don't make it in time, I'll need you on overwatch."

"Whatever you say. You're the boss. I'm just the hired help."

"You don't really feel that way, do you?"

He made a clicking sound with his tongue. "I've lived my whole adult life on teams, but I've never shown up and been instantly accepted like this until you picked me up in Alaska. I've gotta say, it feels a little weird."

"What's weird about it?"

He scratched his chin where his beard was growing back in after his first shave in twenty years. "It's Hunter."

"Hunter? Have you got a problem with him?"

He threw up both hands. "No, I'm cool with him. He's obviously hard-core, and I've got a lot of respect for that, but I get the feeling he thinks I'm his replacement. I figure I'm temporary help, at best, until he comes off injured reserve."

I squeezed my eyelids closed and reopened. "This isn't the time or the place for this discussion, so I want to put it to bed now, and we can discuss it in more detail when we get home if you want, but this is how I see it."

He twisted in his seat as if I had his full attention.

I said, "You're a full member of the team. You proved your mettle on the ice in the Alaska mission. You're a gun-toter, just like the rest of the team, and we're glad you're here. You fill some holes we had, and no matter what happens with Hunter, you'll still be a full member of the team."

He lowered his chin. "Are you sure the rest of the guys feel the same?"

"If they didn't, you wouldn't be here. Listen . . . Here's the nuts and bolts of it. Clark isn't supposed to be operating. He's blown-up and blown-out. His spine looks more like the framework of a skyscraper than a stack of vertebrae. He's got no business out here in the field. Part of it is stubbornness and refusal to admit he's too old and beat-up to play in the majors anymore, but the reality of it is the fact that we need him. We're a six-man team. That's the way we train and the way we operate."

"I get that," he said. "And it's not Clark I'm worried about."

I said, "Hold on. Let me finish. Hunter got the bad end of a deal on an op down in Cuba. He and I stepped off a cliff that felt like it was a mile high. I came out of it okay, but he almost didn't make it back. He's on a long road to recovery, but he is recovering. Tony, Clark's brother, is out of the game for good. We got him hurt too badly to ever put him back on the roster. So, work those numbers. You're not taking Hunter's place. You're taking Tony's spot, and we still need to push Clark out and take on another operator. That's not going to be easy, but you need to get it through your head that you're not temporary help. Your spot on the team is solid, and everybody's happy about that."

He stared between his boots for a moment. "Thanks, man. I appreciate that. I know we should've had this talk back at Bonaventure, but you know how operators are. We aren't good at talking stuff out."

"Don't worry about that," I said. "Just keep your head on straight, and keep me alive. It's time to open a tab, and I like your bartender approach better than dealing with that one-man brute squad."

He reached behind the seat and pulled his SR-25 rifle from its bag. "I'll be on top of that truck if you need me."

Kodiak slipped from the vehicle and scaled the box truck. Once he was settled into position, he set his sat-com to active broadcast so I could hear him without him pushing the PTT button. "I'm in position with a good line of sight through the front door all the way to the bar."

"Wish me luck," I said as I stepped from the vehicle and thumbed my active broadcast.

Kodiak said, "You don't need luck. You've got me."

His confidence reminded me of the thundering question that never left my skull. *Why me? What forces conspired to throw me into the blender with some ice and vodka and then pour me into the tumbler that was my life? I wasn't qualified to lead a horse to water, let alone a team of operators into some of the most inhospitable corners of the globe. No, I wasn't qualified, but I would never quit.*

I locked eyes with the three-hundred-pounder from thirty feet away, and although we probably didn't share a common language or anything resembling similar backgrounds, both of us were doing exactly the same thing inside our heads:

His left knee twists a little to the inside. That's a weakness. His right hand is scarred and swollen. He's probably right-handed. His nose makes far too many turns between his brow and his upper lip. He likely doesn't guard his face well in a fight. His eyes never stop moving. He knows almost every threat in his environment . . . almost.

I didn't break my stride as I continued my confident stroll toward the door. Once within reach, I slipped a folded twenty into

Brutus's palm, but apparently, the cover charge for American spies was a little higher than twenty bucks.

His dinner-plate-sized hand landed squarely in the center of my chest, stopping me in my tracks. He stood from his tortured wooden stool and glared down at me. "American?"

I shrugged but didn't give him an answer.

He must've liked my non-answer because he dropped his hand and said, "*Girenime ökünmäň.*"

Whatever he said didn't sound like a question, so I kept walking, and he didn't follow. I was inside, but something told me getting out may be the tougher of the two pursuits. Hopefully, the rest of my team would arrive before I had to fight my way back onto the street.

The bar wasn't what I expected. For some reason, I thought it would look like a Texas honky-tonk, but I couldn't have been more wrong. Compared to the exterior of the building, the interior was immaculate. Nothing was out of place. Music played, but there was no jukebox. It sounded like an Indian sitar, but I couldn't be sure. Nine tables dotted the floor, and the dim glow of overhead lights showed the floor to be clean and completely free of sawdust. So much for a cowboy bar. I was in a Turkmen lounge, but I doubted they had PBR on tap like the cabbie suggested. His other prediction was spot-on, though. Five unmistakably Eastern European beauties worked the tables, pretending to be infatuated by the rugged, "separated" men like Kodiak.

I didn't look so different from the men sitting at the tables. I was lean, bearded, clearly not from Central Asia, and definitely a long way from home. I tried to look like I belonged in whatever that place was, but I'm not sure anybody from anywhere truly belonged in that lounge.

Taking up a position near the end of the long, well-polished bar, I glanced through the open front door, but the interior light made it impossible to see anything happening on the street outside.

Although I couldn't see out, Kodiak could clearly see in. He said, "Move two feet to your left, and I'll have the best line of sight. If everything is cool, give me a little scratch."

I dug my fingertips into my beard and took a step to the left. Kodiak said, "Perfect. Do your thing, Doc."

The bartender was occupied with a task at the other end of the bar, so I turned with my back to the long bar and faced the room. Everything was eerily quiet. The conversations that were underway remained muted and unanimated. The more I studied the room, the less it felt like any bar I'd ever seen. None of the faces looked local. It reminded me of an airport bar full of weary travelers and homesick vagabonds.

A knock came on the bar behind me, and I spun to see the bartender impatiently waiting for my order. I leaned down and softly said, "Whiskey on the rocks."

The wiry-framed man frowned and swept an open hand across the collection of empty bottles on the mirrored shelf behind him.

I said, "They're all empty. What do you have?"

He continued waving his hand across the collection that would've been a lot of fun at a shooting gallery. I was beginning to believe I was the only person in the bar who had no idea what was happening, so I repeated my order. The man sighed as if I were annoying him and waved me around the end of the bar. I followed his instructions and his outstretched hand until I saw a two-layer shelf beneath the bar with at least fifty bottles without labels, and each bottle bore a handwritten number. The man touched an empty Wild Turkey bottle on the back bar and directed my attention to the small number 14 printed on the cap. Then, he pointed back beneath the bar and touched the clear bottle bearing the same number.

The lightbulb came on. I turned and surveyed the bottle collection until I found the old familiar shape of Jack Daniel's Single Barrel. "I'll have that."

At that moment, Kodiak said, "Tilt your head if everything is copacetic."

I tilted and headed back around the bar. The man had the whiskey poured and waiting by the time I slid back onto the barstool. I said, "Thank you. Can I open a tab?"

He cocked his head in an odd display and frowned with his narrow eyes. Finally, he shook his head in small, sharp jerks, so I slid a twenty across the bar and waited for my change. It didn't come. In fact, there wasn't a cash register in sight, and the bill went straight into the bartender's apron pocket.

I made a mental note to watch other transactions before I ordered my second drink. Watching closely in the mirror, I cupped my hand around the tumbler, hiding its contents, and raised it to my lips. I made a show of enjoying the taste and smell before slipping the glass over the back edge of the rail and pouring most of the whiskey into the empty sink. That same motion, twice more, left my glass empty and my tongue convinced that whatever the man poured, it had never come from Lynchburg, Tennessee, and probably tasted a lot like everything else beneath the bar.

I repeated the order twice more for a grand total of sixty bucks in the man's apron pocket. When he came back when my third glass was almost empty, I slid Teresa Lynn's picture across the bar and shielded it with my left hand to keep curious eyes from noticing the photo. The bartender refused to look down at the picture and recoiled as if I'd shown him a king cobra.

The addition of a much larger American bill made the photo a little less frightening for the man, and he made short work of snatching the hundred from the bar and sliding it into his pants pocket beneath the apron. He took a quick glance at Teresa's picture and shook his head.

I tapped a finger on the picture. "Look again. I need to find this woman."

He flipped the picture over and slid it back across the bar. An instant later, a fresh drink landed in front of me, and he stood, anxiously awaiting another twenty. I returned the picture to its original faceup position and tapped it a little more aggressively. The man pulled a towel from his waist and tossed it across the picture, then stepped back and clapped both hands over his head.

That got Brutus's attention outside the front door, and the monster sprang from his stool and spun on a heel. He could close the distance between us in four or five strides, but I didn't want to do anything to disrupt the quiet calm of the room. I snatched the picture from beneath the towel and shoved it into a pocket. With a continuation of the same motion, I pulled another twenty from my stash and dropped it on the bar.

Thankfully, the bartender raised one hand and nodded to Brutus, stopping him three strides from catching a 9mm bullet in the face and a .308 in the spine from my backup sniper on top of the box truck. Brutus returned to his stool, and the bartender disappeared through a curtain at the other end of the bar.

Kodiak said, "That wasn't cool at all."

I wanted the whiskey in my tumbler to find its way into my belly to calm the nerves I'd stirred up, but I needed my wits about me for whatever was coming next. But when it did come, I wasn't ready for the message or the messenger.

Chapter 17
Like a Thief in the Night

Kodiak said, "It looks like a really good time to make your exit."

He was right, but I wasn't ready to walk away from the spot my gut believed was the right fishing hole. The bartender was far too nervous to be innocent. His eyes said he'd seen Teresa Lynn, but his resistance said he wasn't interested in getting involved. I wasn't going to move until he came back with a better explanation than siccing the bouncer on me.

Before my persistence paid off, a dark-haired, dark-eyed man stepped between me and my sniper. "Whatever you're doing is the worst thing you could do in this place. Walk away now, and I'll make them believe you're okay and you're with me. Go now."

His Israeli accent was unmistakable, and the slight bulge beneath his shirt screamed Mossad, and I was instantly more intrigued than before.

What could a mute bartender, a giant freak of nature, a nearly silent bar, and an Israeli intelligence officer possibly have in common?

From my vantage point in the cheap seats, it looked like the answer to my unspoken question was the face of the woman in the picture now tucked hurriedly in my pocket.

I took one more look into the mirror behind the bar. Nothing except the Israeli and the bartender were out of place. The minor commotion I'd caused didn't seem to bother anyone except those two, and that left me full of even more questions.

I looked into the Mossad officer's coal-black eyes. "Walk me out."

He huffed. "Not a chance, Yankee. You walk out alone, tip the bouncer, and keep walking. I'll find you."

I didn't like it, but for a reason I'd probably never know, the Israeli felt strongly enough about the situation to intervene on my behalf—at least I assumed his intervention was on my behalf. Perhaps that pistol beneath his shirt was destined to be my gallows. Only time would tell.

I took some of his advice and walked away. Brutus didn't get a tip, and I didn't keep walking. Instead, I found a nice little pile of trash that would make a lovely hidey-hole while waiting for my new Jewish friend to begin his game of hide-and-seek. Thankfully, the trash was dry and relatively devoid of smell.

I spoke barely above a whisper, "Kodiak, keep an eye out for him."

"For who?" came his reply.

In that single, grammatically incorrect question, the greatest weakness of Dr. Mankiller's bone conduction device became glaringly obvious. It could not pick up ambient sound not created by the vocal cords of its host. Kodiak hadn't heard a word the Israeli said.

"There's a Mossad officer about six feet tall and two hundred pounds with a full black beard who'll come out that door any minute. I won't be able to see him for several seconds after he emerges, but I need to know which direction and how fast he's walking. Got it?"

"Got it," Kodiak said. "But how do you know he's Mossad?"

"You'll understand as soon as you see him."

I squirmed until I was as comfortable as I would ever be on the filthy ground behind a pile of unidentifiable junk. The minutes dragged on, and the Israeli didn't come through the door. I concluded that even if he were a Mossad officer, he was likely just trying to scare me away from whatever his mission was inside the bar. I had clearly gotten in his way, and he needed me off his playing field.

According to my watch, I'd been hunkering in the same position for almost twenty minutes when I called Kodiak. "Do you see anybody matching the description still inside the bar?"

"Negative. I saw your man, but only his back when he approached you at the bar. I've not seen him since. I can move and scan the room if you want."

"That's not necessary," I said. "He's not coming. Let's move out. I'll meet you at the truck."

I never heard Kodiak's reply. Instead, I felt the muzzle of a small pistol pressed just beneath my right ear and heard, "Who are you, and what are you doing in Dashoguz?"

I threw my hands to the ground to push myself to a standing or kneeling position. If I was going to die, I wanted it to happen while I was fighting back. I prayed I didn't die while sitting on my butt behind a pile of garbage. My efforts were wasted, and my motion was halted when the toe of my attacker's boot landed sharply against my spine, just above my belt. That blow would've been enough to keep me down, but those Israelis don't believe in doing anything just enough. They take a lot of pride in going above and beyond. His kick hurt and sent lightning bolts down both of my legs, but the blow from the butt of his pistol against my spine, just below my skull, sent stars circling my head, and my arms turned to noodles.

"I asked you two questions." His tone wasn't threatening. It was merely matter-of-fact and confident.

I wiggled my fingers in an effort to get enough feeling back in my arms to spin and sweep his legs, but the two million pins pricking my flesh told me it would be some time before either of my arms was available for a fight. All I had left was my ability to talk my way out of the situation, but talking to the gunman wasn't what I had in mind.

I said, "Why are you pressing a gun against my head?"

The aggressor laughed. "Nice try, American, but your sniper isn't going to hear you. He's having a little nap."

The voice belonged, without a doubt, to the same man who'd encouraged me to leave the bar. I was in a situation I didn't like at all.

"Is he dead?" I asked.

"Maybe. Do you want to join him?"

"No. What do you want?"

He said, "You know what I want. I want to know who you are and what you are doing here."

"Why does that matter to you if you're just going to kill me anyway?"

He continued in the same confident, measured tone. "Who are you, and what are you doing here?"

It was time to switch gears and appeal to his sense of brotherhood. "We're on the same team."

"I don't have a team," he said. "I work alone . . . always."

"I meant to say we're allies."

His tone harshened, but only slightly. "Allies don't stick their boot in another man's op. Are you American CIA?"

I told the truth. "No, I'm not CIA, but I am American, and I'm searching for another American. I didn't intentionally step on your operation, whatever it is. I just need to find my target and take her home."

As soon as the word *her* fell from my tongue, I could've stabbed myself in the throat.

The man said, "What makes you think you'll find Teresa Lynn here?"

I'd failed at every critical junction of my operation so far, and it looked like that wasn't on the verge of changing. "How do you know—"

He didn't let me finish. A second kick and a pair of strikes to my neck left me barely better than useless. I gagged in a violent effort to catch my breath, and my ears rang as if I'd spent the last ten minutes inside a clanging bell.

When I finally filled my lungs with air again, I choked out, "Stop doing that."

"Answer my questions, and I'll stop."

"I answered your questions. I'm an American looking for Teresa Lynn."

"But you're not CIA?"

"No, I'm not CIA, but if I were, I wouldn't tell you."

The man said something, but Singer's voice inside the bones of my skull drowned out the Israeli's voice. "Chase, if you want me to shoot him, pick up your left hand and put it right back down where it is."

Kodiak may have befallen the Israeli's attack, but our Southern Baptist sniper had shown up at exactly the right moment. Instead of moving my hand, I said, "No."

The Mossad officer said, "No? What do you mean, no? I asked who you work for. No is not an acceptable answer."

I said, "I told you we're on the same side. I'm not here to—"

Before I had to finish whatever my statement was going to be, the man growled like a wounded bear and collapsed to the ground.

I threw myself forward against the pile of garbage with the intention of using the trash to pull myself onto my still-tingling foot, but little did I know the Mossad officer wasn't going to be my most terrifying ghost of Christmas past.

Before I could scamper onto my knees and ultimately to my feet, the thick, round form of a high-caliber weapon landed against my left shoulder blade. The voice that accompanied the heavy muzzle both surprised and thrilled me.

She whispered, "Who are you, and why are you showing my picture to everyone you meet?"

"Don't shoot me, Ms. Lynn. I'm here to help you."

The Mossad officer's body convulsed on the ground somewhere behind me, and I couldn't decide if Singer had put him down or if it was CIA Case Officer Teresa Lynn who took him out.

"Did you kill the Israeli?" I mumbled with my face pressed against the trash in front of me.

"He isn't dead," she said, "but he'll wish he were when he wakes up. What you feel in your back is half a million volts if I pull the trigger. You'll spasm first, your heart will flutter, every drop of saliva your body is capable of producing will turn to white, milky foam, and of course, you'll ruin that nice pair of pants."

It was Singer's voice that told me what I already knew. "That's Lynn, Chase. Don't let her escape. We're moving in."

I tried to make a sound that would keep my team at a safe distance because I was concerned about my pants. The sound left my throat as a garbled moan, no matter how hard I tried to lift my head from the pile of rubbish.

The next sensation I experienced was bizarre in every way. Lynn jammed a finger inside my left ear, fished around as if digging for part of my brain, and then did the same to my right ear. "Where are your coms?"

"I don't know. Maybe your friend from Mossad has them."

She drove the Taser deeper into my ribs and added the remainder of her weight to her knee in the small of my back, where our Jewish representative had inflicted more pain than I wanted to deal with.

In a whispered voice I'll never forget, Teresa Lynn said, "You've been lied to. You've been sent here to stop me from doing what's right. You don't understand how deeply you're drowning in something you'll never understand. Walk away, pretend you never heard my name, and retire to your nice little life on the North River with your beautiful wife, Penny. You do not need to die here to protect those men from the just deserts of their tyranny. You do not need to die here."

I don't remember the five hundred thousand volts that surged through my flesh that night.

Chapter 18
Heart to Heart

When I returned to the land of the living, breathing, sentient creatures, my head had obviously been crushed in a vise and every muscle torn from my bones and shredded. As bad as my body felt, my prosthetic leg took the brunt of the shock Teresa Lynn's Taser delivered. The complex electronics inside the mechanical leg melted like they'd been hit with a torch. In an instant, one of the most sophisticated prosthetics on Earth was reduced to a useless, inflexible, six-pound relic that belonged in the pile of trash outside the strangest bar I'd ever seen in a corner of the world where I should've never been.

"Is Kodiak okay?"

"I'm fine, boss. I'm sorry I let you down. I never saw the guy. When I came to, Mongo was hefting me into the truck."

"Did he take your rifle?"

"No, that's what's crazy. He didn't take anything. In fact, he closed the ejection port and made sure the gun was well hidden beneath my body."

I groaned as I tried to sit up. "Everything about this op is crazy. Nothing makes sense yet. How long have I been out?"

Clark pointed across the hangar to a body in the fetal position with a full beard and jet-black hair. "Not as long as that guy."

"That's the Mossad officer who got the drop on Kodiak and me. He's good. Very good."

"He's very unconscious is what he is, and your girl, Teresa Lynn, got the drop on him, too."

As my vision cleared, I found Singer. "Did you see her coming?"

The sniper shook his head. "I was on the Israeli, and I caught a glimpse of the barbs hitting his back, right where my crosshairs were. He had you pinned down, and when Lynn hit him with the Taser, he melted like butter. By the time I pieced it together, she was on you. I thought you'd give the order to put her down, but I couldn't understand what you were saying."

I replayed the attack in my head and said, "She had my face crammed against the pile of garbage, so I couldn't speak."

Singer said, "Yeah, I figured that out, but by that time, she'd already Tased you and vanished."

"Vanished? How does anybody vanish from you? You were under nods, right?"

"Yeah, I had the night vision on, but I'm telling you, man, she just disappeared. Poof. Gone."

I tried to recreate the events and slow down the scene in my mind, but the more I thought about it, the more questions I had, so I backed up in time and turned to Kodiak. "Did you get Tased?"

He pointed toward the limp body on the floor. "No. He came out of nowhere and hit me with something. It might've been a blackjack, but I never really saw it. I remember catching a glimpse of him the instant before he hit me, but the next thing I remember was Mongo throwing me in the truck."

"Why didn't they kill us?" I asked.

Clark snapped his fingers. "That's the six-million-dollar question."

I shook the cobwebs from my head. "I'm pretty sure that's not how that saying goes, but I get your point. They obviously weren't working together, otherwise, she wouldn't have Tased that guy. Let's wake him up."

Singer said, "Not before we cuff him."

As usual, Kodiak was first to move. He had the Mossad officer flex-cuffed and tied at the knees before Mongo could get the smelling salts from his kit. Our giant rolled the man onto his left side and emptied a bottle of water in his face. He stirred but didn't come back to consciousness, so Mongo broke open the ammonia pack and waved it beneath his nose.

That did the trick. He squirmed, pulling against his restraints, and shook his head from the powerful smell. As he blinked away his blurred vision, the man took in the world around him and blurted out something that sounded like a question in a language none of us recognized.

"Sit him up," I ordered.

Mongo took the man by his shoulders and situated him on his butt.

I took a knee in front of him, placing myself close enough to his face to make him uncomfortable. "Was that Hebrew?"

He continued blinking. "Where am I?"

"Now we're getting somewhere," I said. "It looks like the tables may have turned a little since you and I last spoke. At this point, the good guys—that'd be us—have the upper hand, and I'd like to start with a few questions. If you choose to lie to me, your situation, and your degree of comfort, will deteriorate quickly. Let's start with your name."

The man twisted his head to wipe his nose against his shoulder. "Water."

I leaned even closer. "Is that your name or a demand?"

He closed his eyes and took a long, deep breath. "My name is Imri Nazarian. May I please have some water?"

I extended my hand behind me, and someone slapped a bottle of water into my palm. I spun off the top and held the bottle to his lips.

He drank until water ran from the corners of his mouth, then he pulled away, sighed, and said, "Thank you."

With the touch of a button, I had Skipper on the line. "I need you to run a name through Israeli intelligence. Imri Nazarian."

Seconds later, she said, "Imri Nazarian . . . Born September first, nineteen eighty, former Israel Defense Force commando, officially listed as missing in action in Syria in July of two thousand six, presumed dead by the Israeli government, family paid death benefit."

"Distinguishing marks?" I asked.

Skipper said, "Checking now . . . Okay. Severe burn scars on left lower leg, bullet entry and exit wound right bicep and left side below his bottom rib."

I shoved the man onto his back and yanked up his pant leg. If the scar was telling the truth, our new friend had endured a nasty burn.

"How did that happen?" I asked.

He shrugged. "I fell asleep while smoking in bed."

I jerked open his shirt and pulled it down over his bicep, revealing an obvious bullet wound. His side bore the same type of scar.

I said, "Thanks, Skipper. Get on the horn with your contact in Tel-Aviv, and let them know we've got their boy rolled up in Turkmenistan. Ask them what they want us to do with him."

"Okay, stand by."

Imri blurted out, "Wait!"

I said, "Are you still there, Skipper?"

I could almost hear her smiling through the phone. "It worked, huh? Mr. Nazarian doesn't want Tel-Aviv knowing he got jammed up by a bunch of Americans, does he?"

"That appears to be the case. Delay that call while I explore our new friend's willingness to cooperate."

"I'm standing by."

I pulled the man's shirt back over his shoulders and dragged him back into a seated position, then I checked my watch. "You've got sixty seconds to convince me why I shouldn't have my analyst make that call to Tel-Aviv. And . . . go."

He eyed the half-empty water bottle on the concrete floor and licked his lips. I gave him another drink, and he started talking.

"Are you guys Delta or SEALs?"

I checked my watch again. "Forty seconds."

"Okay, okay . . . Whoever you are, you're chasing the same ghost as the rest of us. None of us knows exactly what she has to do with this war, but everybody wants to talk to Teresa Lynn. She may be the only person on Earth who knows the truth about any of this."

"What are you talking about? Who else is looking for her?"

He cocked his head as if he expected me to know more than him. "Are you serious? Do you really not know what's going on?"

"Keep talking."

He twisted his shoulders. "Would you mind cutting these cuffs off? You don't really think I'm foolish enough to try to fight my way out of here against six of you, do you?"

I nodded toward Kodiak, and he drew his knife. Singer stepped to the side, sat on a stack of aircraft tires, and laid his M4 across his lap. Disco took several steps backward and drew his pistol.

With his hands free, Imri rubbed his wrists where the flex-cuffs had cut into the flesh. "Thank you."

I let out an exasperated sigh. "Stalling is the second-worst thing you could do right now. The absolute worst decision would be to stop talking completely. I don't have the time or the patience to deal with procrastination. Now, talk, or my analyst makes a phone ring in Tel-Aviv."

He said, "We're on the same side of this thing. CIA, Mossad, MI-Six, and even the Saudi General Intelligence Directorate want to get their hands on this woman."

"How many of them want her dead?" I asked.

His eyes narrowed. "The Saudis, probably the Brits, and definitely the CIA. She killed the first CIA team who came to get her. That's what got our attention."

"By *our*, you mean Mossad." He nodded, and I asked, "How do you know she killed the three case officers?"

He furrowed his brow. "Case officers? You mean they weren't clandestine services?"

He was either a master manipulator, or he truly didn't know the dead CIA officers were merely case officers from Lynn's own station. Either way, I could earn some goodwill by admitting that morsel. "They weren't CS. They were just case officers from the embassy."

His eyes shot to the ceiling as he processed the information before saying, "That makes it slightly more understandable. Taking out three clandestine services guys isn't something most of your case officers could pull off."

I couldn't resist stepping through the door he opened. "That still doesn't explain how one fifty-something female deputy chief of station could take out a thirty-something IDF commando turned Mossad officer . . . like you."

"I deserved that, but what are you going to do with me now?"

"I'm going to release you back into the wild, but you should know we have your fingerprints, a DNA sample, and a nice collection of photographs of you in our custody. If you don't want your prime minister to hear all about your little adventure with the sloppy Americans, you'll stay out of our way while we do our job."

His expression didn't change. "Just so you know, I was trying to save your life last night."

"By shoving a pistol against my head?"

"No, inside the restaurant. There are only three kinds of people who frequent that little spot—guys like me, guys who won't live much longer, and clumsy Americans who show up in a taxi. And from my perspective, you're in two of those categories."

"Thanks for the tip," I said. "Now, one of my men would like to have a heart-to-heart talk with you about a blackjack, so the rest of us are going to step outside and get some air while you and he work that out."

Singer stood, slung his rifle across his shoulder, and said, "Cut his legs free before you start. It's just not fair if he can't run."

Kodiak reached into his pocket and pulled out a long, flat strap of leather with a lead weight in one end, flipped it into his palm with a flourish, and sliced the binding from Imri Nazarian's knees just as the rest of us stepped through the door of the hangar and into the bright morning sun in Central Asia.

Chapter 19
Entry Wound

When Kodiak emerged from the hangar, he didn't appear to have lost the conflict, so I asked, "Is he still alive?"

He examined the Israeli's blackjack in his palm before slipping it back into his pocket. "As far as I know. We came to an understanding. I thanked him for closing the dust cover on my rifle before shoving it into the sand, and I put him in a taxi."

"It looks like you came away with a souvenir."

"It was the least he could do. So, what's next, boss?"

"First, stop calling me boss. Second, we need to take a closer look at our prey. It seems she's a little feistier than we anticipated."

We reconvened back inside the hangar and got Skipper on the horn. "Tell us what you've got," I said.

Skipper ruffled a stack of papers and began her briefing. "I dug a little deeper and put together a dossier on our Ms. Lynn. She's a graduate of the Naval Academy, Naval War College, and the Federal Law Enforcement Academy. She left the Navy after nine years and went to work as a military liaison to the Central Intelligence Agency. She kept that post for eleven months before being selected to attend Camp Peary—aka 'The Farm'—for clandestine service training. She battled her way through the boys' club, mostly in Eastern Europe, and served as chief of station in Rabat. Her tradecraft was so solid that the CIA brought her back to the farm as an instructor for eighteen months before her assignment in Morocco."

I said, "So, we're not dealing with a bureaucrat. This woman is an honest-to-God spy with the scars to prove it."

"It looks that way," Skipper said.

I groaned. "That makes me guilty of underestimating my target."

Clark said, "Don't feel lonely, Chase. I think we're all in that same boat with you."

Why does everything I touch in this op turn into garbage?

Skipper broke up my little self-pity party. "If nothing else, we've learned she's still in Dashoguz, or at least she was last night. That means she may have gone to ground, but she's not underground."

"It means something else, too," I said. "She's extremely well connected. She knew I was flashing her picture around town, and she knew how to find me."

Kodiak said, "I'd put money on the bartender. When he left the bar, he was probably going to the back to call Lynn and let her know about the American asking questions about her."

"I thought that, too, but something the Israeli said may have changed my mind. He said one of the three types of people who hang out in that restaurant is other guys like him. I don't know if that means they're mostly Israeli or they're mostly spooks. My money is on the spooks. Everybody in the place looked like they could be an Agency asset."

"If that's true," Clark said. "Anybody in that bar, or restaurant, could've made the call. She could be working with any of them or any combination of them. I doubt it was our boy Mossad, though. She put him down hard."

"You're right," I said. "And she used two different weapons. She hit him with the Taser from several feet away, but she nailed me with a direct-contact stun gun. I'd say the Israeli got the worse of the two hits based on the length of time he was out."

Mongo said, "Neither of those Tasers is an off-the-shelf item. Somebody built those for her, and I doubt it was the office of technical service at Langley."

I said, "Let's find out. Skipper, is Dr. Mankiller around?"

Skipper said, "She's downstairs with Penny, Maebelle, and Grayson. Hang on, and I'll get her."

Skipper was back in seconds with our new hire. "Hey, guys. What's up? It's Celeste."

I said, "We need to know about Tasers at the Agency."

"What do you want to know about them?"

"How powerful are they, and how long should a healthy adult male need to wake up from unconsciousness after getting hit?"

"Wait a minute," Celeste said. "Stun guns and Tasers don't render a victim unconscious unless he has some underlying medical condition. It might happen if the victim had a pacemaker, but the shock alone can't knock out a healthy adult."

I glanced around at my team, and everyone was leaning in to listen.

"I'm afraid you may be mistaken," I said. "I got hit with one that took me out for about six hours, and a guy a little younger than me and probably in better shape was out longer than that. Plus, the person who hit me with it said something about it being half a million volts."

Celeste said, "First, I call BS on the half a million volts. Even if you could power up a handheld device to half a million volts, the prongs would have to be several feet apart instead of an inch or two. Second, it's not the voltage that matters. It's the amperage. Most Tasers and stun guns are between forty and sixty thousand volts and three to five milliamps. If you were going to knock somebody out, it would take ten times that amperage and prolonged exposure. I mean, like minutes of exposure, and it would be almost impossible to provide DC power in a handheld device sufficient for that prolonged application."

"You're the expert," I said, "but I'm telling you. She put me and a Mossad officer out cold with two different types of Tasers."

"You're mixing your phraseology a little. A Taser is a weapon shaped like a pistol that fires a pair of barbs at the end of a pair of leads from several feet away. When the device is used in direct contact, it's called a stun gun."

"Whatever you call them, they put us down like rabid dogs."

"Where did she hit you?"

"Above my left kidney."

"Do you have a medic with you?"

"Yeah, both Mongo and Singer are medics."

"Cool. Have one or both of them take a look at the contact site and tell me what they see. Better yet, have them take a close-up picture of the contact site and send it here."

I turned and lifted my shirt, and Mongo took a knee behind me.

He pulled out his penlight and shone it on the burn left by the stun gun. After a few seconds of scrutiny, he said, "I don't believe it."

"What?" I said. "What is it?"

"There's a hypodermic needle mark in the center of the contact site. She didn't shock you to sleep, Chase. She slipped you a Mickey."

I said, "Well, Dr. Mankiller, it looks like you're earning your salary already. By the way, the coms work great, except when we're face-down in a pile of trash."

She ignored the compliment. "We need a blood panel."

"A blood panel?" I asked.

"Yes. You do want to know what kind of drug she used, don't you?"

"I'm not sure it matters at this point."

Celeste huffed. "It matters to me. We might want to use it in the future, and it's possible you may have a reaction in the next twenty-four hours. If that happens, we definitely want to know what drug she used so we can come up with an antidote."

"As much as I like that idea, there's no way to get any blood-work done over here. We're in the middle of a pit bull fight, and neither dog seems to know what they're fighting over."

"I don't know what that means, but what about the Mossad agent? Can he get bloodwork?"

"We cut him loose, and I don't know how to find him again."

"Well, next time you get drugged, try to ask the attacker for her recipe before you go down."

"I'll keep that in mind. Thanks, Doc. But I've got another question. If she did slip us something, she couldn't have done it with the Taser. There's no way to deliver a syringe through the air with the barbs, is there?"

"No, definitely not, but the barbs could've been designed with hollow cores that could be filled with the drug. Although that's possible, it's highly unlikely. It would be too risky. A lot could go wrong, like the barbs getting caught in clothing and not delivering the drug. That's just one problem. I could come up with dozens more. What's more likely is that she took down the Mossad agent with the Taser, approached while he was twitching on the ground, and jabbed him with a preloaded syringe."

"That's possible," I said, "but I don't remember her doing anything other than hitting me with the stun gun."

"From what you describe, it's likely that the syringe is built into the case of the stun gun and auto delivers when the probes are pressed against a target."

"I'll buy that."

"Any other questions?" she asked.

"Just one. Do you think the CIA provided those tools to her, or did she acquire them through some other source?"

She made a popping sound with her lips. "I can't say for sure, but I've never heard of the Agency deploying any kind of Taser or stun gun to case officers. That doesn't mean they didn't, but I've never heard of it. My bet would be she sourced them on the black market, but I'll do some poking around and see what I can find."

Clark said, "We've got work to do, so if there's nothing else . . ."

Skipper said, "I don't have anything else for you."

"I guess that means we're all caught up. We'll check in within eight hours."

I disconnected the link and rubbed my wound from the stun gun. "Something tells me we'll have Tasers with built-in narcotics dispensers when we get home."

Singer said, "That Dr. Mankiller is going to be worth her weight in gold. Between her brain and Mongo's, not even the sky is the limit. They'll have us teleporting by the Fourth of July."

Mongo gave him a playful shove. "It won't take us that long."

"Let's get back to work," I said. "We've got a lot of ground to cover before Teresa Lynn has enough time to teleport herself out of Turkmenistan."

"Wait a minute," Mongo said. "I just thought of something. We need to inventory everything that broadcasts a signal and check you for bugs."

Clark screwed up his face. "Why?"

He said, "If she's good enough to Tase and drug two of you in seconds, she's good enough to plant a tracking device or nab a piece of our gear that can find us in an instant."

I stripped down to my shorts, and everyone took turns scouring my clothes until we were convinced there was nothing broadcasting bluegrass music from my collar. We laid out our coms gear and double-checked that every piece was accounted for.

Mongo leaned against a barrel and scratched his chin. "I don't get it. Why wouldn't she bug you?"

I climbed back into my clothes. "Maybe she did, but maybe whatever she's using to track me is another tech services gadget we don't know anything about yet."

"It's possible," he said. "But I'm pretty current on tracking devices. The limiting factor is power right now. We can build a transmitter almost too small to see, but it still needs a battery, and those aren't getting any smaller anytime soon."

I suddenly felt as if a thousand spiders were crawling all over me. "I think it makes sense for you to get on the phone with Celeste and see what she has to say about an undetectable tracking device."

Mongo said, "Sure. Maybe I'll learn something. She's pretty squared away, and it's nice to finally have somebody around who's smart enough to keep my attention."

Clark grabbed a pea-sized rock from the hangar floor and bounced it off Mongo's skull. Just wait 'til I tell Irina that Celeste is the only one who can keep your attention."

The big man threw up his hands. "Wait a minute now. That's not what I said."

Clark waved a hand at each of us. "That's what I heard, and you guys heard it too, right?"

Mongo shook his head. "Go ahead. Laugh it up. I'm going to make a phone call, and then I'm going to plan a slow, painful death for every one of you conspirators. Well, not Singer. He gets to live because I know he'd never tell a lie on me."

Chapter 20
Where is Here?

"Was that thunder?" I asked as we pushed open the hangar's rolling door.

Clark stopped what he was doing and turned to the sky. "It's thunder all right, but it's the man-made kind."

Seconds later, another roar pulsed through the air, and I said, "That doesn't sound like artillery fire."

Clark said, "No, that's definitely air-dropped munitions, and it's way too close to feel comfortable."

As I scanned the horizon for plumes of smoke, four gray fighters raced overhead. "Those are MiG-twenty-nines!"

Mongo watched the jets pass. "You're right. The Uzbeks have twenty-four of them, and according to the report I read, they're all in service and capable of delivering payloads of anything they can hang underneath them."

"Why would they bomb Dashoguz?" I asked.

Always the voice of reason, Singer said, "Maybe because they're at war."

"But civilian targets?"

He shrugged. "We don't know enough to say if there are any military targets in or near the city."

I spun to look for the departing MiGs against the western sky, but they were out of sight. "Somebody get Skipper on the horn."

I continued piercing the horizon behind squinted eyelids until four dark specks dotted the blue sky. "They're turning back!"

Every eye turned to the sky except for Clark's. He was busy on the coms. He said, "Got her."

Skipper's voice filled my ears, "Go for op center."

"The Uzbeks are bombing Dashoguz with MiG-twenty-nines. Have there been any other reports of bombings?"

Her fingers danced across her keyboard. "Affirmative. Early reports say the Turkmen dropped munitions on eleven military and civilian targets within eighty miles of the border, just before sunrise this morning."

"That makes this a retaliatory strike by the Uzbeks."

An eerie feeling of dread consumed me as I scanned the airport. A few civilian airplanes sat in rows on the parking apron, but nothing was moving on the airfield. The question that leapt into my head hit me like a hammer.

What would I hit if I were trying to cripple a city?

I yelled, "They're going to hit the airport!"

Without a word, everyone ran for the fence line, but I couldn't keep up. It felt like I was dragging an anchor. The harder I pumped my legs, the slower I moved. I looked down, expecting to see my boots sinking into the mud, but what I saw was far more horrific. The titanium, aluminum, and electronics that had been my right shin, ankle, and foot, were nothing more than dead weight. The anchor I was dragging suddenly became clear. If I survived the next sixty seconds of my life, a spare prosthetic waited for me in my auxiliary gear bag in truck number one.

Another glance into the sky showed the MiGs as far more than four specks on the horizon. They were well-defined silhouettes coming hard and fast.

My team was at least a hundred yards ahead and still sprinting. Of all the insanity that could've invaded my thoughts in that moment, the picture of a cartoon peg-legged pirate wouldn't leave my head. I pounded my dead foot against the earth with every second stride and tried to overcome my burden by demanding more of my healthy left leg. It didn't work. Instead of increasing my speed, it sent me into a listing, clumsy drift to the right. The distance between my team and me grew with every stride, and the roar of the MiGs grew louder with every passing instant. What lay in the coming seconds was a fate my mind couldn't fathom and a consequence I'd never wish on my most hated enemy.

Driving my legs even harder, my lungs burned, and my every sense begged to be with my team until I watched Mongo turn to see me so far back. I'll never know why the big man became my personal guardian angel so many years before, but the decision he made in that instant flashed like a neon sign over his head. He never hesitated. Instead, he planted a foot and pivoted, turning his massive body in one stride to sprint back for me. He made three loping strides before I could get enough air in my lungs to bellow, "No! Keep running!"

I'll never know if my screams fell on deaf ears or a defiant determination to rescue me. When the coming hell was over, the difference wouldn't matter.

The sound of the MiGs' roaring engines may have been the last real sound I heard that day, but I'll always believe it was the torrential explosion of the five hundred pounders tearing into the concrete and steel of the airport, hangars, our trucks, and the bloodthirsty earth beneath my feet.

In an instant that seemed to last an eternity, every sensation melted into one soul-shaking eruption of unimaginable force, sending my body, mind, and consciousness into an endless abyss of darkness, heat, and cacophony of boundless sound thundering down on me simultaneously. In that moment, all of creation turned her back on me and hurled me through time itself until nothing existed except ever-deepening darkness, crushing agony, and ultimate abandonment.

Maybe I was unconscious for a breath, or perhaps a thousand ages. The passage of time was an abstract concept lying somewhere beyond my reach.

Are my eyes open?

Is that the sound of my pounding heart forcing my life's blood through a thousand wounds and into the absent world outside my chest?

Why doesn't it hurt?

Am I alive, dead, or lost somewhere between the absolutes?

One breath ... move a finger.

The breath came, but the finger wouldn't respond.

Another breath ... taste for blood on my lips.

The breath came, and my lips tasted of dust, dirt, and sweat. The taste of iron didn't come.

Perhaps my face and head aren't bleeding.

One more breath ... move a leg.

When that breath came, with it came a thousand daggers piercing my body from within. I bellowed from the depths of my soul, but no sound came from my lips. Instead, it felt as if I were forcing my very life from my body with every desperate attempt to cry out.

The animal inside me lusted for a clean, dry breath and a chance to survive, but my heart lay terrified in its bloody pool, crying out to God to end the torturous agony. Perhaps I was damned to endure the pain for all eternity in utter darkness, fear, and emptiness. Perhaps I'd fallen from Earth and into ultimate separation from goodness and light and life. Perhaps this is Hell—the only just end to a man like me. Perhaps the lives I'd taken and ordered to be destroyed were reaping their horrid revenge on all I would ever be. Perhaps I would never again hear the soft, gentle sounds of Penny's breath on my skin as she slept in my arms. Perhaps I'd never taste the sweet air of the evening breeze blowing from the ocean. Perhaps I'd never again feel the relief of laughter and the freedom of temporary peace. Perhaps I was no more.

As I battled between the hope of being alive and the terror of being dead, time passed without me. I suppose I lapsed into and clawed my way out of consciousness a thousand times, each time awakening to find my darkest fears exploding behind my eyes. Unsure if I were awake or lost in the chaos of a dream, I focused with ultimate intensity on the mechanism of my right hand. The multiple surgeries and almost endless rehab I endured when the surgeons and therapists pieced back together what remained of my wrist and hand so many years before filled my conscious mind. Nothing inside my body had the strength and rigidity of that appendage. If any part of me could survive whatever torment I'd befallen, it would be that mechanical, man-made part.

To my delight and utter disbelief, some part of that extremity moved.

Was it a finger? Could it have been the thumb?

Joy and elation filled the tiniest empty corner of the void, and the reality of my imprisonment lost its fangs. I was alive—at least temporarily—and I wasn't in the timeless Hell. Instead, I was trapped by some force, be it gravity or the Earth itself, but I was alive.

Every inch of my body seemed to be in a life-or-death battle, with every other ounce of me, to claim the ultimate pain. My hope remained with the sole part of me I could move: my mechanical right hand.

As I lay in the darkness, unsure if I were blind or simply encapsulated inside debris and earth, I clung to the moving finger—or perhaps, fingers—of my right hand and tried to replay the events that brought me to my predicament. Often, the chaotic mind only needs one tiny string attached to sanity to find its way back from a darkened chasm of delusion, and those fingers were my only string.

Keep it together, Chase. It's bad, but you're breathing. As long as you're breathing, we can work everything else out. Let's start with the vision.

I closed and reopened my eyes several times, hoping to see a difference . . . any difference. Darkness consumed me, regardless of the position of my eyelids, but with great effort I could pick out glowing orange and red orbs with my eyes closed tightly. I hoped that meant my eyes were still communicating with my brain.

Okay, let's move our jaw.

I wiggled my chin, anticipating the feeling of a sword piercing my skull when I did, but the pain didn't come. The chin moved left, then right, in what felt like one- or two-millimeter sweeps. Then I let my mind work its way back to my hand, and two fingers moved together.

If I could've done a backflip in celebration, I would've never stopped. Moving my chin and at least two fingers at the same time felt like the greatest victory of my life.

As the muscles in my face grew tired from wiggling my chin, I made a bold decision.

Let's try to move the whole head.

If my neck isn't broken, it might be possible to move my noggin even slightly. Fearing the scorching pain, I gathered my courage and raised my head a fraction of an inch, but it definitely moved. Left and right wouldn't happen, but up and down in tiny motions did.

I found myself exhausted after the exercise, and the pull of unconsciousness tugged at me from somewhere in the darkness. I battled but lost. When I came back, a new agony consumed me: thirst. I worked hard to force my thoughts away from water, but no matter how much I tried focusing on anything else, my parched lips cried out for relief.

Could thirst mean blood loss? Could I be bleeding to death and not realize it?

It was possible, but worrying about something I couldn't control was wasted effort to the highest degree, and I banished the thought of blood loss from my head.

"Jawbone!" I'd yelled the word, but when it reverberated through my ears, it sounded as if I were a mile away in a canyon.

If I still have a jawbone, I still have coms.

I was still in communication with Skipper when it happened . . .

But what happened? What put me in this situation?

It didn't matter. I was certain I'd been talking with Skipper when it happened, and Dr. Mankiller's magic bullet was still glued to my jawbone. If I could make a sound, maybe, just maybe, Skipper could hear me. I tried in desperation to form a word, any word, but everything came out as a groan or a whimper I couldn't hear.

Am I making sounds at all? Is there any chance anyone can hear me?

My breathing quickened, coming in spasms as panic dug her vengeful talons into what remained of my mind.

Calm down, Chase. Easy. You're alive. What if I'm the only person left alive? What if everyone is dead or trapped like me? What if . . .

If it's possible to be thankful for unconsciousness, I was. When it ended, I wasn't panicking, and nothing hurt that wasn't already hurting when I fell asleep.

How long was I asleep? How long have I been here? Where is here? I'm cold.

Shivering came, and with it the realization that my mind and body were not incommunicado. Muscles only shake when ordered to do so by the brain.

I'm definitely alive.

Is that a horse? Is he laughing at me?

As if standing at center stage with the spotlight glistening off his red-brown hair and blond mane, Pecan, Penny's favorite horse, stood laughing at me while pawing at the floor.

Why is he laughing at me? Why isn't he helping me? Why is he here? Where is here?

Before any of my questions could be answered, the spotlight drifted away, and every muscle of my body relaxed in surrender. The shivering ceased, and the obsidian realm absorbed me as if I were nothing more than a morsel on her tongue.

Chapter 21
You're Not Skipper

"Chase, op center."

Skipper? Yes! That's definitely Skipper. Answer her! Answer her, Chase.

I drew in the deepest breath my confinement would allow and concentrated on the three words I beseeched my mouth to say: "Go for Chase."

Did I say it? Did I hear it?

"Chase, op center"

Why can't she hear me?

Her voice echoed inside my head, time after time, but I couldn't know if it was really Skipper trying to call me or if my delirious mind was imagining it. Was her voice another figment of my imagination like Pecan was?

I'm hungry. How long have I been like this? Why am I not thirsty?

My education should've allowed me to understand what was happening inside my head, but everything seemed like a train wreck in the Everglades. I couldn't tell the difference between what I wanted and what was actually happening. Darkness, isolation, fear, pain, hunger, thirst, injuries, and a thousand other conditions I didn't want or need combined to blur the line between reality and fantasy.

There has to be a way to determine what's real and what my brain is dreaming up.

"There you are, my Chasechka. Why are you hiding from me? I am looking for you for so many days, and here you are, just beneath my nose."

Anya? No! She's not real. Keep it together, Chase.

Her beautiful broken English that laced through her native Russian took me by the hand and led me back to the days when I'd first encountered her—the long, blonde hair; those smoky, hypnotic blue-gray eyes; the smile that seemed to exist only for me; her flawless Eastern European skin kissed by the Caribbean sun; the way she emerged from the shower wearing nothing but my T-shirt; her wet hair hanging across her shoulder; the razor-sharp edge of her knife slicing through my flesh, opening my body to drain the life from within. The murderous spine behind the heart-stopping beauty.

Get out of my head!

"But why, Chase? I love you. I should be in your head and in your heart. That's where I belong."

Penny?

"Yes, Chase, it's me. Who else would it be? Come home to me, Chase. Wherever you are, come home to me."

Her hypnotic North Texas drawl felt like a warm, welcoming blanket on a cold, dark night, and I found myself reaching for the sound of my wife's voice through the endless midnight veil around me. "Penny, tell them where I am. Tell Clark and Mongo. Tell them I'm alive."

Reality was gone. Nothing was real, and I was left to die alone in my insanity, my delusion, my isolation surrounded by the ghosts that were destined to spend all of eternity wafting through

my consciousness. The only remaining reality was the final submission of my mind to the cruel, relentless void.

* * *

Time either passed, or it didn't. To me, it was all the same. The
fear and desperation were gone, and the thirst and hunger were
distant memories lost somewhere astern on a limitless sea, until . . .
Is that light?

It was yellow and distant, but it had to be real. It was flawed
and wavering, but it was light. Earthly light. Tremors of pain exploded through my spine as if the relief of a great burden had been
lifted, leaving behind the misery of freedom.

*My arm. I can move my arm. I can move both arms! What's
happening to me?*

Hands slid across my body, probing and advancing, pressing
and retreating. The same hands cupped beneath my right arm and
hip and rolled my nearly lifeless form onto my back. The light was
real and assaulting, and the brightness blinded me more completely than had the darkness of the world from which I'd just
been dragged.

Everything hurt, and I labored in a wasted effort to raise my
arm to shield my tortured eyes from the glowing, burning orb. Although my command for my arm to move fell on deaf muscles, a
darkened silhouette slid between my face and the light. There was
no detail to the form, only a black, two-dimensional shade.

I tried to speak, but my lips were frozen together by dehydration, and perhaps drying blood. As my eyes adjusted to the flood-
ing light, small details emerged. Shoulder-length hair, narrow
shoulders, small hands.

Who is this person?

Fingers pressed against the flesh of my neck, checking for a pulse, and then a hand rested against my chest, feeling for the rise and fall of my lungs. Next, a bottle neck touched my lips, and cold, welcome, life-giving water trickled into my mouth. I tried to swallow, but the tiny stream felt like a firehose, and I coughed and gagged. The spasms through my abdomen hurt, but not like daggers. The pain was subsiding, and my eyes were clearing and focusing.

A woman? What is she doing here? Who is she? Is she helping me or taking me prisoner?

She cradled my neck in the bend of her elbow and slid her thigh beneath my neck, allowing me to rest my head on her lap. When the water bottle returned, I swallowed the first sip, then the second, and the ravenous thirst returned. I lapped at the stream of water like a dog until the flow was exhausted.

A glance down my body proved that most of the big parts were still attached, except for the prosthetic. What had been a modern marvel of medical science had been transformed into a useless, brittle appendage, and then devoured by the beast that had been my attacker and undertaker.

As the world slowly transformed back into something my feeble mind could understand, the face above me looked like someone I should know, perhaps someone I *had* known, but recognition lay just beyond my reach. Her lips moved, but no sound came from them. The lips seemed to form the words, "Where are you injured?"

The self-assessment I began at some point in the previous hours, seconds, or days continued. The fingers curled and opened, elbows bent, knees worked, head moved, and I said, "I don't know."

At least, that's what I tried to say. Just like my rescuer's lips, mine refused to generate sound.

She spoke again, but for me, there was nothing but silence. Then, she poured water onto the bottom of her shirt and wiped my face. The cool water and soft cotton of the shirt felt great against my skin, but my thirst cried out for the shirttail to touch my lips. She could apparently see my desire, and she opened another bottle. Forcing myself to drink slowly, I finished the bottle and sat up with my abs screaming in protest.

The woman kept one hand on my back, supporting me through the range of motion. Although standing was out of the question, my mind yearned to find my team. I mouthed, "Where are my men?"

She looked away and said something, but I could only hear a faint rumble, so I touched her cheek with my fingertips, turning her face toward me. "Say that again."

She spoke, and sound came, but not sounds that created words —just chaotic, garbled sounds. I focused on her lips and made a circling motion with my index finger, encouraging her to repeat what she'd said.

"Can you read lips?"

I nodded, and she asked, "How many men?"

I held up five fingers, and she slowly shook her head.

"Are they dead?" I asked in desperation.

She shrugged. "I don't know, but you're lucky to be alive."

"I have to find my men."

She scowled. "You have to sit still until we know how badly you're hurt."

"Who are you?"

"I'm the woman you've been chasing."

The mission crept its way back into my skull. "Teresa?"

She nodded. "Are you Defense Intelligence?"

"No, I have no Agency affiliation."

Her face turned to what could've been anger. "You're a contractor?"

"Not really," I tried to say. "I'm . . . we're . . . never mind. We're here to bring you home."

She laughed and then wiped the smile from her face. "Is that so? You're not in any shape to bring me anywhere."

"Where's my leg?" I asked without meaning to.

She glanced down at my stump. "I don't know."

I groaned. "I have another one in the truck inside the hangar."

She laughed again. "I just spent two hours digging you out from beneath what's left of that hangar. There's no truck."

"Yes, there is. There are three of them inside the hangar."

"The Russians blew the hangar to hell and back. If there were trucks inside, they're destroyed, just like everything else on the airport."

I said, "No, not the Russians. It was the Uzbeks."

"That's what Putin wants you to believe, but it's not true."

"Why can't I hear you?"

She said, "The initial blast probably destroyed your eardrums. Can you hear anything?"

I concentrated and listened intently. "I hear high-pitched tones and a roar like rushing water. When you speak, I hear something, but it sounds like a record being played backward."

"Your eardrums are definitely blown. We need to get you to a medical facility. You've probably got massive internal injuries, but nothing appears to be broken."

"How long?" I asked.

"How long for what?"

"How long was I buried?"

She checked her watch. "About five hours."

I reached for the sat-com on my belt but found only filthy, torn cloth where my radio should've been. "I need to talk with my analyst."

"Your analyst? You're a contractor with an analyst?"

At least, that's what I thought she said. Her constant scanning of the environment made it challenging to continue reading her lips, but I had respect for her situational awareness.

"Do you have a sat-phone?"

"I do," she said, "but I'm not giving it to you until I understand who and what you are."

"My name is Chase Fulton. I'm in command of a six-man team of operators here to bring you in out of the cold."

To my surprise, she laughed again. "Out of the cold? I'm out in the cold because my agency started this war."

That can't be what she said.

"Say that again, and look at me this time."

She locked eyes with me. "My station chief started this war, then dispatched three case officers to murder me. Is that why you're here as well?"

"No, I'm here to pick you up."

"And deliver me to whom?"

Instead of admitting I didn't know, I asked, "What did you do to get the Israelis after you?"

"The whole world is after me, Chase Fulton. The Israelis just happen to be the best at finding spooks like me. What's his name?"

"I didn't say the Israeli is a man."

"They're always men," she said. "They're always tall, dark, and handsome, as if they were just sent over from central casting. What's his name?"

"Imri."

She raised her eyebrows. "Ah, Imri Nazarian. He's one of my favorites. Was he the other guy I rocked to sleep the other night?" I nodded, and she said, "Thought so. Where is he now?"

"I don't know. We woke him up, interrogated him, and cut him loose when we discovered he was on our side. But none of that matters. I need to find my team, and that starts with you giving me your sat-phone."

"We'll get to that," she said. "But first, I need to know who's signing your check."

I sighed, and a wave of pain shot through my body like lightning. I spasmed and finally settled back into a position that didn't feel like fire shooting down my spine.

"That looks like it hurts. I've got some morphine, but not before you come clean about who you're working for."

"I don't want the morphine. I want to find my team."

"Tell me who you work for, and I'll help you find your men."

I let out a long breath. "I work for a quasi-governmental agency known as the Board. They work in the best interest of the American people. That's who I work for. Now, give me the sat-phone."

"Not quite yet. Who decides what's in the best interest of the American people?"

I changed tactics. "You do, and you know they're never going to stop coming for you until you're dead. So, if you want to stay alive, I'm your best shot at that target. Give me the phone, and all of this will be over."

She pulled a sat-phone from her pocket, bounced it in her palm, and gave another appraising glance. "God help me if you're really my best shot at getting out of here alive. From the looks of things, you probably won't even get that done for yourself. Here's the phone, but I think I'll do the talking. Give me the number."

Chapter 22
Another Pocket Dump

I refused to let myself believe my team was dead. I was little more than a worthless, one-legged casualty. Finding my team meant making whatever sacrifice Teresa Lynn required of me, and in that moment, nothing was more important than laying eyes on my brothers-in-arms. I gave her the number to the op center back at Bonaventure, and she pressed the phone to her ear.

Seconds later, she said, "Is this the analyst?"

I couldn't have heard Skipper, even if Teresa Lynn had put the call on speaker, so I was left reading lips to catch maybe half of one end of the conversation.

"Who I am doesn't matter. Who I *have* does. I have a man claiming to be Chase Fulton. Is he yours?"

She listened, and I imagined what Skipper was saying. Whatever it was, it was likely laced with impatience.

Teresa said, "Which of his legs is missing?"

Clever, I thought. She's vetting Skipper by asking details about me.

Apparently, Skipper passed the test until Teresa asked, "Who do you work for?"

Based on the length of time Teresa sat, silently listening to whatever Skipper was saying, she was getting an earful about having the audacity to call *her* op center and demand answers.

When the barrage was over, Teresa said, "That won't work. He's deaf from the explosion."

Whatever Skipper said made Teresa give in and put the phone on speaker. "She wants to hear your voice."

I leaned close to the phone. "Skipper, it's Chase. Do you have locations on the rest of the team? We got separated just before the bombing."

I immediately focused on Teresa's lips, relying on her to repeat whatever our analyst said.

It was Skipper's turn to get some answers. She said, "If you're in danger, tell me what position you played on the football team."

For the first time in hours—maybe days—I smiled. "I'm not in danger, and I played baseball for your dad."

The inquisition was over, and I repeated, "Do you have locations on the remainder of the team? I'm alone."

"I've got locations on their sat-coms, but I can't raise anybody on the net."

Teresa repeated everything Skipper was saying, or at least I believed she was repeating what Skipper said.

Teresa said, "Yes, this phone can receive text messages."

A few seconds later, she held the front of the phone toward my face as the GPS coordinates of the team's sat-coms scrolled across the screen.

"Can you plot those on a chart?"

Teresa said, "Give me a minute."

A few seconds later, she brought up a map of the Uzbek–Turkmen border with a flashing icon northeast of the waterway that formed the boundary between the two countries.

I said, "They wouldn't have moved back across the border without searching for me."

Through Teresa's lips, Skipper said, "From the looks of the satellite tracks, they were taken shortly after the blast."

I could hear weak sounds coming from the speaker, but it was impossible for me to identify them as Skipper's voice. I was left with no choice other than trusting the CIA case officer who'd been trained to lie, deceive, and misdirect everybody she encountered.

I had a thought, and I couldn't keep it in. "Is Dr. Mankiller handy?"

Teresa nodded, "She says yes."

"Good. Have her talk Teresa through connecting her sat-phone to my bone conduction device."

Teresa listened and typed furiously on the small keyboard of the phone until Celeste's voice resonated in my head. "That should do it."

I said, "I've got you loud and clear, Celeste. How do you hear me?"

"You're loud and clear, also," she said.

Skipper's voice soon replaced the tech's. "Chase, can you hear me?"

"I hear you, Skipper."

"Are you really okay? Are you being held captive?"

"No, I'm not being held captive, but I'm not okay. My hearing is shot, my prosthetic is gone, and I'm pretty beat up from the blasts."

"Can you trust Teresa Lynn?"

"I don't know yet, but she's all I've got until we find the rest of the team."

"But what about your leg?"

I instinctually stared down at my stump. "I've not figured that one out yet, but I'm working on it. Let's get back to the team. Did they move out in vehicles or on foot?"

"They were definitely in vehicles, but it looked like whoever took them confiscated their sat-coms and carried them in one vehicle together. It could've been a truck or a van, but I can't imagine a force large enough to overpower and grab our guys in one vehicle."

"Okay, get to work on their location. We need to know what's there, what it's made of, and how secure it is."

"I'm on it," she said. "Tony and Hunter are here, too. They're both geared up and ready to deploy if you need them."

The thought of plunging Hunter and Tony into the terrifying circus I'd built halfway around the world sickened me, but having either or both of those men by my side would increase the odds of my success exponentially.

My mission had changed in an instant. I no longer cared if I repatriated Teresa Lynn. The sole focus of my world was getting my team, my brothers, out of wherever they were being held, and I would give every last drop of blood in my body to make that happen.

Teresa gave me a punch to the shoulder. "Are you okay? You got quiet."

"I'm okay. I'm just thinking. Give me a minute."

"Are you talking to me?" Skipper asked.

"No, no. I was answering Teresa. Do you have a plan to get Tony and Hunter over here?"

"I'm working on that."

I said, "You need to know something. Teresa believes the MiGs who dropped the bombs aren't Uzbeks. She thinks they're Russian."

"What? Russian? No way! Why would she think that?"

"I don't know, and I don't have time to walk through it with the two of you. I'll put you back on with her, and you can sort it out. Right now, I have to find a foot and a ride back across the border."

I handed the phone to the CIA case officer. "Tell Skipper about the Russians while I find something I can turn into a foot."

Teresa took the phone, disconnected it from my bone conduction device, and stuck it to her ear.

I found a broken timber that would have to work as a crutch. Hopping around on one foot wasn't going to cut it. After a dozen hobbling steps, I learned the angle and started to move more efficiently.

The airport was destroyed beyond description. Of the dozen buildings that stood prior to the attack, only two remained relatively unharmed. Everything else was leveled.

Two minutes into my search for a makeshift foot, the trauma of my injuries reared its ugly head in the form of vertigo, nausea, and tunnel vision. I leaned heavily on my crutch and tried to focus on the horizon, but it was no use. The contents of my stomach—mostly water—made its way back out of my mouth, and I found myself on one knee, trying to shake the cobwebs from my skull. The world around me spun in unlevel orbit, leaving me confused about which way was up. I slowed my breathing, squeezed my crutch, and willed myself to stand again. The motion took every ounce of strength and determination I could muster, but I did it.

Moving more slowly, I plundered piles of debris until I found a short piece of wood with a protrusion about a foot from one end. I sat, positioned the protrusion against the metal rod extending from my stump, and ground my way into the knot until the rod was embedded in the wood at least half an inch. I then pulled my belt from my pants and wrapped it twice around the part of the timber that continued up the outside of my leg. I dug the belt into the flesh so deep that I wondered if I'd lose even more of the leg after turning my belt into what was essentially a tourniquet to hold the timber in place.

The crutch helped me get back on my feet, and I hobbled around like Captain Peg Leg as I adjusted to the feel of the field-expedient prosthetic. It wasn't even close to the same sensation of walking with the robotic foot that lay in waste somewhere beneath a pile of airport debris, but it had to do.

I worked my way back to Teresa, who was still on the phone with Skipper. When I reached her side, another episode of dizziness crushed me, and I grabbed her arm to keep from going down. She dropped the phone and caught me, easing me carefully onto a bucket that made a nice place to land.

"Are you okay?"

"Stop asking me if I'm okay. No! I'm not okay, but I have to keep moving. It's just a little vertigo. I'll be better in a few minutes."

She scooped the phone from the ground at her feet. "Sorry. Your operator just had an episode. We have to move, but we'll check in when we're headed for the Uzbek side."

Teresa pocketed the phone, and I said, "Did you make her understand why you think it's the Russians doing the bombing?"

"I told her why it was the Russians and how I knew, but whether or not she understood, I don't know."

"Trust me. If she didn't understand, she'll dig and sniff until she does."

"This vertigo of yours . . . Did you have it before getting blown up?"

"No, it's new, but it's only happened twice, and the second time was much milder than the first."

"Milder doesn't matter. Vertigo is a potential symptom of a serious head injury. If it happens again, you tell me immediately."

"If it happens again, you'll most likely know by my inability to stay on my feet . . . or foot."

She studied the makeshift prosthetic and slung her pack to the ground. "Let's get rid of that belt. It looks more like a tourniquet than anything else."

She pulled a roll of duct tape from her pack and replaced the belt with tape. The upgrade felt much better and actually held the wood in place far better than the belt.

"Thank you. We need to have a talk before this goes any further."

She looked up. "So, talk."

"You used the word *we* on the phone with my analyst. You and I weren't a *we* before I got blown up. In fact, the last time *we* met, you were Tasing me and injecting me full of something that left me in the spirit world for several hours. We're not exactly bosom buddies."

She pointed toward my stilt. "You're an American stuck in a war you don't understand. Your team either abandoned you for dead, or they've been captured. I'm a case officer for the American CIA. I can't exactly leave you out here on your own. We may not be allies, but our shared geographical and geopolitical circumstances give us at least a common enemy, and that's not a bad place to start."

I said, "In that case, I'll consider you a friendly asset until we agree to step up our relationship to the next level."

"Fair enough."

"Since you're an asset, do you know where we can find a vehicle to get us back across that waterway?"

She stared out across the ruined airport. "My truck took a direct hit, and yours didn't fare much better. The only thing I've seen on this airport since the bombing is an old helicopter. That pilot of yours would sure come in handy."

"I can fly it."

She laughed. "It's Russian, so all the instrumentation is in Cyrillic, and you're having a vertigo episode every few minutes. I don't think putting you at the controls of a chopper is a great plan."

"Do you have a better one?"

She huffed. "Any plan is better than that one."

"Are you suggesting we walk across the border and assault a temporary prison with a wooden leg and some duct tape?"

Before she could answer, the world wound itself up and turned into a tilt-a-whirl again. I spread my feet apart and braced against my crutch.

"It's happening again, isn't it?"

I held up a hand. "Yes, but it's not bad. It's getting better."

"Can you read Cyrillic?"

"Sure," I said. "Can't you?"

"Of course I can. But I can't fly a chopper. I've got a few hours in fixed wings, but no rotor time."

"Take me to it."

"The chopper?" she asked.

"Yes, the chopper. How far away is it?"

She motioned to the southwest. "It's about half a mile that way between the only two buildings still standing."

I leaned down and hefted her pack, but she grabbed it from my hand. "I'll take that, and I think this might be a good time for a pocket dump."

"I agree." I've got a switchblade, an ink pen, an empty holster, and two Glock magazines."

"I came a little more prepared. I've got a pair of Makarov pistols, a cut-down AK-Forty-Seven, duct tape, water, a sat-phone, two knives, a compass, and a map."

"You must've been one heck of a Girl Scout."

She said, "Nope, just a Naval Academy grad turned spook."

Chapter 23
I Have the Controls

"Take me to the helicopter."

"I'm not getting in a helicopter with you while you're having seizures . . . or whatever those episodes are."

"Fine," I said. "Just show me where it is, give me your AK, and watch me fly away. I'm going to get my men."

Her demeanor didn't change, but she walked a little faster than I was capable of accomplishing. "Keep up, contractor."

"Slow down, expat."

She spun on a heel and stuck a finger in my face. "Listen to me, you little wannabe! I've been operating covertly since before you could wipe your own butt. I've been shot, cut, burned, left for dead, and beaten to within an inch of my life all over the world in places you've never heard of. I've given everything I had, and then some, to a country that has now turned its back on me and sent little weasels like you to find me. I gave up a family, a nice cushy job in the Navy, and a normal stateside life. I'm the very definition of a patriot. Expats leave because they *want* to leave. I left because my country demanded it of me. So, next time you think you want to call somebody an expat—especially me—I recommend shutting your mouth and showing a little respect."

Dr. Fulton, psychologist extraordinaire, showed up. "Look, I'm sorry. I didn't mean it that way, and I'm sorry it came out like that. You're under an enormous mountain of stress, and I understand your need to get some of that pent-up frustration out in the open."

She took a step even closer to me. "What is this, some kind of touchy-feely, hold-my-hand counseling session? We're not doing that. I don't have any loyalty to you. I don't owe you anything. I'm helping you because your team doesn't deserve to be held prisoner in somebody else's war. That's it. Once that's done, you'll never see me again. You got that?"

Dr. Fulton put his diploma and license to practice back in the drawer and unleashed the South Georgia redneck that lived somewhere inside of him. "Now, you listen. You're not the only one who's been all over the world getting torn apart because you believe in something bigger than yourself."

I pointed toward my cobbled-together prosthetic. "I've got one foot, half a dozen bullet holes, an injury that left me unable to father a child, a team that demands more of me than I've got to give, and five brothers who are likely being held as POWs. If you want to get in my face, do it with facts, not some fairy tale dancing around in your head about a *contractor*. You got that?"

She took a step back, turned around, and slowed her pace. Neither of us said a word until we reached the helicopter.

She was right. It was indisputably old, Russian, and probably nowhere near airworthy.

I stuck a finger toward the decrepit machine. "Is that it?"

"That's it. I tried to tell you, but you wouldn't listen."

"Let's see if it'll start."

She said, "Oh, it'll start. I saw it fly three or four times in the past week."

I held out a hand. "Okay, then. Give me a couple of bottles of water and one of your guns."

She lowered her chin and started another tirade, but a new episode of vertigo demanded my attention. I clenched my jaw, breathed in through my nose and out through my mouth, and stood my ground. Ultimately, I stayed on my feet—or foot—but Teresa was right.

"You said you have a few hours of fixed-wing time, right?"

She nodded. "Yeah, but it's been a long time."

"It's like riding a bike. I can teach you to fly this thing in ten minutes."

She unshouldered her pack, drew a battered 9mm Makarov pistol from a side pocket, and stuck it in my hand. "Take this, and promise me you'll shoot me in the head if we're going to crash. I don't want to limp away from a helicopter wreck with a braindead pilot."

I shoved the Makarov into my holster that once held my Glock. "I thought you said you weren't getting in a chopper with me."

"That's old news. You won't survive half an hour without me."

She rounded the old bird and climbed into the left seat while I propelled myself into the right seat, dragging my peg leg behind.

She was right, again. Everything had originally been written in Cyrillic, but most of it had been worn off from decades of use, and from the looks of it, abuse.

"Okay, let's light the fires."

There was no checklist, so I was left to stumble my way through the startup procedure of a helicopter I'd never seen with two dozen unmarked switches over my head. I searched the panel until I found the switches with the most wear on the console around them. The most used switches were probably exactly the ones I needed. My procedure wasn't straight out of the manual, but two minutes later, the rotor was turning above our head. We pulled on a pair of headsets, and I burst into laughter as I yelled into the mic. "I guess there's no reason for me to wear a headset, huh?"

She turned to face me and pushed the microphone away from her lips. "Keep it on. That way, I'll be able to hear you, even if you can't hear me."

With my real foot, I stepped on the left pedal and propped my piece of lumber on the right. "Here we go."

If Teresa Lynn had been Catholic, she would've crossed herself at that moment, but instead, she gripped the edges of her seat as if they were her only lifeline.

I waited for every needle in the cockpit to climb into the green arcs, and I pulled enough pitch with the collective to lighten the load on the skids. Everything seemed to behave like a relatively healthy flying machine, so I kept pulling and adding enough pedal to keep us from spinning out of control. The makeshift foot was awkward, but I learned to make it work as we taxied away from the hangars.

When we reached what had been a taxiway, I pulled the mic against my lips. "Ready?"

She gave me a nod, and we climbed away from the bombed-out airport and headed northeast.

Once in cruise flight, I said, "Put your left hand on the collective control beside your seat and your right on the cyclic stick."

She did as I instructed, and I took her through the basic functions of each control. She learned quickly and soon had us flying relatively straight and level.

"Now, put your feet on the pedals and coordinate your turns using the cyclic and the pedals."

We did a few turns, and she caught on quickly.

"That's all there is to cruise flight, so if I have an episode, you take the controls and keep us flying in this direction."

"What if we're in the process of landing when you freak out?" she asked.

"I recommend unbuckling your seat belt before we start to land."

She furrowed her brow. "What? Why?"

"So you can jump out instead of dying in a fiery crash with me."

She brought up the map on her tablet and motioned out the window toward the coordinates Skipper gave us for the team's sat-coms location. "It looks like about ten or fifteen degrees to the left will take us directly to the site."

I made the turn just as the waterway and border between feuding countries passed beneath our skids. "When all of this is over, you'll need to make me understand why Russia is involved with any of this."

"I'll try . . . if we survive."

She jabbed a finger at the windshield and probably said something, but I couldn't see her lips. A wall of sound poured through my headset, but nothing about it sounded like any language. It was just a garbled mess.

"Look at me and say that again."

She faced me. "That two-story building right there must be the place."

I flew directly over the structure at two thousand feet to give both of us a bird's-eye view, and what I saw tied my gut in a knot. "I don't like it. It's wide open in every direction. There's no way to approach undetected."

"Agreed," she said. "But we need to get as much intel as we can. How many vehicles did you count?"

"I got nine, including the heavy trucks to the west."

"I counted ten, but it doesn't matter. Nine is just as bad. We've got two pistols, part of a rifle, and three feet between us. There's no way we're storming that building and surviving."

In that instant, the world outside spun to the right in a violent and uncontrollable run, and I crushed the right pedal in a wasted effort to stop the spinning. The controls felt heavy and sluggish. No matter how hard I pulled or pushed, it felt as if I were fighting an enormous rubber band. A glance to my right explained the resistance in the controls.

Teresa was wrestling the controls just as hard as I was, and the reality of my vertigo fell on me. Forcing myself to release the controls, I leaned back and drew my legs beneath my seat. I had to stay off the stick and pedals until the episode passed, but everything inside me was screaming for me to fly the machine.

I couldn't tell how much of the spinning was the result of my vertigo and how much was Teresa's rookie flying, but I made a decision I would soon regret.

I closed my eyes in an effort to isolate the motion in my head from the motion in my gut. It took only seconds for my inner ear and my stomach to start a holy war with each other, and my head won the battle. I emptied the contents of my stomach out the door and wiped my mouth on my sleeve. When I looked out the windshield, we were still airborne, the spinning had stopped, and we'd gained a few hundred feet in altitude.

"Nice job," I said. "Sorry about that."

The intensity on her face said she didn't have the time or patience for conversation.

I wrapped my fingers back around the cyclic and collective and slid my feet back onto the pedals. "I have the controls."

She didn't react, so I shook the stick and said, "I've got it, Teresa. You can let go."

She reluctantly surrendered the controls, and every muscle in her body relaxed after being drawn into knots.

"How long was I on my little joyride?"

She said, "I don't know, but it felt like an eternity. Let's get this thing on the ground before you kill us both."

"Okay, but where are we?"

"I didn't make any turns once I got you to let go of the stick. We kept flying in the same direction for maybe two or three minutes."

"Okay, that's good," I said. "We'll put down in that spot behind those trees to the right."

I flew a descending arc to the east and touched down behind the concealment of a semi-circular clump of trees. The rotors kicked up a wall of sand and dust, but I stuck the skids to the ground before we browned out completely.

"Well, that was exciting," she said.

"Just another day at the office for us contractors."

Chapter 24
Quick Reaction Force

The rotors spun to a stop overhead as we stepped from the cockpit, and I said, "Let's talk tactics."

Teresa Lynn rounded the front of the chopper and took a knee in the sand facing me so I could read her lips. "If we assume the best possible scenario, there's two shooters per vehicle for a total of eighteen to twenty gunmen in that building. They're likely armed with AKs, and they're likely to have body armor. I'm all about dynamic entry with our hair on fire, but with our limited weapons and low ammo count, we've got no chance inside that building."

"Those are exactly the odds we face every time we deploy."

She shook her head. "I doubt it. Going in there with just the two of us is suicide. If we were armed to the teeth and you had two good feet, it would still be impossible to survive a two-man direct assault on that place."

She was right, but knowing my team was chained to a wall inside that place made my blood boil. "I'm getting my men out of there, no matter what it takes."

"I get it," she said. "But if you and I get killed one foot inside the front door, what do you think will happen to them? Do you have a QRF in place?"

"Really? Do you think I'd be out here trying to kill us in a stolen chopper if I had a quick reaction force hiding somewhere, just waiting to rush in and save the day? We're here completely black. The State Department will disavow any knowledge of us if our presence ever becomes known."

She said, "They've got five American prisoners of war, so I'd say your presence is already well known."

"None of my guys will talk. They'll take the beatings and the waterboarding, but they won't divulge anything."

"You've got a lot of confidence in a bunch of civilians."

"Those guys aren't civilians. They're warriors of the highest caliber. Green Berets."

She frowned. "Your pilot was Special Forces?"

"No, he's the exception. He's a retired A-Ten driver, but he's been in the trenches with us long enough to deserve a beret of his own."

She said, "Academically, that's cool, but we're talking real-world stuff in there. This isn't training and practice. This is the part when dead bodies start piling up."

"You're right. And those bodies aren't going to be my guys. I'm going in there if I have to clear that place, room by room, by myself. If the roles were reversed, that's exactly what any one of them would do to get me out of there."

"I get it. I do. I'm just asking you to slow your roll and think about our asset list."

"We've been through this," I said. "I know what we've got to work with, and I'm willing to—"

She held up her hand. "Stop. I'm not talking about the gear in my pack. I'm talking about other assets in the area."

"What other assets?"

"Remember that little bar full of guys who didn't look like they belonged in Central Asia? You know, the one where I tucked you in, sang you a lullaby, and kissed you goodnight?"

"I don't remember it playing out quite like that, but yeah, I remember."

"Those guys are assets. Especially your Israeli friend."

"What are you talking about?" I asked. "I can't exactly parade back in there and start taking applications."

"You don't have to. All you have to do is get that analyst of yours . . . Skipper, is it?"

"That's right."

"So, all you have to do is get her to start making phones ring in stations all over the world until she gets somebody to answer."

I said, "I've got a better idea."

"This ought to be good. Let's hear it, Cowboy."

I pointed to her pocket. "Rig that phone for my bone conduction again and find me the number for Tel-Aviv."

She slid the sat-phone from her pocket and slowly shook her head. "I don't want to, but I like you a little more every time you open your mouth."

"Hey, I'm a likable guy."

The episode that took me wasn't the typical merry-go-round ride. This one was a fireworks show on the inside of my eyelids. I fell backward toward the chopper and collapsed against one of the skids, feeling as though I was falling and tumbling while lights flashed in every direction.

Teresa yelled something and grabbed my shirt with both hands. She shook me until I opened my eyes to find her only inches from my face.

"Keep your eyes open and focus on me! Breathe, Cowboy, breathe!"

I recovered and shook off the ride. "That one was special."

"Let me guess. Flashing lights?"

"Yeah."

"We have to get you to a hospital, Chase. You've got a concussion or a TBI. The next time you go down, you may not get back up."

I made a curling motion with my hand. "Phone."

She thumbed in the number and laid the device in my palm.

It worked, and I heard the phone ringing on the other end through the electronic connection inside my head.

A deep, resonant voice answered on the fourth ring. "Abrams."

"Listen and don't hang up."

"Who is this?"

"Just listen. You have an operative in Dashoguz using the name Imri Nazarian. Do I need to describe him for you?"

Abrams said, "Who is this?"

"Who I am isn't important for you, but it will be for Nazarian. I need him on this phone inside of three minutes. Can you make that happen?"

"Whoever you are, I'm hanging up if the next words out of your mouth aren't your name."

"American is my name, and I have Teresa Lynn."

Silence filled the line, and I believed my device had lost its connection with the sat-phone. "Are you still there?"

Abrams said, "I'm here. Just wait."

After an eternity, a new voice came on the line. "Who is this?"

I growled. "If Abrams didn't brief you on who I am and what I have, you should fire him and find somebody who knows how to pass intel up the chain."

"What do you want?"

"I want to talk to the man calling himself Imri Nazarian, and I want his QRF for a hostage recovery operation ASAP."

The voice said, "I need to know who you are and who you're working for before this goes any further."

I took a long breath and blew it out. "I'm hanging up now. MI-Six will answer on the first ring and hand me a squad of SAS before I can say bangers and mash."

The man said, "Wait! Give me your coordinates."

"Right . . . So your team can hit me and take the package. I've been in this game way too long to fall for that. Here's what's going to happen. You and I are going to hang up. Then your man, Imri Nazarian, is going to call me within three minutes while you summon a quick reaction force. The QRF doesn't have to be made up of Israelis, but you guys are the best in the world, so that would be my preference. This doesn't need to be contentious. We're on the same side of this thing. I want my team back, and you want to debrief Teresa Lynn. Everybody gets what they want, and the good guys get to go home and sleep in their own beds tonight."

His one-word answer was the best I could've hoped for. "Fine."

Less than a minute later, Teresa's sat-phone rang in my palm. I accepted the incoming call and said, "Go."

"American?"

"Imri?"

He said, "I suspected it would be you who answered. Brief me up."

"First, I need to know where you are."

"I'm on the border near Mayli-Dzhengel."

Teresa was listening in and immediately went to work pulling up a map. She shoved the tablet toward me. "That's forty clicks southwest."

I gave Imri our coordinates for the suspected building where my team was being held.

He said, "Give me a second to plot it."

While he was doing the math, I said, "Tell me about your QRF."

"It doesn't really qualify as a quick reaction force. It's four trigger-pullers who all speak Yiddish and never shut up. They're loud, but they're hard-core when they go to work."

"How far out are they?"

"They're still on the Turkmen side, but they've got a capable vehicle. If I plotted your position correctly, they can be there in two hours. I'll make it in about an hour."

Teresa checked her watch and mouthed, "Your head injury will have you out of the game in less than four hours."

I said, "I've got a strange question, but can any of your Yiddish-speaking trigger-pullers fly a helicopter?"

"I don't know. Why?"

"Because I just happen to have one."

"A bird is pretty useless without somebody who can fly it."

"I *can* fly it, but I got beat up pretty badly, and my head's a little wonky. I'd like to put somebody at the controls who only sees one of every object in front of him."

"I'll see what I can do. Can you defend your position until we get there?"

"No. You get to work finding a pilot, and I'll get the chopper to your QRF. Have the pilot rendezvous with us at their location."

He grunted. "I thought you said you couldn't fly."

"No, I said I *shouldn't* fly, but my men shouldn't be getting waterboarded inside a building, either."

Imri provided the coordinates for his team of shooters, and Teresa plotted it. For the second time that day, the turbines in the ancient Russian helicopter whistled to life, and we were airborne over the border.

Fifteen minutes into the flight, I said, "You have the controls. It's happening again."

"I have the controls," she said.

I dealt with a massive wave of nausea and the feeling of a spike being driven into the base of my skull. My vision darkened, and shards of electricity shot down both arms. I shook off the episode and slid my hands back onto the controls. "You really need to learn to land a helicopter."

She rolled her eyes. "I'll add that to the list of things I need to do right after surviving the afternoon with you."

The coordinates Imri provided put us in a remote area with only one small hut and a few trees. A heavily armored vehicle was parked beneath the shade of the best tree in the area, but the sun was still winning the battle.

I touched down without issue, and an assault team, fully kitted out, sprinted for the chopper. Their size, dark beards, gear selections, and sense of urgency made them exactly the team I was hoping for. They hit the chopper at a run, and every man mounted up as if he'd done it a million times.

One of the shooters stuck his head into the cockpit and said something I didn't hear, but Teresa got it.

She said, "This seat is yours."

She abandoned her perch, and an olive-skinned man with dark, deep-set eyes slid into her seat. He pulled on Teresa's headset and adjusted the mic.

I watched for his lips to move, but he was obviously waiting for me to talk first, so I said, "Listen closely. I'm Chase, but I'm deaf. I can read lips, and I've got a custom device that helps me hear the sat-phone. That's it. When you talk to me, get my attention, and look directly at me so I can read your lips. Got it?"

He stared through me. "Got it."

"There's one more thing. I'm having mini seizures every half hour or so. That's why I needed a pilot."

His full beard mostly hid his lips when he spoke, but I picked up most of what he said. "I've never flown this particular bird. In fact, I don't even know what it is, but I can get the job done."

I imagined his accent based on the shapes he formed when he spoke.

I said, "We're picking up your officer in Mayli-Dzhengel. Do you know where that is?"

He nodded and took the controls. His skill in the chopper was obvious long before we leveled off in cruise flight, and he handled the machine as if it were an extension of his own body. We made a hot extraction on the outskirts of Mayli-Dzhengel and were back on our way with Imri safely aboard in seconds.

I pointed toward the building where I suspected my team was being held. "That's our objective. I've got five men in there, and we suspect up to twenty bad guys."

He gave a nod, dumped the collective, and flew an arcing descent at well over a thousand feet per minute. Before I realized what was happening, we were on the ground, and Israeli commandos were pouring from the Russian chopper like bolts of lightning. In an instant, they had a security perimeter set, and I was alone in the cockpit.

I shut down the flying machine and slipped from the seat and onto the rocky ground with my timber foot and screwed-up head ready to brief the assault and get my team back.

Chapter 25
CQB the Israeli Way

Close-quarters battle is one of the most unpredictable and danger-ous tasks an operator performs. Mastery of the skill set requires thousands of hours of repetitive training, honing physical move-ment as well as mental preparedness. The psychology of bursting into a room with a four-man team of gun-toters and eliminating every threat in the room is a head game most people will never play, and for that, they should be eternally thankful.

Surprisingly, we didn't draw any obvious attention when we fell out of the sky and deployed armed operators all over the sandy, rocky terrain. Our capabilities had increased dramatically in the previous hour. Instead of an assault force consisting of a one-legged knuckle-dragger and a senior CIA case officer, we were now stronger by five. Four hard-core commandos loaded to the teeth and obviously more than capable of the mission that lay ahead. We'd also added a Mossad officer, but his tradecraft hadn't fully re-vealed itself yet.

I took a knee in front of the team and began the briefing. "First, you need to know that I'm deaf, so if you want to talk to me, get my attention and face me so I can read your lips. When we hit the house, I'll be on sat-coms linked to a hearing device im-planted in my skull."

The commandos didn't react. They merely continued listening as if my condition were a common element of their day-to-day lives.

"Now that we've got that out of the way, we're pulling five Americans out of that building. They are Clark—blonde hair and beard, five ten, two hundred pounds. Mongo—impossible to miss at six eight and three hundred pounds. Disco—five ten, one-eighty, graying hair and beard. Singer—African American, six feet two-ten. And Kodiak—red hair and beard, five eight, one-eighty."

The look in their eyes told me they were committing every detail to memory, and I continued. "We estimate eighteen to twenty hostiles, all armed, but not likely very well trained. Don't let that make you sloppy, though. These guys were able to roll up five hard-core operators, so there's obviously strength in numbers. Is everybody tracking so far?"

Heads nodded, so I kept talking. "If my team isn't injured, they're capable of joining the fight once they're liberated, so hand them a weapon if you can."

I'd almost forgotten about the episodes, but I was promptly reminded when everything in my field of vision was instantly reduced to a pinpoint of light on the distant horizon and my body felt as if it were tumbling inside a clothes dryer. I braced off against the ground with both hands until the seizure faded.

"Sorry about that. I took a nasty head shot earlier today, so I'm dealing with some of the aftereffects. Any questions?"

The shooters talked among themselves for a minute before the pilot asked, "Where are we sending your guys when we find them?"

I said, "I'll be the fifth man in each stack once we're inside. I'll take control of each man when you find and free them. If they're wounded, I'll send them out to my partner." I motioned toward Teresa. "If they're still in the fight and you can arm them, I'll dispatch them to clear the opposite side of the building once we have at least two of them."

The Israeli pointed toward my wooden peg leg. "You're going in with that?"

"It's all I've got, so yeah, I'll be the fifth man in your stack."

Another operator asked, "Are we putting down the hostiles?"

Again, I was immediately thrown into a decision to take the lives of men who were fighting a war in which they were little more than pawns.

"Do you have zip ties?" I asked. The man nodded, so I said, "If they're a direct threat, put them down. If not, zip them up, and we'll deal with them once the building is clear."

Imri, the Mossad officer, spoke in what I assumed was Yiddish, and then turned to me. "They'll comply with your instructions to the limit of their own safety. If they encounter numbers they can't manage, they'll eliminate them and move on."

"I've got a better idea," I said. "You and I will become five and six in the stack, and we'll help manage any encounters with more than four bad guys."

He turned back to his QRF and explained the new plan. When he was finished, he said, "Let's hit 'em."

Teresa programmed a spare sat-com to communicate with my bone conduction transceiver, and I tucked it into my belt.

With communication checks complete, I pulled Teresa aside. "I left you out of the clearing op for a reason. It'll take us twenty minutes or more to secure that house and liberate my team, if everything goes perfectly. That'll give you plenty of time to disappear if that's what you want to do."

She looked up at me and mouthed, "Understood."

Believing I'd never see Teresa Lynn again, no matter how diligently I searched, I turned away and focused on the daunting task at hand. Clearing that house against twenty armed militiamen without getting any of the good guys hurt or killed would be hard enough, but the horrifying fear of not being able to keep myself alive during a neurological episode in the middle of a gunfight was all-consuming.

Hobbling toward the structure, I felt a hand on my arm, and I turned to see Teresa standing only inches away. She said, "I need to know one thing before I go."

The pain in her eyes spoke volumes about the weight of the coming question, so I stood, waiting for her lips to move. When she finally spoke, her words were like a dagger dividing truth from everything else. "Are you loyal to the American people . . . or the American government?"

I pointed across my shoulder. "I'm loyal to those five men and everybody they love."

She nodded and turned away, but her question has never left my mind. I've heard it a million times in the midst of battle, in the quiet moments when peace almost felt permanent, and especially in those moments when I questioned every decision I'd ever made.

The entry team moved silently like a snake through the sparse wisps of grass and across stony stretches of coarse sand until they reached the front door of the structure and pressed themselves against the wall. I finally caught up and took my place as the number five man in the entry stack. Number one made a fist and raised it to the side of his helmet, signaling for the breacher to open the door.

That sent the fourth man forward with his shotgun raised to his shoulder with two breaching rounds in the tube. Number one held up his hand and then touched his finger to his lips. The breacher lowered the shotgun and knelt in front of the door. He worked the knob with a gloved hand, but it wouldn't budge. Finally, he retrieved a wedge and a rubber hammer from his kit and leaned against the door. With the wedge between the jamb and the door, he tapped with the rubber mallet until he created enough space to separate the locking mechanism from the jamb, and then he silently pushed the door inward an inch.

Sliding his tools back into his kit, the breacher withdrew a long, flexible cable from a pocket and slipped it into the cracked door. At the opposite end of the cable was a small black-and-white screen giving the team a grainy picture of what waited inside the door.

The number two man squeezed the first man's shoulder, telling him the stack was ready to move. Number one paused long enough for everyone to raise their rifles into the ready position. Man two elevated his barrel over the shoulder of man one, and three and four positioned their rifles at the low ready. I press-checked my borrowed pistol and glanced back to see Imri with his rifle raised high.

I didn't like not having a rifle, but the disadvantages of carrying a pistol into a room-clearing op were outweighed by the ease with which I could help my men back to the exit if they were injured.

Number one eased the door inward, lifting upward on the knob to take the weight off of the hinges that were likely old enough to squeak like an alarm under the weight of the heavy door. The stack moved through the door with practiced confidence and skill. Every man knew precisely where his sector of responsibility lay, and he covered it as if his life depended on it. Before the day was over, everyone's lives would depend on the professionalism and skill of the fearless commandos.

Once inside, number one broke right and pushed through a blanket hanging over a cased opening, and the tempo of the operation tripled. Man two followed and broke left, keeping himself near the wall and remaining well clear of the door to the next room. Once the six of us were inside the room, the man who'd been number two moved into the lead position, and the stack re-formed on him.

Even through my deafened ears, I could hear the sounds of a radio or television playing from somewhere in the building, and I was thankful for the noise. Although we were working as quietly as possible, the gig would be up the instant we encountered another human, especially if we had to put him down.

We pushed into the second room with speed unmatched by any team I'd ever worked with. The Israelis did everything with such precision and flawless timing that it was hard to believe they weren't somehow reading each other's minds.

I hobbled, trying to keep the sound of my temporary wooden foot striking the concrete floor to a minimum. The rubber soles of the commandos' boots made them silent, but I didn't have that luxury.

The second room was clear, and we pushed onward, moving through every doorway like a well-oiled machine. I studied the way each man positioned his feet, head, and weapons as they moved. As strong as my team was, the Israelis were better, and I had every intention of taking some of their tactics back to Bonaventure and training my team the Israeli way.

The first four rooms offered no targets or prisoners, but the sense of urgency didn't change. We continued our push through the building as if every corner hid a threat, and when we reached room number five, that mentality paid off. The fiberoptic camera went through the door first, and number one held up three fingers and then pointed to sectors inside the room. Peacetime was over, and the true close-quarters battle was about to begin.

Number two squeezed number one's shoulder, the pause came, weapons moved to the ready positions, and forward we went. Number one broke left and put two suppressed rounds into the chest and one in the face of his man against the far wall. Number two broke right and eliminated a target on the back wall with the same three-shot technique. Man number three pressed his trigger three times before he was fully inside the room, and long before the entire stack was through the door, three bad guys lay in puddles of their own blood.

Disco sat on a wooden chair with his forearms flex-cuffed to the armrests.

I stepped forward, sliced the flex-cuffs, and whispered, "Are you hurt?"

He looked up with surprise and relief consuming his face. "I'm okay. Give me a gun."

The breacher handed his shotgun to Disco. He took it, press-checked for a round in the chamber, and tossed the sling across his shoulder. Our six-man stack had just grown by one, and we'd soon be forced to break into two elements.

The stack stopped with every man covering either the entrance we'd come through or the only other door out of the room, and number one leaned against Disco. Although I couldn't hear the conversation or get the angle to read their lips, I was confident my chief pilot was briefing the element commander on what he knew about the rest of the structure.

I collected the three AK-47s from the dead militiamen, handed one to Disco, and shouldered the other two. The breacher reclaimed his shotgun and slid it back into his pack.

It took maybe ten more minutes to clear the first floor of the building, and we discovered four more men, but the rest of my team was nowhere in sight.

A stairwell is the ultimate fatal funnel. Once committed to the narrow, ascending space, the team would be vulnerable to ambush with every step. Man one led the way, taking every tread in ultra-slow motion and leading with the muzzle of his rifle. To that point, every shot that had been fired came from the suppressors mounted on the muzzles of the commandos' rifles. Even though they were quiet, they still made enough noise to be heard through thin walls. Hopefully, the concrete structure of the building dampened enough of the rifles' reports to avoid alarming the remaining men upstairs.

We reached the landing in the stairwell and turned the corner with number one's rifle panning the space above him. I'll never know where the first unsuppressed round came from, but even my deaf ears heard it. Instead of retreating like most mortals would do, man one and man two advanced, laying down fire as they moved. Commands came in Yiddish through their coms and through my bone conduction device, and I was the only person in the stairwell who didn't understand a word of it.

Imri shoved me against the wall and stepped around me with his rifle raised. Disco followed with his requisitioned AK pressed to his shoulder. My Makarov pistol and I were all but worthless in the fight, but the rest of the team pressed onward, silencing the guns at the top of the stairs.

We now owned the first floor and stairwell, and eleven of the suspected twenty militiamen were dead or dying and disarmed, but the element of surprise vanished with the silence we'd enjoyed downstairs. Our mission had just become a dynamic clearing operation, and the pace increased to match the deadliness of our new lot in life.

The team cleared rooms in seconds instead of minutes, and bullets flew in every direction. Armed with a Russian AK-47, I joined the fight until the world in front of me rolled upside down.

Have I been shot, or is this another seizure?

I didn't feel the old familiar sensation of a burning entry wound, but that didn't mean I wasn't hit. Bullets sometimes pass through muscle, fat, and soft tissue, doing little damage other than opening a vein or artery. Those could occur, failing to produce enough pain to override the adrenaline flowing through my system.

I was suddenly cold, confused, and completely incapable of focusing on anything in front of me. The world was inverted, blurred, and trembling . . . until it all turned to black.

Chapter 26
Immortality

When I came to, Imri Nazarian was hovering over me with his hand on the center of my chest. I stared up at him until he came into focus. "Where was I hit?"

He took my right arm in his hand and lifted it far enough for me to see the pressure dressing he apparently applied to my hand. Half the bandage was soaked dark red, but it wasn't dripping. He laid my wounded hand across my chest and touched his finger to his lips. I obeyed the command to be quiet, but I couldn't resist pressing on the bandage with my left hand in a wasted effort to find the wound. There'd been enough blood to soak the dressing, but apparently not enough to kill me.

Imri moved to the doorway of the room we were in and peered down the hallway. My hearing hadn't improved, but the deafest of men could hear and feel the gunfight raging just down the hall. The thunder of the AKs roared over the pops and hisses of the suppressed 300 Blackouts the Israelis were firing. I lay there listening to the fight, and everything inside of me wanted to be in it with my men and the men who'd unselfishly volunteered to rescue them. Lying on the floor while my brothers-in-arms were under fire was not something I was capable of doing.

Imri kicked an AK toward me and stepped back inside the room. I watched his lips through his beard, and I think he said, "Stay here and stay quiet. It's getting bad. I'm going in."

Without waiting for me to respond, he tightened a strap on his plate carrier, pulled his magazine for a round count, and stepped through the doorway. I rolled over and reached for the Russian rifle lying beside me, but the bulky dressing on my right hand prevented me from gripping it. I scooped it up with my left hand and stood, a little dizzy, but thankfully, I wasn't going down.

I pulled the magazines from the other AKs on the floor and shoved them everywhere I could find a spot on my body. Without unloading and reloading each magazine, I had no way to get an accurate round count, but I placed the heaviest mags in front and stepped to the door. One of the Israelis was sitting in the hallway with his back against the wall and firing shots through an open door. From my vantage point, I couldn't see if he'd been shot or if he'd fallen during the breach. In that moment, it didn't matter. The man was in a gunfight on my behalf, and I was doing nothing to help him. That was about to change.

I shook my head, trying to clear my vision, and clomped down the hall. When I got to the commando, he glanced up at me, revealing a badly broken nose and likely several more breaks in his face. His left eye wasn't visible, and his right was barely open, but he looked straight at me, showing no sign of recognition. He just kept firing back into the room. When his rifle ran dry, he dropped the empty magazine and reached for a replacement, but his ammo pouch was a black hole. He let his head fall backward against the wall, and I grabbed the collar of his plate carrier vest.

Struggling backward with every stride, I dragged him down the hall and into the room where I'd been. He was badly injured but still conscious, so I stuck an AK in his hands and dropped a mostly full magazine onto his lap. "I'll be back."

He didn't put up a fight, so I headed back down the hallway. I wasn't certain how to join the fight without having both sides shooting at me. I scanned the hall for possible threats and saw none, so I cut the pie around the door casing of the room into which the injured Israeli was firing. The first two bodies I identified were two of the commandos who were shooting for their lives.

Completing my pie, I committed and stepped into the room. I yelled, "Friendly by the door!"

If they heard me, neither man acknowledged my presence. They kept their eyes trained downrange and bullets in the air. Firing left-handed, I threw myself into the fight. My field of fire was narrow, but it was just enough to give us the upper hand and allow us to push ahead.

We moved through the next doorway just in time to see Mongo explode from the chair that was supposed to confine him. I didn't see the move he made to destroy the simple piece of furniture, but I had a front-row seat for the gladiator show that came next. The giant sent a descending elbow into the skull of an unsuspecting rifleman, and the man withered to the ground, likely having departed this world.

Mongo spun on a heel, ripped the wooden arm of the chair from his wrist, and sent two blinding shots to the gunman's head who'd been pouring lead toward me. The gunman went down hard, and Mongo gave him a love tap with his bootheel, just in case he needed a little more affection.

The two Israelis took out the two remaining shooters in the room, and that gunfight reached its end, but the war was far from over. We pressed forward to join the rest of the pieced-together team. The good guys were slowly winning, but the scene awaiting us at the northern end of the second-floor hallway was more than any of us could've expected. Black smoke boiled from at least three doorways, and four gunmen dived through a pair of open windows to escape both the flames and our onslaught of gunfire.

"How many do we have?" I yelled at the top of my lungs. I couldn't hear any response, so I grabbed one of the Israeli commandos and spun him to face me. "How many do we have?"

"How many what?" he mouthed.

"My team!"

He held up three fingers and yelled, "Is David alive?"

I pointed down the hallway behind me. "He was when I left him, but I think he took a round to the face. I parked him in the first room on the left."

Mongo roared through the door on my right and straight through the wall of orange flame and blinding smoke. The giant vanished into the abyss of the fire before I could stop him, and one of the Israelis followed him into the hellish realm, bent on saving the remaining members of my team.

I shook off the coming seizure and pressed myself against the wall of the hallway as I played out a mental roll call. Mongo and Disco were alive, but who was the third man the Israeli said we had? Clark, Singer, and Kodiak were still missing in my head.

Nearing panic, I scanned every inch of the second floor I could see, but I couldn't find anyone. Two doors remained closed on the side of the hall that wasn't an inferno, so I threw myself against the first door and crashed through as if it were made of paper. The room was empty except for a pile of filthy blankets in one corner. I pumped four rounds into the blanket, just in case one of the militiamen had chosen to bury himself there instead of making the leap through the window.

Back in the hallway, I reoriented myself and clomped to the next door, but it was clearly made of something far heavier than the previous one I'd breached. I bounced off the door twice before sending a burst of full-auto fire into the knob and lock. That did the trick, and I was in.

The room appeared to be a storeroom of some kind with enormous bottles of water, ammunition, boxes, and rolls of brown paper. With the inventory of the storeroom locked in my skull, I ran as fast as my lumber leg would carry me back into the previous room and gathered up the blankets that were now full of holes from my AK. I lugged them back to the storeroom and threw them on the floor. Sidestepping the pile of blankets, I reached for my knife, only to find an empty pocket where it should've been.

Think, Chase . . . think!

With my one good hand, I raked four heavy bottles of water from the shelf and opened up on them with my rifle. The contents of the plastic bottles came pouring from the 7.62mm entry and exit wounds I'd delivered. With the bottles empty and the blankets soaked, I threw one across my head and gathered the others in my arms.

Mongo and the commando braved the wall of flames unprotected, but they'd never survive the furnace if they stayed more than a few seconds. I collided with Mongo first and shoved a soaking wet blanket to him. Although I couldn't see an inch in front of my face, I had to find the Israeli. Mongo yanked another blanket from my arms and shoved me to the left. I assumed he was trying to shove me back out the door, but I couldn't have been more wrong.

After stumbling three strides to my left, I collided with someone on their feet, and I stuck a blanket against his chest. He took it, grabbed my hand, and placed it against his plate carrier. We moved as one through the room with our soaking blankets doing all they could to protect us from the flames and smoke. In an instant, my training in finding and rescuing victims of a fire flashed back, and I dropped to the floor. The Israeli did the same, and the world opened up in front of us. The smoke and flames were a foot above our heads, and we had a few feet of visibility in front of us. I low-crawled with him, keeping one hand on the wall and the other outstretched in front of us. I held his webbing with my left and probed the darkness with my wounded right hand. Ten feet into our search, I felt a leg, but the person attached to it showed no re-action when I grabbed and shook it.

"I've got one!" I yelled, and the Israeli tossed a blanket across him.

Unwilling to wait any longer, I rolled onto my back and dragged the person onto my stomach while I backpaddled across the floor. Finding the door was a challenge, but when I broke free of the smoke, I discovered that we were back in the hallway. I sat up and pulled the blanket from the victim I'd dragged from the flames. His eyes were closed, and his clothes and hair were singed. I wiped his face with the corner of a blanket and stuck my fingers on the side of his neck. A faint but regular pulse pounded beneath my fingertips, and I said a silent prayer of thanks for Singer, our Southern Baptist sniper, for being not only eternally immortal, but apparently also fireproof.

He coughed, gagged, spat, and clawed at the air as if drowning.

I took his face in my hands. "You're out of the fire. You're safe!"

His lips moved, but I couldn't hear his deep baritone. The words he formed when he pointed back toward the fire cut like a knife. "Kodiak! Clark!"

"I'm going back in for them," I said as I pulled the blanket back across my head.

Before I could crawl my way back to the door, a pair of bodies collided with me, shoving me back into the hallway. I tried to ma-neuver out of their way, but my clumsy effort only worsened our entanglement. When the three of us rolled clear of the smoke and soaked blankets, the filthy face of the Israeli emerged with Kodiak in his arms.

Gasping for clear air, Kodiak yelled, "Clark!" and almost before his next breath came, Mongo burst from the second door, sending shards of wood in every direction. His momentum carried him across the hall and into the opposite wall. The crash looked like a freight train hitting a mountain, and the big man fell to his knees. He dumped the limp form of a shackled and flex-cuffed man who looked far too old to be on a mission like this one.

Clark was unconscious, but his chest rose and fell in rhythmic waves.

Disco moved in, cut Clark's hands free of his flex-cuffs, and rolled him onto his side. "He's got a good pulse. I think he's going to be okay."

"We've got to get out of this building," I yelled.

Those of us who could walk—even me—helped those who couldn't down the flight of stairs where the chaos had begun and out the front door. The thought that wouldn't leave my head was of the men who leapt from the second floor after starting the fire.

Once outside of the burning structure, I hobbled around the building, hoping to see at least a couple of militiamen with broken legs beneath the windows, but instead, I found four men—two appeared to be corpses with bullet holes through their skulls, and the other two were sitting back-to-back and tied together. Standing over them was an American with a cut-down AK-47 aimed at the knees of the bound men.

"It looks like you caught a couple of keepers there. What do you plan to do with them?"

Teresa Lynn looked up and showed me her lips. "I plan for these two to be exhibit A and B when I testify before Congress in a few days. Would you mind giving us a ride back to the States, Cowboy?"

Chapter 27
Identify Friend or Foe

I considered the implications and complications of forcefully taking two Uzbek militiamen back to the United States. Would they suddenly have a collection of Constitutional rights on U.S. soil? Would I be guilty of violating more international laws than I could count?

"I'm not sure I'm the right bus driver to get your prisoners back to the States. We aren't officially here."

Teresa said, "They aren't my prisoners. Do you speak Uzbek or Turkmen?"

To my surprise, I heard some sound coming from her mouth, but it was still too garbled to make out without reading her lips.

"No, I speak Russian but not Uzbek or Turkmen."

Her smile said that must've been the answer she wanted because she waved the muzzle of her AK across the two men and said, "The same is true for them."

"What?"

She nodded slowly. "You heard that correctly. These two, and probably all the dead guys in that building, are Russian nationals."

I held up a finger. "Don't go anywhere."

It took two minutes of wading through the triage scene before I found Clark. He was burned, covered in black soot, but still breathing.

"We need to talk."

He looked up at me from behind his bottle of water. "I need a minute to catch my breath, College Boy."

"It can't wait," I said. "Did you notice anything about the guys in the building?"

He huffed. "Yeah, they were a lot better gunfighters than I expected."

"Exactly, and I just learned the reason for that. They're Russian regular Army, not Uzbeks."

"What? How do you know?"

I took a knee beside him. "I don't have all the pieces yet, but according to the case officer, the Kremlin is behind this war nobody understands."

He furrowed his brow and took in the scene around him. "I don't know if I'm buying it, but keep talking."

"We have to debrief Teresa Lynn. That's the only way we're going to get all the facts."

"Come on, man. When was the last time you heard a CIA case officer spew facts?"

"She's got a lot to lose."

"Yeah, and she probably thinks getting you on her side is the best way to keep from losing all of it."

I glanced back across the gritty earth between us and Teresa. "I don't know. Something tells me she's the only one telling the truth in this thing."

He took a long drink of water. "Okay, you're the boss, but you've got a lot of injured soldiers to deal with before we can play grown-up spy."

"When you catch your breath, go talk to her. Tell her who and what you are, and then listen to her."

He examined the remaining water in his bottle. "All right. I'll give it a shot."

Mongo was the easy one to spot. Regardless of how filthy he was, picking him out of a crowd was never challenging.

"How bad is it?"

He didn't look up from his patient, but he said something.

I laid a hand on his shoulder. "I'm deaf, so you need to look at me so I can see your mouth."

He turned his head. "It's bad. The Israelis are critical. We've got to get them to the next level of care or they're not going to make it."

I found Disco and Kodiak sitting on the ground and using each other as backrests. "Are you guys okay?"

Disco nodded and held up a twisted hand. "I scored a couple of broken fingers, but we're okay. Whoever those guys were, they weren't amateurs."

"Yeah, I know. I'm piecing that together now. The theory is they're Russian regulars."

Kodiak said, "That would explain it."

I asked, "Where's your buddy, Imri?"

Kodiak raised his water bottle and pointed toward a crowd of three men. "I think he's one of them."

Kodiak was right. Imri was cleaning and dressing the wounds of his commandos.

I took a knee beside him. "Let's get you and your men out of here and in the hands of some real doctors."

Imri wiped his face with a sleeve and grabbed my collar. "Look around. Do you see any trauma centers or emergency rooms?"

I ignored his grip on my shirt. "Look, I understand you're angry. You have every right to be. I put you and your men into a gunfight I underestimated, and we're all lucky to be alive."

He gave me a shake. "You're damned right you did. You told me we were hitting a team of militia, not Spetsnaz."

I looked back at the burning building. "I don't have a hospital to give you, but I've got the next best thing. Where's your pilot?"

Imri motioned toward the man I'd dragged out of the firefight with a bullet in his face.

"Here's the plan," I said. "My pilot is going to fly you and your men to the airport in Nukus. I've got a jet there. At least, I hope it's still there. You tell me where we're going. I've got fifteen hundred miles of fuel, so pick something friendly and close." I returned to Disco. "Can you fly?" He nodded, and I said, "Good. Where's Singer?"

"Right behind you."

I turned to find our sniper only three strides away. "We've got to move. The Israelis are in bad shape, and you're the lightest medic we've got. Let's go."

Disco fired up our stolen helicopter while the rest of us loaded the most serious casualties onto the chopper. Mongo would add too much weight and bulk to the flight, so Singer had to play flight nurse. All five Israelis and Teresa's two prisoners made the first flight to Nukus while the rest of us licked our wounds and put as much distance between ourselves and the burning building as possible. Nobody, except Teresa, was uninjured, but everyone could walk better than I could. Watching them outpace me reminded me of the final seconds prior to the explosions that left me buried and unconscious and my team in the hands of the Russian Army.

We finally stopped about half a mile from the fire, near a grove of small trees. The shade was a welcome relief, and our helicopter soon appeared on the northern horizon. Disco put it down a hundred yards away, and we climbed aboard.

I joined Disco in the cockpit. "Was our jet still there?"

"Yeah, but our security contingent must've gotten a better offer. They were nowhere to be seen."

"Let's go," I said, and he put us in the wind.

The flight to the airport gave me just enough time to run through every terrible decision I made on the mission, but not enough time to come up with solutions for any of the disasters I'd created.

By some miracle from God, the *Grey Ghost* was safe and sound, right where we'd left her. By the time we got on board, Singer had IV bags hanging and a makeshift mobile hospital up and running in the cargo area of the cabin.

Even though some of my hearing was returning, I was in no shape to fly, so Clark slithered into the right seat, and I sent Imri forward.

I said, "Tell them where we're going, and pick some place with jet fuel."

Imri made his way to the cockpit and discussed the plan with Disco and Clark while Mongo and Singer cared for the most injured among us.

We were soon climbing away from Nukus International Airport in weather that couldn't have been more opposite to the horrible conditions we endured on our arrival. Blue skies stretched for hundreds of miles in every direction, and that was the first good omen I'd seen in days.

When Imri returned to the main cabin, he said, "We're going to Ben Gurion."

I scowled. "Did you say Ben Gurion?" He nodded, and I drew a mental map. "That puts us over Iraq, Iran, Syria, and Jordan, and it has to be more than fifteen hundred miles."

He gave me a slap to the shoulder. "Relax and trust your crew, American."

"If we don't get shot down, we'll run out of fuel somewhere over Jordan."

Imri said, "According to your man named Disco, he's got a plan."

* * *

Three and a half hours later, we touched down at Tel-Aviv's Ben Gurion International without any bullet holes or empty fuel tanks, and I couldn't wait to hear how we'd pulled it off. A fleet of ambulances waited inside the enormous hangar, where a ground crew towed us after we taxied to the ramp. Once inside, the hangar doors were moved back into place, leaving just enough space for the ambulances to escape. We opened the hatch and deployed the airstairs.

Two men who looked a lot like Imri raced up the stairs and surveyed the scene inside the plane. One of the men spoke in what must've been Hebrew, and Imri followed the two of them off the plane. Medical crews followed and removed the wounded Israelis, leaving my team, Teresa Lynn, and two suspected Russians wondering what would happen next.

Clark and Disco climbed from the cockpit, wearing the same look as me.

Disco said, "Do you think there's a chance we might get a little gas somewhere around here?"

A third man in a well-worn suit and no tie climbed the stairs and studied every face still on the plane. I almost laughed when I realized what the man must be thinking. The contents of our jet were anything but typical. Six filthy men covered in soot, sweat, dirt, and dried blood, two similar-looking men who just happened to be handcuffed together, and one relatively clean American woman holding a cut-down AK-47 stared back at him.

When he spoke, he didn't form words I could read on his lips, so Clark answered by pointing at me. "He is, but he doesn't hear so well these days, so I'll have to do."

Before the man could begin questioning Clark, I said, "Wait. I have an idea."

I dug through the pallet of backup gear and came up with a sat-com rig and remote microphone. I programmed a transceiver to communicate with my bone conduction device and clipped it to my belt. Handing the other transceiver to the man, I said, "Stick this radio somewhere, and clip the mic to your shirt."

He examined the device and hesitantly followed my instructions. "What is this?"

"It's a long story," I said, "but rest assured nothing is being recorded. This just allows me to hear you."

"What happened to you?"

The twelve-year-old boy in me wanted to crack a joke, but instead, I motioned toward Teresa's prisoners. "It would appear the Russians happened to us."

"Who is the woman?" he asked.

I grimaced. "That answer depends on several factors, not the least of which is who you are."

"I am Asher Katz of the Israeli Mossad. The woman is American?"

I met Teresa's eyes, and she gave me the faintest shake of her head. "Perhaps American, perhaps something else."

Asher said, "And the rest of you are CIA clandestine service, yes?"

"Most certainly not," I said.

The man made a motion resembling a slight bow. "Very well, then. The medical officers will care for your wounded." He stared down at my hand wrapped in a bloody pressure bandage. "That includes you, and then we will talk."

Without another word, he pulled off the mic and radio, handed them to me, and descended the stairs.

With the com gear in my hands, I turned to Clark. "We never called Skipper."

"Relax, College Boy. I briefed her up. She arranged all of this and got us safe passage through a little unfriendly airspace."

I said, "She told me Tony and Hunter were standing by to deploy if necessary."

"We handled that, as well. They're safe and sound at Bonaventure."

I nodded toward the airstairs. "What's going to happen here?"

He glanced at Teresa. "That's up to you and her."

Asher was right. His medical team took extremely good care of us. We showered, changed clothes, and almost looked human again. Other than a few superficial bullet wounds, some burns, a few broken fingers, and dehydration, we were mostly in good shape. The wound to my hand and wrist wasn't as minor as I'd hoped, but other than a few stitches to close the skin, I'd wait until I could get to Dr. Ham at UAB to repair or replace the mechanical components. I was due for a new foot, as well, so the trip would be a dual-purpose visit. In the meantime, I pulled a simplified version of my mechanical foot from our backup gear and fit it to my leg. Walking with the foot was easier but still not as good as the electronic version.

The two suspected Russians were well guarded while they showered and received treatment for their injuries, and I took the opportunity to pull Teresa aside. "How do you want to play this?"

She sighed. "Right now, I trust the Israelis a lot more than I trust anybody at Langley."

The expression she wore said she'd reached the limit of her ability to keep the secrets that made her Langley's favorite target at the moment.

I said, "Get me one of those radios, and let's have a conversation."

Chapter 28
The Facts

One of the medical staff gave us a small room that appeared to be relatively private, and I handed the coms to my favorite CIA case officer. "Let's hear it."

She clipped the mic to her collar and started talking without preamble. "The chief of station in Tashkent was caught in a Russian honeytrap. Do you know what that means?"

I couldn't hold back the chuckle. "Oh, I know far too well what that means. I've still got honey in places I can't wash off."

"And you're still in the game?"

"It's a long story, and it sort of worked itself out, but we don't have enough time for me to tell you the details."

She said, "Okay, but promise me you'll tell me if we get out of this alive."

"Alive?" I said. "The Israelis are our allies. We're not in any danger here."

"Don't be naïve. We're in enormous danger. The U.S. and Israel are allies, but the CIA and Mossad are bedfellows. The relationship between the two services is stronger than you can imagine. It's likely we're being recorded and piped directly to Langley."

"Then why are you talking?" I asked.

"I'm talking because you didn't shoot me on sight."

"Why would I have done that?"

She said, "Chase, there's an unofficial kill order against me. The three officers the chief of station sent to find me were there to put a bullet in my brain and leave me to rot."

"Is that why you killed them?"

"They didn't give me any choice. The chief was so deep in bed with Moscow that he corrupted the entire Tashkent station by convincing them I was the Russian mole. When he dispatched me to the border, he thought I'd be killed in the initial fighting."

I stopped her. "Let's talk about the fighting. Which side really started the war? Everybody knows the first mortars came from the Turkmenistan side, but that's too simple."

"You're learning," she said. "Putin wants to rebuild the former Soviet Union to its previous strength and glory. What better way to do that than to have former Soviet republics crumble under war? The KGB started that war for the sole purpose of allowing the Kremlin to step in at the final hours and broker a peace agreement by absorbing Turkmenistan and Uzbekistan back into Russia."

"Hold on," I said. "There's no such thing as the KGB anymore."

She rolled her eyes. "There you go being naïve again. Just because they call it the SVR now doesn't mean it isn't the same demon with a new cloak. They're still corrupt. They're still brutal. And most of all, they're still under Vladimir Putin's thumb. It's still the Komitet Gosudarstvennoy Bezopasnosti, no matter what label you stamp it with."

"Okay. Keep talking."

"It's the oldest play in political propaganda. Everybody knows you never let a tragedy go unexploited, and Putin is the reigning world champion of that game."

I squeezed my temples and tried to fathom how a baseball player from Georgia ever found himself locked in a tiny room in

Tel-Aviv, with an American CIA case officer who was either spinning the grandest yarn in the history of espionage or telling the truth. In that moment, the truth terrified me far worse than the lie. "So, what do you want from me?"

She said, "I want you to listen to two more facts, and then I want you to do what you believe is right."

I nodded and wordlessly encouraged her to continue.

"The U.S. Ambassador to Uzbekistan was a personal friend of the First Lady. That's how he got himself appointed to that posting. He was a good man and a loyal friend to the White House."

"You keep saying *was*... past tense."

"That's right. He was murdered four days ago on his way to the airport in Tashkent."

"Murdered? How do you know?"

She said, "I've been in this game well over half my life. I've got contacts in every corner of Europe and Central Asia. The things I know would melt your brain, so take it from me. He was murdered, and it was made to look like a horrible traffic accident."

"Why?"

"Come on, Chase. You're smarter than that. The ambassador was flying home to brief the president on what was happening inside the CIA in Tashkent. Putin couldn't let that happen. Open your eyes. It's all right in front of you."

I wanted to believe every word, but I'd lived through too many lies and deceit from intelligence operatives to take Teresa Lynn at her word without verifying what she was saying through sources I trusted. I pushed away from the table. "Stay here. I'll be right back."

When my hand landed on the doorknob, she said, "Wait a minute. You haven't heard the second fact yet."

I couldn't imagine anything she could say that would keep me from walking out that door and putting Skipper to work verifying everything Teresa told me, but when I turned back to tell her to wait, she said, "Dr. Robert Richter taught me everything I know about how humans behave when logic and reality no longer sleep in the same bed."

Invoking my mentor's name nearly brought me to my knees. "What did you just say?"

She wore the blank expression of a woman who'd played her last trump card. "You don't need me to say it again. I knew him, too, and he was more than just a teacher. You of all people understand exactly what I'm saying."

Dr. Robert "Rocket" Richter had been the most influential person in my life, with the possible exception of my own father. Dr. Richter was an Air Force fighter pilot, a covert operative in the Cold War years, the best psychology professor I ever met, and the man who brought me into the world of espionage and service to my country.

"How did you know Dr. Richter?"

"Have a seat, and I'll tell you everything."

Am I being toyed with?

Only time would answer those questions, and nothing outside that room could've pulled me away. Instead of sitting, I leaned on the table with my fists. The clean bandage and dressing on my right wrist and hand starkly contrasted the dark wooden table, and I realized the truth never lay in the dark or the light. It hovered somewhere between the two in a realm that is so easy to overlook.

"If you lie to me, I don't care what happens to you, but if you're telling the truth, I'll take every step with you and put a bullet in anyone who tries to stop you."

She never took her eyes from mine. "I was a Navy lieutenant attending the Naval War College, and a guest lecturer named Dr. Richter spoke for two hours on the validity of the evil of communism. In those days, the world was simpler, and also far more complicated than it is today. Good and bad were the extremes, and it seemed like everyone believed nothing else existed."

She paused for a moment as if remembering the wisdom of my mentor, or perhaps she was formulating the next lie to cross her lips. "Dr. Richter held private sessions with a few of us who were interested. By the end of the two-week period of his presence at the War College, I grew enamored by him and drawn to every word he said. I'll never forget one particular thing he said . . ."

Again, the pause came, but I didn't flinch. When she spoke again, it was like hearing the man I trusted, adored, and loved like a father speak in her voice.

"Communism is a sickness, a disease spread by those who wear its stench like a badge of honor. The Soviet people aren't communists, so don't hate them. They are human victims of tyranny of the highest order. Despise, loathe, and destroy communism at every opportunity. Seek out those opportunities, mine for them, tear through the Iron Curtain with your teeth if you must, but do not do it blindly. Do it with compassion for the people of the Soviet Union. Live the sacrificial life of a liberator, a savior, a standard bearer of freedom, and should you be chosen to do so, die the death of a warrior fighting not to defeat an enemy, but fighting instead to break the chains of socialism and communism binding millions of innocent prisoners of corruption and domination. Fight for them as if they were your very flesh, your blood, your soul, for they did not choose their fate. They merely fell victim to blindness. Tear down that curtain and let the light of freedom flush out the shadows of oppression so the sweet taste of freedom can touch the lips of those whose only crime was being born on the wrong side of that wall."

"You memorized his entire speech?"

She bit her bottom lip. "No, I didn't memorize it. I recorded it and listened to it every day of my life until the words became part of who and what I am. I have no reason to lie to you, Chase. You have the resources to check everything I tell you. Lying to you would only mean having you turn your back on me, and I've come to believe that without you, I would've spent the remainder of my life on the run from people who would spit on the ultimate truths I learned from our beloved Dr. Richter."

I collapsed onto the seat I'd abandoned and pinched the bridge of my nose, trying to ward off the coming explosion inside my head.

"Are you okay?"

I tasted something bitter and harsh rising in my throat. Shards of light flashed behind my eyes, and pulses of electricity ran down both arms, curling my fingertips into my palms with more force than my muscles could produce. I reached across the table and grasped her arm with what had become little more than a claw. "Get Clark and a doctor."

Clark was first into the room, where I lay slumped over the table and gasping for my next breath while a storm raged inside my head, waging war against my senses. "Chase! What's wrong?"

I tried to look up at him, but my vision was darkening with every ragged breath. I reached out for him like a drowning man and pleaded for the ability to speak one more line. "Protect her. She's telling the truth."

I couldn't know if my words came out clear enough for Clark to hear and understand, but the instant they left my tongue, the coming fog enveloped me, and the silent darkness consumed my body and mind.

Chapter 29
Far from Home

When I opened my eyes, everything in my memory felt like a distant dream, like the imagination of a storyteller, a reality that could've never been. As distant as my past appeared to be, my present felt equally foreign. As the world came into focus, confusion consumed me. I lay in a softly lit room on a comfortable bed with IV lines and electrical cords streaming from my body. The harsh tone of the alarming monitors cut through the veil that was my inability to hear. The sounds felt like ice picks being driven into my skull, but I couldn't tell the direction they were coming from. They seemed to be everywhere, all at once. No other sounds existed until a man and a woman came through a door. They wore scrubs and carried stethoscopes around their necks.

The woman rushed to the source of the alarm and silenced it while the man leaned across me and shone a light into my eyes. When he spoke, he sounded like the public address announcer at a baseball game. His words roared and echoed inside my head, and I recoiled and reached to cover my ears.

The man asked, "Is it too loud?"

I nodded and pressed my palms against my ears.

He lifted a small device attached to the rail on the side of my bed and made some adjustments. "Is that better?"

I shook my head and grimaced against the piercing sound.

He made more adjustments to the device and spoke again. "How's that?"

I nodded and removed my hands from my ears. "What's happening? Where am I? Where's Clark?"

The man's accent was thick, but his English wasn't bad. "I am Dr. Klein, and you are in the neurological intensive care unit of Sourasky Medical Center in Tel-Aviv."

"Why?"

"You were brought here after you suffered a hemorrhagic stroke resultant from a traumatic brain injury. We performed both stereotactic and endoscopic aspiration to relieve the pressure inside your skull. Following the procedures, we placed you in a medically induced coma to allow time for your brain to heal."

"I've been in a coma? How long?"

Dr. Klein checked his watch. "Approximately seventy-two hours."

"Three days? Where's Clark?"

Dr. Klein looked at the woman and asked, "Is there anyone named Clark in the waiting room?"

She said, "I'll ask."

She left the room, and the doctor continued. "How is your vision?"

I focused on his face. "I can see up close, but things across the room are a little blurry."

"That is to be expected. Now, how about your hearing. I'm sorry it was so loud initially."

I blinked, trying to clear the cobwebs. "It was really loud, but it's okay now. You sound electronic, if that makes any sense."

He nodded. "The device you have implanted in your mandible has been paired with this device." He held up the small box from the bed rail. "The implant you have is quite remarkable. The damage you suffered to your eardrum is outside my specialty, but it is likely permanent natural hearing loss. The ENT will discuss that with you."

A commotion at the door caught my attention, and I turned to see Clark scampering to my bedside. "Hey, College Boy. Welcome back. You had quite a nap."

I held up my bandaged hand. "What's going on here? My memory is a little foggy."

He waved a hand. "Don't worry about that. It's minor. We'll get that taken care of when we get home. How are you feeling?"

"Not great. I'm in a hospital a long way from home, and I'm not real sure how I got here."

He leaned in. "You remember the mission, right?"

"I'm not sure. The doctor said I had a stroke."

Clark chuckled. "Yeah, that's putting it mildly. You actually had a bunch of them, but the nasty one put you in here three or four days ago. I'm not sure what day it is."

"Did we get in a gunfight with some Russians?"

Clark's eyes turned to saucers. "What? No, of course not. Nothing like that happened." He looked up at the doctor. "Would you mind giving us a couple of minutes?"

"Of course not," he said. "Just press the call button if you need us." He left the room and pulled the door closed as he went.

Clark double-checked the door. "You really don't remember the mission?"

"I've got parts of it," I said. "A gunfight and a fire are the flashing neon signs in my head right now. Did that happen?"

"I'm afraid so. It wasn't pretty, but we all made it out. Do you remember the Israeli commandos and Imri, the Mossad officer?"

I sighed. "I don't know. Maybe. I remember a woman. I think she was CIA. Does that make sense?"

He lifted the television remote control from the bedside stand and flipped a button. "Yeah, that makes sense. Take a look at this."

The TV came on, and the screen filled with a view of the United Nations General Assembly. A voice said, "The UN passed the resolution condemning Russia's involvement in Uzbekistan and Turkmenistan by an overwhelming majority of one hundred fifty-five in favor, five against, and twenty-three abstaining."

I tried to smile. "It's starting to come back to me. Where's the CIA woman? Was her name Teresa something?"

He checked the door again. "Yeah, her name is Teresa Lynn, and the Israelis are taking good care of her while the whole thing flushes out. It turns out she knew Dr. Richter."

Bells went off inside my head as the memory of the speech Teresa recited poured into my brain. "When do you think they'll let me go home?"

Before he could answer, the door burst open, and the most beautiful woman I've ever seen came in with tears in her eyes and her hair dancing in a windstorm above her head. "Chase! How long have you been awake? Do you need anything? Where's the doctor? Do you need another blanket?"

I reached up and took Penny's perfect face in my hands. "I've got everything I need right here, and I'm going to be fine."

She leaned down and kissed me as if she hadn't seen me in decades, but she quickly pulled away. "Whoa . . . You could really use a toothbrush."

I laughed and squeezed her hands as the door to my room took on the look of a clown car at the circus. People kept coming through the door in what seemed like an endless stream, and the team lined the wall beneath the television with relief on their faces.

Singer gave me a wink and folded his hands in front of him.

I mouthed, "Thank you," and he nodded.

Dr. Klein would probably take the credit for saving my life, but the prayers Singer sent up on my behalf will forever be the reason I survived. Everyone should be lucky enough to have a Singer in their lives.

Skipper stepped beside my bed and took my unbandaged hand. "It's good to see you awake, Chase. You had us pretty scared."

"Yeah, I guess I did. Sorry about that. But you didn't have to come all the way over here. I was in good hands."

She gave my hand a playful slap. "What are you talking about, silly boy? There wasn't a thing on this Earth that could keep us away. We're family."

Tony, Skipper's husband and my teammate whose gunfighting career ended because of an injury a lot like mine, stepped beside his wife and looked down at me. "Sucks, doesn't it?"

"It sure does. But maybe I can learn to paint like you."

He put on his brother's grin. "You can probably learn, but you'll never be as good as me."

Hunter, my partner and dearest friend, was next. He just stared down at me and tried to keep one persistent tear from finding its way from his eye.

I laid my hand on his and nodded slowly. "Me, too, man. Me, too."

He leaned back and fanned the air in front of his face with a hand. "Penny's right. You do need a toothbrush."

A trio of nurses pushed their way into the room with looks of fear on their faces. One of them said, "Uh, I'm sorry, but you all can't be in here. We only allow one visitor at a time."

Everyone agreed Penny should stay while they made their way to the waiting area. She took my hand in hers and gave me that irresistible smile I love so much. "We're still breaking the rules."

"What are you talking about?" I asked.

She pulled my hand across the bed rail and placed it against her stomach. "It's not just you and me anymore, Chase. You're going to be a father."

Author's Note

First, I must thank you for allowing me to be your personal story-teller for another edition of Chase's adventures. I don't have the words to adequately express my appreciation for your support of my work. Thanks to you, I get to do what I love and share it with so many friends. I often say I don't want fans. I want *friends* who enjoy my work. That's what I consider all of you to be, and I treasure our friendship.

Let's talk about the Russians. By now, you probably know how much I love using them as the bad guys. That's probably the result of having grown up during the Cold War and being taught that Russian paratroopers would likely one day drop from the sky to take over America. I'm thankful that invasion never happened, but it did instill some thoughts into my head that have turned into stories you seem to love. Dr. Richter's speech, as recited by Teresa Lynn in this story, is exactly how I feel about the Russian people. They are not the bad guys. They are the victims of bad guys, and I harbor no ill will toward them. I do, however, have a great deal of ill will toward the ideologies of communism and socialism, and I will continue to write stories of freedom prevailing in the face of tyranny.

Of course, the war between Uzbekistan and Turkmenistan is entirely the product of my overactive imagination. To my knowledge, those two nations have never disagreed about anything, and they've certainly never lobbed mortars at each other. They just happen to be the two former Soviet republics I chose for this story because they were roughly the same size and shared a long border that was convenient for my fictional tale. As far as I know, they are wonderful neighbors to each other. I meant no offense to either nation or any of their citizens.

Now it's time to talk about the flying. As you probably know already, I'm a huge aviation enthusiast, and I've been a pilot for nearly forty years. My passion for flying machines and the people who get to sit up front are elements I will always pour into my storytelling. I try to keep the cockpit action as real as possible, but I had to stray a little to make this story happen. The faked emergency decompression incident would not work in reality. The procedures I described are plausible and were the product of a collaboration with a dear friend of mine, Gary Bray, who is a senior airline captain and retired Air Force C-130 pilot. I often turn to him when it comes to the operation of aircraft above and beyond the limit of my knowledge and ability. Likewise, the flight from Nukus to Tel-Aviv is pure fiction. The current geopolitical climate of the region wouldn't permit such a transit, but again, I needed the route to hold the story together, so I made it all up . . . just like I always do.

I doubt that anyone from Langley reads my stories, but just in case, let's talk a little bit about the CIA. I have no direct personal knowledge of any corruption at any level within the Central Intelligence Agency. I've never been directly employed by the Agency, and I never expect to be invited to do so. Like the Russians, the CIA is an easy target for fiction writers like me. The Agency is shrouded in mystery, intrigue, and downright lies. Because so few people have any real idea what happens behind the walls of Langley, writers like me get to make it up, and I love doing just that. I suspect, much like most federal government agencies, there is some degree of corruption, mismanagement, and lack of efficiency in the CIA, but that doesn't make a very good espionage story. It's up to me and my fellow writers to take advantage of the veil of mystery the Agency hides behind and bring you stories that only serve to further the intrigue with the CIA. I have no animosity toward the Agency or any of its employees, but that doesn't stop me from having a bit of literary fun at their expense.

I said on many occasions that most of my characters are based on people I've known throughout my life and had the privilege of working alongside. That remains true, and if you and I have ever had a personal conversation, we've likely talked about some of the real people my characters are based on. Teresa Lynn's character is based not on a mysterious spy, but on the traits of my sister, who happens to be named Teresa Lynn. I treasure, adore, and love Teri beyond description. She played a major role in my childhood and continues to be one of the most wonderful people in my adult life. She even plays a role in the production of these stories when they become audiobooks. When I created the fictional character of Teresa Lynn, I was thinking of my sister and her remarkable strength and resilience. She has endured personal loss and tragedy in her life that would destroy most people, but instead of succumbing to the heartbreak and giving up, she finds new reasons to see life as a beautiful gift rather than a collection of curses. She is sacrificial beyond limit for those she loves, and our country would be well served to have a million just like her in the CIA and every other field. I love her dearly, and I hope she approves of her namesake's performance in this story.

I want to discuss two underlying themes within this book. The first is traumatic brain injury (TBI). So many of our fighting men and women suffer TBI and are never treated for their condition. Modern warfare demands a great deal of our warriors, and we often expect them to be almost superhuman. After suffering a TBI, soldiers, sailors, and airmen often fear seeking treatment because of the effect it may have on their careers. In my opinion, that is a tragedy. We already ask too much of our brave service members. Expecting them to live with the crushing symptoms of TBI is too much to ask. I hope we can remove the stigma and turn the numbers around. I want our heroes to receive the treatment and care they need and deserve without fearing what it may cost them. If you or anyone you know is suffering from an untreated TBI, please seek medical attention from a competent provider.

The second issue I need to discuss is hearing loss. It is extremely common among service members who've experienced the chaos of combat. Explosions, weapons fire, aircraft, and machinery noise are all routine hazards of modern warfare. Service members are issued hearing protection, but it isn't always sufficient or available when it's needed most. This leaves many current and former warfighters with the condition of hearing loss. In most cases, it can never be reversed, but it can be treated. I once believed going deaf meant the world around me would slowly grow more and more quiet, but as I've learned through my personal battle with hearing loss, that isn't what happens. Instead of growing softer and quieter, the sounds of the world around me have become utter chaos at times. I find conversation in restaurants and other crowded settings to be nearly impossible. I learned in the early days of Covid that I had been reading lips without realizing I was doing so. When everyone around me suddenly began wearing a mask, I discovered that I could no longer understand anything they were saying. I sought help through the VA and received it in the form of excellent hearing aids that have changed my life. They've allowed me to continue flying and to have conversations with family and friends, as well as enjoy music and television again. I'm extremely thankful for the availability of such high-quality hearing aids through the VA, and I encourage you to seek care for your hearing loss if it's an issue in your life, regardless of the source of the loss.

I used a horrific event in this story to bring the subject to light, but it is rarely a singular event that leads to hearing loss. It is, most often, prolonged exposure to unsafe levels of noise. I will likely explore this condition even more as the series continues, and I hope including it in my stories will help raise levels of awareness of the availability of care and devices that help mitigate the devastating effects of hearing loss on a person's quality of life. While we're on the subject of hearing loss, I believe it is my responsibility to address one particular issue that almost prevented me from seeking care. When I realized I was going deaf, I was embarrassed, and the thought of hanging chunks of electronic equipment behind my ears was absolutely unthinkable to me. I couldn't let the world see me wearing hearing aids. I believed everyone would see them as if they were donkey ears protruding from my head. People would laugh and make fun of me for wearing them. I couldn't possibly endure such ridicule. I've since learned that most people share those feelings of unnecessary embarrassment when it comes time for hearing aids. I encourage you to put away that silly fear and irrational shame. Almost no one sees the hearing aids, and those who do often have questions about how they work and if they might be right for them. Ultimately, I'm extremely happy that I chose to treat my hearing loss with high-quality hearing devices that have dramatically improved my quality of life.

And of course, we have to talk about the dramatic ending of this story. In *The Devil's Chase*, book number seven in this series, Chase endured an injury that left him incapable of producing children. That has played a minor role throughout the storyline of the series since both Penny and Chase expressed the desire to have children. Their inability to do so has proved to be convenient for me in that a child would dramatically complicate their already overwhelmingly complicated lives. I've enjoyed keeping them childless because it makes my job as the writer a lot easier. Now it's time for confession. Forgive me, for I have no idea what I'm doing. I don't have a clue how I'll deal with Penny's pregnancy. I don't know how well Chase will heal from the injuries he suffered in this story. Most of all, I don't know how I'll manage including a baby in the storyline. As with most elements of every story I write, I suppose I'll just make it up as I go along.

Thank you again for allowing me to take you to parts of the world most people can't spell. The series is far from over, and I still have so many stories to share and adventures to experience. I sincerely appreciate and treasure your support for my work, and I vow to never stop giving one hundred percent effort to create stories that leave you feeling as if you experienced the adventure, rather than simply reading it . . . because that's what you deserve.

—Cap

About the Author

Cap Daniels

Cap Daniels is a former sailing charter captain, scuba and sailing instructor, pilot, Air Force combat veteran, and civil servant of the U.S. Department of Defense. Raised far from the ocean in rural East Tennessee, his early infatuation with salt water was sparked by the fascinating, and sometimes true, sea stories told by his father, a retired Navy Chief Petty Officer. Those stories of adventure on the high seas sent Cap in search of adventure of his own, which eventually landed him on Florida's Gulf Coast where he spends as much time as possible on, in, and under the waters of the Emerald Coast.

With a headful of larger-than-life characters and their thrilling exploits, Cap pours his love of adventure and passion for the ocean onto the pages of the Chase Fulton Novels and the Avenging Angel - Seven Deadly Sins series.

Visit www.CapDaniels.com to join the mailing list to receive newsletter and release updates.

Connect with Cap Daniels:

Facebook: www.Facebook.com/WriterCapDaniels
Instagram: https://www.instagram.com/authorcapdaniels/
BookBub: https://www.bookbub.com/profile/cap-daniels

Also by Cap Daniels

The Chase Fulton Novels Series
Book One: *The Opening Chase*
Book Two: *The Broken Chase*
Book Three: *The Stronger Chase*
Book Four: *The Unending Chase*
Book Five: *The Distant Chase*
Book Six: *The Entangled Chase*
Book Seven: *The Devil's Chase*
Book Eight: *The Angel's Chase*
Book Nine: *The Forgotten Chase*
Book Ten: *The Emerald Chase*
Book Eleven: *The Polar Chase*
Book Twelve: *The Burning Chase*
Book Thirteen: *The Poison Chase*
Book Fourteen: *The Bitter Chase*
Book Fifteen: *The Blind Chase*
Book Sixteen: *The Smuggler's Chase*
Book Seventeen: *The Hollow Chase*
Book Eighteen: *The Sunken Chase*
Book Nineteen: *The Darker Chase*
Book Twenty: *The Abandoned Chase*
Book Twenty-One: *The Gambler's Chase*
Book Twenty-Two: *The Arctic Chase*
Book Twenty-Three: *The Diamond Chase*
Book Twenty-Four: *The Phantom Chase*

The Avenging Angel – Seven Deadly Sins Series
Book One: *The Russian's Pride*
Book Two: *The Russian's Greed*
Book Three: *The Russian's Gluttony*
Book Four: *The Russian's Lust*
Book Five: *The Russian's Sloth* (2023)
Book Six: *The Russian's Envy* (2024)
Book Seven: *The Russian's Wrath* (TBA)

Stand-Alone Novels
We Were Brave
Singer – Memoir of a Christian Sniper

Novellas
The Chase Is On
I Am Gypsy

Made in the USA
Middletown, DE
25 February 2024

50323766R00151